Christmas can be a lonely time of the year for those serving their country far from home—or it can be a time of new discoveries. Will four couples find romance or heartbreak while on Christmas duty?

About-Face by Jill Stengl—Lt. Cathy Guillard hides a secret crush on Capt. Tim Falkirk, a fighter pilot of dubious reputation who now professes faith in Christ. His first Christmas as a Christian holds great meaning for Tim, and he asks God to make him worthy of the pretty, prim, and proper lieutenant who seems impervious to his charm. Their professional and personal interaction convinces Cathy of the change in his life, but she still hesitates to trust him. Tim's close brush with death in a flying incident shocks Cathy into recognizing her love for him.

Outranked by Love by Tammy Shuttlesworth—Hayden Jacobs and Lacey White meet while stationed at the same air force base. Hayden was raised to believe that power and status are the most important things in the world, while Lacey knows that life can be happy without money or things. Will Hayden find a true power to believe in and will Lacey find purpose in life after a medical discharge? Can there be a Christmas wedding?

Seeking Shade by Paige Winship Dooly—Special Ops Agent Nick McLeod is sent to rescue Shade Matthews, his former fiancée, who is being held captive in the Caribbean by a band of drug smugglers. He only has a few weeks until their formerly planned Christmas wedding to find, rescue, and convince Shade that he still belongs at her side. Will he win Shade's heart once more?

A Distant Love by Janelle Burnham Schneider—Capt. Katrina Falkirk is determined to serve her year as a peacekeeper in Israel's Golan Heights with distinction and without entanglement. Yet while doing her part to contribute to Christmas celebrations for those unable to leave the peacekeeper camp, she finds herself unwillingly intrigued by the provost marshal, Capt. Brian Smith. Katrina's determination to avoid heartache sends her to the England home of her brother, Capt. Tim Falkirk, where Brian finds her and convinces her to trust him with her heart.

Christmas Duty

Four Stories of Love in the Armed Forces

Paige Winship Dooly
Janelle Burnham Schneider
Tammy Shuttlesworth
Jill Stengl

BARBOUR
PUBLISHING

About-Face © 2003 by Jill Stengl
Outranked by Love © 2003 by Tammy Shuttlesworth
Seeking Shade © 2003 by Paige Winship Dooly
A Distant Love © 2003 by Janelle Burnham Schneider

ISBN 1-58660-846-0

Cover image © Greg Copeland

All Scripture quotations, unless otherwise indicated, are taken from the HOLY BIBLE, NEW INTERNATIONAL VERSION®. NIV®. Copyright © 1973, 1978, 1984 by International Bible Society. Used by permission of Zondervan Publishing House. All rights reserved.

Published by Barbour Publishing, Inc., P.O. Box 719, Uhrichsville, Ohio 44683, www.barbourbooks.com

Our mission is to publish and distribute inspirational products offering exceptional value and biblical encouragement to the masses.

Member of the
Evangelical Christian
Publishers Association

Printed in the United States of America.
5 4 3 2 1

Christmas Duty

About-Face

by Jill Stengl

Chapter 1

A s Capt. Tim Falkirk rose from his desk, rubbing his aching back, another pilot paused in the office doorway. "Brief in the auditorium in fifteen minutes."

"Thanks, Hal," someone at a desk behind Tim acknowledged. "Now get lost."

Tim checked his watch. Two-fifteen. Where had the day gone? Busting a flight crew on a check flight ranked among his least favorite tasks, but filling out reams of paperwork afterward was even worse.

"Hey, Captain Falkirk! Good to see you, Sir. When did you get back from Turkey?" Hal Redmond, a young pilot, leaned against the door frame.

"Wednesday. RAF Lakenheath sounded like 'home, sweet home' to me until I got here. You say the brief starts in fifteen minutes?" Tim's stomach rumbled. "No lunch again."

"So grab a candy bar. Trust me, you won't sleep through this brief. Wait 'til you see the new intelligence officer. You'll be drooling."

Five minutes later, Tim took a seat in the auditorium, chewing the last of a peanut bar from the vending machine. The man seated in front of him turned, leaned his forearm on the theater seat's back, and assumed an amiable expression. "Glad you're back in England, Falkirk. We're short on instructors and have a bunch of new pilots coming before Christmas. The experience rate has bottomed out." Captain Lofty's given name was Ken, and he had the shiny plastic hair and smile to match it.

"Tell me something I don't know," Tim responded. "I've been back two days and already led two training flights."

"So how was good ol' Incirlik Air Base? Hit on any babes this trip?"

Tim's smile froze. "I thought we believers were supposed to encourage one another to good works."

Ken's grin resembled a smirk. "Oh, yeah. You're on the good guys' side now. I keep forgetting. Let me know when you start leading prayer meetings. That should prove interesting." He abruptly faced front.

With friends like you. . . Propping the bridge of his nose against two fingers, Tim closed his aching eyes.

Someone sat down beside him. "You can't sleep yet, Tim; the meeting hasn't started." Capt. Jason Thomson, a weapons system officer, or "wizzo" in military vernacular, and one of Tim's roommates, poked him in the ribs.

Tim stirred. "Wake me if it gets interesting. I expect a long nap. Got any food on you by any chance? All I've had since breakfast was a candy bar."

"Sorry. Rotten day. Why didn't you stop for lunch? I did."
Jason glanced around. "What stinks? Oh, hello, Lofty."

Frowning, Tim shook his head. "Knock it off."

A female officer paused beside Ken Lofty's row. Ken indicated the open aisle chair. "I saved you a spot, Cathy."

She slipped into the fold-down seat and gave him a fleeting smile. "Thanks."

"Not nervous, are you?" Ken leaned close.

Tim saw the lieutenant's head tip away from Ken Lofty's.
"A little."

"Our new intel chick," Jason informed Tim without bothering to lower his voice. "Isn't she a hammer? Mrrr-row!" He yowled like an enamored tomcat.

The young woman twitched but did not look over her shoulder. Tim admired the way she had slicked her blond-streaked hair into a fat bun. "Love the freckles," he said before stopping to consider his comment.

"She's got plenty to love." Jason slid down in his seat and bumped the back of her seat with his knees. "C'mon, Lieutenant Guillard. You could at least greet the best wizzo in USAFE. What have I done to deserve your cold shoulder?"

Ken Lofty turned to glare. "Have you two been at the bar already? Leave the lady alone before she nails you on harassment charges. I'm her witness."

"Like anyone would believe you."

"Drop it, Jase," Tim said.

Jason abruptly sat up. "You're right. It's hopeless. Not even you could score with Lieutenant Guillard. She's one of those uptight religious chicks."

"Religious? As in Christian?" Tim gave the lieutenant's starched shoulders another look.

Captain Lofty and Lieutenant Guillard consulted together, then rose and moved to different seats.

"So have a great USAFE day," Jason called after them. "No great loss. Yep, you guessed it: Chatty Cathy is a Bible-thumper like our lofty Kenny." He gave Tim a wary glance. "That's right; I'd forgotten about your religious infection. We all thought you'd recuperate at Incirlik."

"It's terminal."

Jason lifted a brow. "The last thing we need around here is another Reverend Lofty. Heard you've been going to one of those prayer groups. What's with that? Trying to impress some babe with your spirituality?"

Swallowing his irritation, Tim shook his head. "I want to learn what the Bible is about. I'm interested in God."

Jason gave him a blank look. "You're taking this thing too far."

Before Tim could answer, the meeting was called to order. One after another, heads of various sections of the squadron gave their briefings, complaining about forms being improperly filled out or items not being turned in. The flight commanders discussed upcoming holiday parties. Tim's eyelids grew heavy. More than once his chin bounced off his chest.

Again Jason elbowed him in the side. "Wake up. Here she comes."

Someone let out a wolf whistle, and laughter drifted

around the room. Tim blinked and sat up straight. Lt. Catherine Guillard mounted the steps in front. He could see her hands shaking as she arranged her notes, yet when she began to speak her voice was clear. One stray lock of hair bobbed near her cheek while she talked.

"Gorgeous, eh?" Jason whispered.

"She's all right. Looks about fifteen. Seems to know her job, though."

When Jason made a lewd comment behind his hand, Tim's fists clenched. "Don't talk that way about a lady."

"What's with you? Heard one too many political correctness lectures? Her first few weeks, we razzed her unmercifully. She learned fast. Today, I'd guess, we will learn in under five minutes all there is to know about a new weapon system."

He was right. When the meeting ended, Tim remained seated while everyone around him rose and began to talk. "Staying for First Friday?" Jason asked. "The wives are planning to decorate the squadron for the holidays. We could help hang mistletoe."

"Don't think so. I'm beat like a bad dog. Got to get some sleep before I keel over."

"You look bad, now that you mention it. Get on home, but don't use up all the hot water. Guess you've had too many late nights and too much scotch—if such a thing is possible. Or was it the wild Bible meetings that did you in?" Grinning, Jason punched Tim's shoulder before moving down the aisle to join the flock of men surrounding Lt. Catherine Guillard.

When the aisles cleared, Tim rose stiffly to his feet.

Although a warm bed sounded like heaven at the moment, he didn't look forward to going home. *Home. That's a joke.* As if the bachelor pad he shared with Jason and Lt. Adrian Hill deserved the name.

Wives and children were arriving at the squadron for the monthly First Friday party. Ladies walked past, carrying brown bags and steaming covered dishes toward the pub. Tim's stomach growled. Pausing in the hallway, he considered his options, shook his head, and flung on his flight jacket. His fist connected with something, and he heard a gasp of pain. Startled, he spun around.

The intelligence officer leaned against the wall, holding one hand over her mouth.

"Are you all right? I didn't know you were there."

"It was my fault for trying to slip past you from behind." Tears glistened in her blinking eyes. "I'll be fine in a minute." She produced a tissue from her pocket and pressed it to her mouth.

"Let me see." He pulled her hand away from her face. "There's blood—I gave you a fat lip!" He took the tissue and dabbed at her mouth. "I'm so sorry!"

"I'll get her a glass of water," a helpful wife offered.

"Thank you, but honestly, I will be fine." Her voice sounded breathless. Tim saw her glance around at their gathering audience. "I just bit my lip." The hand in his grasp made a weak attempt to be released. She seemed to sway.

Tim wrapped an arm around her shoulder. She stiffened but did not pull away. "Come into the lounge and sit down.

It shouldn't be crowded yet," he said. "Where's Lofty?"

"He had to leave."

Moments later he was elbowing his way between people in the pub, trying to clear a way to the vinyl couches. One officer, roaring with laughter, backed into Tim and slopped beer on the carpet. Tim caught himself with one hand on the bar just in time to keep from crushing the woman he was trying to protect. Bodies jostled them from all sides. Rock music pounded an irregular beat. Delicious food aromas blended with the reek of beer and the stench of sweaty flight suits.

The lieutenant spoke, but shouts of people trying to converse above the stereo system drowned her out. Tim bent down, and her voice tickled his ear. "I'm so thankful we beat the crowds." Turning quickly, he caught a twinkle in her eyes.

"Ingrate," he said. She was so close. One little squeeze and her forehead would touch his chin. He wanted to rest his cheek against her shiny hair; but her hands flattened upon his chest, maintaining a circumspect distance. Now her eyes delivered a mistrustful admonition.

Tim found a place on a lumpy vinyl love seat and pulled her down beside him, resting his arm behind her on the back cushion. Her small hands clenched together in her lap, and her short fingernails whitened. Straight as a pool cue she sat. He respected her reserve yet perversely yearned to break it. "Feel any better? Relax, Lieutenant. I don't eat little girls for supper."

She sucked in that swollen lip and winced. "I think I'd better go."

He couldn't resist taking hold of her chin and inspecting

her tremulous mouth at close range. "A bit puffy but not bad. Hmm, not bad at all." As he relaxed back on the sofa, she relaxed along with him, staring into his eyes as if hypnotized. "That's better. So tell me about yourself, Lieutenant. Where are you from?"

"Thought you weren't staying for First Friday," a slurred voice accused. Jason stood over them, beer stein in hand. "Hey, no fair. I saw her first. Anyone sitting here?"

"There's not enough room—" Tim began to protest, but Jason wedged in on the lieutenant's other side. Crammed between two large men, the lieutenant almost disappeared into the crack between cushions. "You're squashing her." Tim took her hands and pulled hard. Lieutenant Guillard sprawled across his lap, tried to push herself up, slipped, and fell face first against his chest. He gripped her shoulders and held her close for only an instant before helping her up, wary of flailing elbows.

Once on her feet, she lifted both shaking hands to her disheveled hair. "Excuse me," she gasped in horror.

"Look, she's blushing!" Jason exulted. "I didn't know blushing women still existed."

Lieutenant Guillard gave them one scathing look and stalked away.

Both men watched her go. Their eyes met. "Whew! Is it just me or was there a sudden heat wave?" Jason fanned himself. "Score one for the legendary Falkirk. That was one original way to cop a feel."

Heat poured into Tim's face and sweat beaded his forehead.

"I gotta get out of here." Leaving a snickering Jason on the love seat, he rushed toward the doorway, pushing and shoving without apology.

❧

Cathy was halfway down the long hallway when she heard him call. "Lieutenant, please wait. I'll walk you to your car."

Slowly she turned. Captain Falkirk looked like a guilty puppy, lacking only the wagging tail.

"Leave me alone."

"I promise not to touch you. I'm truly sorry for what happened back there. I know you're a believer, and I wouldn't offend you for anything."

Cathy studied his pleading brown eyes. He appeared sincere, but his type never was.

He sucked in a deep breath. "You probably don't know that I'm a believer in Jesus."

"That's not what I've heard."

"You've heard about me." His shoulders sagged. "Didn't know I was so notorious. My reputation is bad, but God is changing me."

Her heart gave an extra thump. Absently she started walking toward the exit. "When did. . . ? How long. . . ?"

"Last summer I went back to the States for my cousin's wedding. Had a couple of long talks with my sister while I was there. She answered all my religion questions—and when she didn't know the answers, she wasn't afraid to say so. She told me to check out the Bible for myself. I started seriously thinking about God and eternity and the meaning of life, and things began to change."

"Really?" Despite her doubts, Cathy couldn't help hoping.

Captain Falkirk opened the heavy squadron door for her. "Almost every day I have to claim as my own that verse about old things passing away and all things becoming new. It's tough to change a lifetime of thought and behavior patterns."

"Do you have Christian friends here?" Cathy asked as they passed through the gate in the chain-link fence separating the squadron from the car park.

"Not yet. I joined a Bible study at Incirlik while I was there. Is there something similar here at RAF Lakenheath? There used to be several Christians in this squadron, but most of them have moved on. I need support, someone to talk with about God."

"We don't have many singles at our church, but a few of us meet together and go on occasional outings. You know Captain Lofty already; he attends. Our pastor, Paul Volkman, sets up discipleship meetings. I'll tell him about you if you want." Even to her own ears, her voice sounded stilted. She clicked the remote to unlock her car.

By the light of the streetlamps, he scribbled the pastor's name on a business card. "Volkman? I've heard of him. Thanks. I'm not glad I punched you, but I'm glad we met. I need friends who don't think I've lost my mind."

Mumbling a farewell, she climbed into her car. Captain Falkirk closed her door and gave a little wave. Before she left the parking area, Cathy watched him climb into his sports car. "Dear Lord, please let it be true," she murmured.

Chapter 2

"Erica, what does 'you-safey' mean?" Cathy poked her head into her roommate's bedroom.

Erica took her eyes off the television long enough to reply. "It stands for United States Armed Forces Europe. Let me guess: Someone told you to 'have a great USAFE day,' right?" She lifted a brow. "So what happened to your mouth?"

"I got in the way while a man was putting on his flight jacket. USAFE. Now I know. How long will it take me to get used to living here? I feel like an ignoramus most of the time, and it's been two months. At least the flight crews don't persecute me during my briefings as much as they used to."

"Honey, you're such a babe in the woods, you'll probably never fit in. I foresee you getting married, getting out of the military, and getting pregnant within the next year or two. You've already got one good-looking pilot eating out of your hand." Erica tapped a long red nail against her lower lip and gave Cathy a frankly puzzled assessment.

"I still have more than a year of active duty to serve." Cathy jiggled the doorknob, studied the window curtains, and shifted her weight to her other foot. "Do you know a guy named Tim Falkirk? He's a pilot in the 494th."

Erica wagged her finger. "Ah-ah-ah! Not for you. That guy is straight scotch and you're a soda pop girl. You stick with Ken Lofty. He's the marrying kind. Leave Tim for gals like me who know how to keep him in line."

"If he's so bad, why would you want him, Erica? You're a Christian like me."

"Nobody's a Christian like you, Cathy. You're too good for the rest of us, but we can always hope some of that righteousness will rub off. Now get lost. This movie is getting to the juiciest part, and I wouldn't want our Pollyanna Pureheart to be shocked."

"Good night, Erica." Cathy went to her own tiny bedroom and lay staring at the ceiling until the wee hours. Her face and body still burned at the memory of one stolen embrace. There ought to be a law against a man being that attractive.

❧

Rev. Paul Volkman laid his Bible on the coffee shop's small table and opened it to the book of Romans. "The passage you're looking for is right here—chapter six." He scanned the page. "I'll start reading here in the middle of verse nineteen. 'Just as you used to offer the parts of your body in slavery to impurity and to ever-increasing wickedness, so now offer them in slavery to righteousness leading to holiness.' Do you understand this?"

Slumped back in his chair, Tim pulled his donut to bits. "I understand the part about being a slave to wickedness. The problem is, even though I know God released me from slavery, I still struggle against sin. I'm afraid I'll slip up just once, and all will be lost."

Paul ran his fingers through his graying hair and nodded. "I understand your concern. Sin is a powerful master and doesn't relinquish control easily. Listen to the last part of that verse again, 'so now offer them in slavery to righteousness leading to holiness.' Jesus once told a parable about a man who was freed from demons, but later on the demons returned to the man in greater numbers than before. Why do you think that happened?"

Tim shook his head.

"Because his life was empty. He never bothered to replace the evil with something good. Do you see the parallel? Once you were a slave to sin. Jesus has freed you, and now you belong to God. From now on you will choose to serve one master or the other. Either you will serve the lusts of your flesh, or you will serve God."

"I must actively serve God to escape bondage to sin."

Paul's gray eyes searched Tim's face. "Exactly. Let's read on. 'When you were slaves to sin, you were free from the control of righteousness. What benefit did you reap at that time from the things you are now ashamed of?'"

Tim snorted. "Nothing but sick memories and a load of guilt. I know God has forgiven me, but the memories don't go away."

"God will heal your mind, Tim. Let's finish reading this passage; then I have another to show you. 'Those things result in death! But now that you have been set free from sin and have become slaves to God, the benefit you reap leads to holiness, and the result is eternal life.' The Christian life is a journey, not an instant fix. You must understand that fact, or Satan will lead you into despair."

Tim took a deep breath and fastened his gaze to Paul's earnest face. "This is exactly what I've needed to hear, Pastor. I was becoming discouraged, I'll admit. But last night Lieutenant Guillard told me about you. God answered my prayer before I put it into words."

"I'm glad you called this morning, Tim. I had two free hours in my afternoon. My wife and daughters were attending a 'girl thing' at church today, and I was at loose ends. It was no coincidence."

"How many daughters do you have?"

"Three. We even have a girl dog," Paul said with a grin.

"You don't seem to mind being outnumbered."

"I don't. My wife and daughters are the greatest blessings I could imagine. By the way, if you don't have plans for supper tonight, you're welcome to join us."

"Sure your wife won't mind you inviting a stranger?"

Paul chuckled. "Not at all. 'The more the merrier' is Sandy's motto."

"Thanks. I'd enjoy a home-cooked meal." Tim twisted his cup, watching the coffee slosh. "I've always avoided marriage. It seemed like a prison sentence, being tied to one woman. I saw no point in it."

"And now?"

"I've been reading what the Bible has to say about marriage, and my feelings are changing. I'd like to have a lifetime friend and partner, someone to stand beside me and encourage me. Someone who needs me."

Paul nodded. "Marriage can be tough, but it's worth the effort and sacrifice. There's nothing better here on earth than the love of a good woman. Now that you're no longer a slave to sin, the concept of commitment and unselfish love is becoming attractive."

"Not long ago I would have laughed at the idea, but now I think it would be great to belong to just one woman and know that she was equally committed to me. I would like to be worthy of a good woman."

"So now we get down to action. How will you exchange slavery to sin for slavery to righteousness?"

"Have any ideas for me, Pastor?"

Paul smiled. "Thought you'd never ask. Let me read this passage in Philippians with you, chapter four, verses four through eight. 'Rejoice in the Lord always. I will say it again: Rejoice! Let your gentleness be evident to all. . . .' "

Two weapon system officers, or wizzos, and a baby-faced pilot lounged at the briefing room table, munching popcorn and propping their boots on vacant chairs while they waited for their flight leader to appear and begin the debrief. Cathy sat straight in her chair, trying to ignore their stares and comments. If not for a strong desire to learn the success of her work, she would have walked out.

"I'm thinking of this girl," Lt. Adrian Hill said in his Tennessee drawl. "She's got a shape to drive you wild."

Tim Falkirk entered, plopped his briefcase on the table, and pulled the video player into position.

The other men continued their oblique discussion. "I know just the woman you mean. She's a little thing, but, oh, so nice," the baby-faced pilot said around a mouthful of popcorn. His following comments bordered on the obscene.

Captain Falkirk interrupted firmly. "Did Lieutenant Guillard give us a good scenario today or what?"

The flight crews agreed. Adrian winked, still chewing with his mouth open. "The lieutenant has many obvious talents."

Falkirk's face was like granite. "She learns fast and works hard. The mission was a success from takeoff to landing. Thanks, Lieutenant. Now let's get to work." He popped a recording of their flight into the VCR and began to write with a marker on the erasable board.

"That's what I needed to know," Cathy said quietly and rose.

"Hey, Lieutenant, join me for dinner tonight?" the younger pilot inquired hopefully.

"No, thank you. Good day, Sir." She addressed the farewell to Tim and made her escape.

"I figured it was hopeless, but a guy's got to try." As the door closed, she heard, "That woman's got blood like ice."

Later that afternoon Cathy stepped out of her office,

already digging in her purse for her car keys, and nearly bumped into Captain Falkirk. "Excuse me, Sir." A blush rolled up her cheeks. He probably thought she was permanently sunburned.

"Lieutenant Guillard, I'm sorry about today. The men around here don't know how to treat a lady. Most of them have never met one before, I'd wager."

She didn't know how to reply.

"You gave us a great scenario. Lots of SAM sites," he said, ending her concern about whether she'd included enough surface-to-air missile sites. "Never let those guys belittle your abilities. You're really good."

"Thank you, Sir."

"I've been hoping you might go with me to the squadron Christmas party this weekend."

Cathy could scarcely breathe. He was overwhelming enough when encountered on a professional basis. Now, when he spoke to her in that voice like crushed velvet, she was lost. "I—I'm already going with someone."

Thick lashes hooded his eyes for a moment. "I figured as much but thought it couldn't hurt to ask. I'll try again another time. Good night."

She watched him walk away. Not just any man looked good in a flight suit. Tim Falkirk was not just any man.

⚓

Ken Lofty pulled out a chair and Cathy settled at the round table, smoothing her frothy blue and silver skirt. A woman sat beside her, introducing herself as Jodee Marker, the wife of a pilot. Cathy vaguely recognized the slender young husband. All over the banquet hall, people claimed seats and chatted. Cathy was already tired of making conversation and nursing her glass of diet soda.

"Mind if I sit here?"

Cathy's gaze traveled up a length of immaculate mess dress to meet Tim Falkirk's puppy-dog eyes. He smiled slowly. Her mouth went dry.

"Where's your date?" Ken asked him.

Tim slid into a chair across from Cathy and Ken. "Don't have one. Mind if I share yours?" His teasing gaze flicked to Cathy's face.

"Who is that?" Mrs. Marker hissed in Cathy's ear. "He's drop-dead gorgeous. How'd you rate two men in one night?"

Cathy could only smile weakly in response. She took a gulp of her soft drink and nearly choked.

"You all right?" Tim asked. Cathy nodded. How could she possibly eat with that man seated across the table?

Tim followed her through the buffet line. "You look like the sugarplum fairy," he murmured while Ken was preoccupied. He picked up a napkin when it slipped from her nerveless fingers.

Back at the table, he chatted easily with everyone seated near him. Ken, on the other hand, monopolized Cathy's attention throughout the meal. She tried to listen while he related his life story, but her mind kept straying to Tim's more interesting conversations with the other pilots seated at their table.

"Thanks," she heard Tim respond when a passing major offered to bring him a drink from the bar. "I'm having cranberry juice."

"But you can't be designated driver." The somewhat inebriated officer scowled. "What's the world coming to when Falkirk don't drink?" He moved on without waiting for an answer.

Cathy couldn't help glancing Tim's way. He looked up from his meal and smiled at her.

When the meal ended and the program began, Tim turned his chair around. Cathy found even the back of his head more interesting than the scheduled entertainment.

To his evident surprise, Tim won a decorated Christmas wreath as a door prize. He immediately bestowed it upon Cathy. "You'll probably enjoy this more than I would."

"What if she doesn't want a wreath?" Ken snapped.

"Thank you. It's lovely." Cathy reached for the unwieldy gift.

Tim grinned. "How about if I put it near the door, and you can pick it up when you leave?"

"Let me take your picture with the wreath," the pilot's wife insisted. "Tim, you come around the table and hold it out to her." She used Cathy's digital camera and snapped several shots.

Cathy could hardly wait to view them on her computer screen at home.

All too soon, Tim excused himself. "Nice to meet you," he told Jodee Marker, shaking her offered hand. "Enjoy your evening." His gaze lit upon Cathy. "You too. Don't forget your wreath."

Cathy thrust out her hand in imitation of Jodee. It trembled noticeably. "Good night."

He gave her fingers a squeeze and held on while addressing Ken. "You're the lucky one tonight, Lofty."

The other pilot glowered. Ken's bad mood remained even after Tim left to mingle with other people. When the band warmed up for dancing, Ken complained about the noise. "Can't hear myself think. Want to dance, Cathy?"

"Thank you, but no. I'm ready to leave when you are. I need to get home. I'm teaching children's church tomorrow morning." They collected their wraps, and Cathy picked up her wreath.

A voice suddenly spoke into her ear. "Merry Christmas, lovely lieutenant. Wish you'd come with me tonight—I would have been the proudest man in the room." Before she had recovered from the thrill of his warm breath on her neck, Tim disappeared into the crowd.

Chapter 3

Thu Friday before Christmas, Tim drove home after work. The car's heater hummed but failed to dispel the winter chill. *Well, soon I'll be back in Turkey, probably missing the cold. At least it feels like Christmas here.* Tim turned in at his driveway and braked sharply to avoid rear-ending a coupe. Every inch of the drive already held a car. Light poured from the house's windows.

"Great. Forgot about Adrian's Christmas party." He backed out and parked on the street. As he emerged from the car and walked up the gravel drive, a sleety rain began to fall. Tim felt the earth vibrate with a rock beat. "This will endear us to the neighbors," he told a nearby shrub. "Sounds of the season."

When he opened the front door, cigarette smoke billowed out. He pulled off his cap and tucked it into an ankle pocket of his flight suit. His leather jacket landed on the coat tree. "Jason? Adrian?"

The living room teemed with bodies. Empty beer cans

cluttered the coffee table. A Christmas tree flashed multi-colored lights. Adrian's enormous stereo system blared. Several people waved. "C'mon in. Get yourself a drink."

"Merry Christmas! I've been waiting for you, Darling." A girl wearing a glittering red dress and far too much makeup caught him by the hand, shoved him into a chair, and plopped into his lap.

Slowly he lifted his hands, started to put them around her, but instead pressed them over his ears. That noise! It seemed to throb in his soul and body, demanding satisfaction.

"What's wrong, Timmy? Got a headache?" She took his face between her hands and kissed him. Her long fingernails knifed him behind the ears. There was a roaring in his head apart from the stereo's din. He sprang to his feet and saw the girl fall away, her mouth and eyes wide. "Ouch! Watch it, you—" She ranted and swore as Tim scrambled to escape.

The front door slammed behind him. Striding down the drive, he lifted his face, letting icy rain scatter the fog in his brain. By force of habit he pulled out his flight cap and donned it. Not that it did anything to keep him dry.

He drove back toward the base, considering his options. It was just past 7:30. *I need to talk to someone. Pastor Volkman. I'll call him.*

Pulling over, he found the pastor's number on a card in his wallet and dialed it on his cell phone.

❧

"It doesn't look as if anyone else will show up tonight. How about we pour the wassail, serve the cookies, and start the movie?" Paul Volkman said.

"How about we skip the movie?" Ken Lofty suggested, running one hand over his golden flattop. "I'd rather play games."

"Oh, no. This is tradition. It isn't Christmas without at least one viewing of *It's a Wonderful Life*," Sandy Volkman said, arranging platters of candy and cookies on her kitchen table.

Cathy used a spoon to pick cloves out of the steaming pot of wassail. "This smells good, Sandy. I've never heard of cranberry wassail."

"It's my invention."

The telephone rang. "I'll take it in my office." Paul left the room.

Ken approached Cathy from behind and rested his hands on the countertop, one on either side of her. "You're beautiful tonight," he murmured. She dropped her gaze to his hairy arms. Ever since the Christmas party two weeks ago, he had behaved as if she were his property.

"Watch it, you two," Sandy warned with a chuckle. "Wait for the mistletoe."

Cathy winced.

"Mommy!" Rubbing her eyes with one fist, a child stood in the doorway. "I can't sleep."

Ken stepped back, and Cathy quickly moved out of his reach.

Sandy looked at her watch and pulled out a kitchen chair. "Come here, Melanie. You can stay up for a little while. But no more cookies." The toddler climbed into her mother's lap, blanket in tow.

Paul returned. "We'll have another visitor soon, a man I've been counseling these past few weeks. Come to think of it, you must know him, Ken. Isn't Tim Falkirk in your squadron? He's attended our church a few times, but he usually slips away right after the sermon."

Cathy felt her heart stop, then pound double-time. *Oh, no!*

Ken's smile froze. "I know Falkirk. Did you say you've been meeting with him? I find that. . .hard to believe."

"Why?" the pastor asked.

"Let's just say he's not a man I'd introduce to my sister. I've tried to witness to him in the past and got cussed out." Ken's chuckle fell flat.

"He's a flirt," Cathy added. "Not the type of man you can take seriously." She sat down beside Sandy, who had buried her face in Melanie's hair.

Paul's voice held a steely undertone. "It's not my place to judge a man's heart—only God can do that—but I consider myself a good judge of character. Tim has given his life to God; he won't turn back. I believe he is genuine."

Ken lifted a brow. Cathy wished she had kept quiet.

"Tim is in need of Christian friendship," Paul continued. "He had forgotten about our singles' fellowship tonight, so I invited him over. He'll be here any minute."

"I think he's a sweetheart," Sandy spoke up. "Our girls love him—he's really good with kids. I keep telling him he needs to get involved in the children's ministry at church.

He's not at all shy, but he's afraid people won't accept him." Her gaze impaled Ken. "Now I understand why."

"I didn't say I won't accept him." Ken took the chair beside Cathy. "I'm just leery about trusting him too much too soon. I mean around women."

Cathy studied her clenched hands. In her haste to conceal her crush on Tim Falkirk, she had slandered him. *Maybe I should leave before he gets here and I make an even bigger fool of myself.*

Sometime during the past few weeks, she had memorized the way Tim walked; now she could pick him out of a group of flight suits half a mile away. The sound of his name being paged over the squadron intercom system set her pulse racing. The quality of any given day depended on the number of times she laid eyes on the man, with bonus points if she actually spoke to him. In her bedside table, hidden from her roommates, were several large photos of Tim at the Christmas party. Tim Falkirk in mess dress—to die for!

Headlights flashed against the kitchen wall, and the Volkmans' dog began to bark outside. "He's here," Sandy said. "Paul, will you let him in while I put Melanie to bed? She zoned out almost as soon as she hit my lap. I need to prod the other two munchkins toward bed while I'm up there."

"Don't let the girls know Tim is here," Paul said. "He needs space tonight."

As Sandy mounted the stairs, male voices sounded at the front door. Cathy drew a deep breath and rubbed her shaking hands down her thighs. Ken popped entire cookies into his mouth, one after another.

"We're in the kitchen," Paul was saying. "Want some wassail? Sandy's special recipe. She baked a bazillion Christmas cookies. Hope you're hungry."

Tim entered, wiping his mouth with a tissue. "Something hot to drink sounds great." He rubbed his hand down his face to remove tissue lint. The shoulders of his flight suit were dark with moisture, and his hair looked equally wet.

He looked from Ken to Cathy. "Hello, Lofty, Lieutenant Guillard. This is the singles' group?"

"A lot of people are away for the holidays," Cathy said quickly. "Do you like old movies?" She hoped her friendly tone didn't sound forced. Her gaze skittered across the room as soon as it met Tim's.

"I doubt this is the kind of flick Falkirk goes for," Ken told Cathy in a stage whisper. "But we've got rules against R- and X-rated movies at our church gatherings."

Cathy stared. "Ken!"

Paul resembled a storm cloud.

"I'm relieved to hear it," said Tim. He settled in Sandy's empty chair beside Cathy. She scented the metallic odor of his flight suit and a whiff of cigarette smoke. His long fingers drummed once on the tabletop. She saw his knee jiggle. "I don't care for modern movies anymore. There aren't many worth watching."

"You're too busy living like trash to watch it. When did you take to wearing lipstick?" Ken asked. "That's not your best shade. I think an earring would better match your tattoo, but if you're into lipstick, what can I say?"

Paul's jaw dropped. He ladled wassail into Tim's cup until it nearly overflowed.

Tim's knee stopped jiggling. Cathy saw Tim's hand slip to his lap and clench into a fist. His voice remained quiet. "You're on a roll tonight, Lofty. All you need is a mike, and you've got a second career as a stand-up comic."

A voice shrilled from the stairwell. "Kenneth Lofty, if you can't keep a Christlike tongue in your head, you leave our house this minute! I've heard enough." Sandy stomped down the last few steps.

Paul recovered from his shock and seconded his wife's suggestion. "I think you'd better go, Ken. If you want to talk later tonight, I'll be available."

Silence.

Ken rose. "Okay, fine. I need someone to pray with me. Will you come, Cathy?"

Chapter 4

Cathy sucked in a quick breath. Must she pray with Ken? Would God be disappointed by her reluctance?

Paul rescued her. "I think it would be best if she didn't. This is between you and the Lord."

"Yeah, right. And a Merry Christmas to you too. Didn't want to watch the stupid movie anyway." Ken picked up his jacket and left.

Tim's knee began to jiggle again. He laid his hands flat on the table, then folded them in his lap. "Sorry I wrecked your party."

"It isn't a party, and you didn't wreck it." Sandy leaned against her husband's shoulder. "Paul, I'm sorry I blew up again. I can't tolerate that man no matter how much I pray about it. I hope you aren't hurt, Cathy. We know you and Ken are seeing each other."

Intensely aware of the man beside her, Cathy said, "Actually, we're just two Christians who sometimes stick together. Ken can be annoying. I thought I was the only person he irritated."

She felt Tim give a snort or laugh. "Hardly."

"Do you really have a tattoo?" Sandy asked.

"Guilty. I got it right after graduating from pilot training. Pilot's wings on my arm. Stupid, I know, but there's not a lot I can do about it now."

"We know that. Paul's brother got a tattoo when he was in the army, and he wishes it were only pilot's wings. Ken was just trying to make you look bad." Sandy grinned at Cathy. "You know what? He sounded jealous."

Cathy looked away, hoping Tim wouldn't follow Sandy's line of thought.

"Do we want to start the movie or just talk?" Paul glanced around for a reaction. "Here's your wassail, Tim." He pushed it across the table. "Want some cookies? Have a dozen. Please."

"I. . .uh. . .if you've got a minute, I need to talk." Tim's hands formed fists again.

"In private? We can go to my office."

Tim chewed his lip. "I want the ladies to hear. Maybe they can help."

Sandy nodded encouragement. "I'm listening. And, Tim, we all know how tough it is to be a baby Christian. We're on your side." She patted his clenched fist.

"Thanks." He glanced at Cathy. There was still a fleck of tissue on his chin and a red smear at the corner of his mouth. Jealousy and curiosity warred within her.

"I share a house with two other bachelors," he began.

"We used to throw wild parties every few months." Cathy saw his Adam's apple bob up and down. "I don't want to be part of things like that anymore, but Jason and Adrian think I'm going through a religious phase, and they're determined to cure me. Tonight was their big Christmas party. When I got home from work, a woman shoved me into a chair and sat in my lap."

He rested his elbows on the table and gripped his hair. "She kissed me, but I ran away, hopped in my car, and phoned you. Now what do I do?"

Cathy almost wished she had left with Ken. Almost.

Tim rubbed his eyes with both hands, rattling on as though he had forgotten his audience. "Most of the time when I'm at the house, I hide in my room to avoid seeing the garbage my roommates put on TV. I read my Bible or one of the books Paul loaned me. It's not much of a life. How can I witness to my friends that way?"

Paul cleared his throat. "Your story reminds me of Joseph versus Potiphar's wife."

"The Joseph in the Christmas story?"

"No, a Joseph long before the time of Christ. You might enjoy reading his story in the book of Genesis. When he was confronted by sexual temptation, Joseph's response was to run. You did the right thing tonight."

Sandy reached across to squeeze his arm. "God was with you, Tim. He always gives the strength to resist temptation when you depend on Him."

Cathy heard her own voice say, "I think you ought to

move out. Find a small flat or house of your own."

"It would be more expensive but worth the price," Paul observed. "Cathy's right. You can witness to your friends from a safer distance."

Tim nodded. "I'm deploying to Turkey in a few days, but I'll look for a place when I get back. I don't mind a drive if I can have privacy."

"Deploying to Turkey? But you just got home." When the Volkmans both looked at her, Cathy realized how distressed she sounded.

"The check pilot who was supposed to go is having health problems. I figured it would be better for me to go, anyway, since he has a wife and kids here and I have nobody."

"You've got lint stuck in your five-o'clock shadow," Sandy told him abruptly. "Right here." She leaned across the table but couldn't reach him. "You get it for him, Cathy."

"Whoever invented tissues should have foreseen how they would shred in a man's beard," he grumbled, turning toward Cathy.

"They're intended for your nose, not your chin," she said. "Now stop talking so I can get it off." Keeping her eyes on his mouth, Cathy managed to pick off the lint without bursting into hysterical giggles or otherwise disgracing herself. She used a napkin to remove the last trace of lipstick from the corner of his mouth. "There."

"Thank you." He gazed at her with those beautiful droopy eyes. No wonder that other woman had wanted to kiss him.

Tim suddenly leaned back in his chair, linked his fingers

behind his head, and stretched with a groan. "Sorry. We did BFM today, and I'm aching in every joint." Cathy heard ligaments creaking somewhere in his shoulders or elbows.

"BFM?" Sandy asked.

"Basic fighter maneuvers. Air-to-air combat." He turned to Cathy. "So tell me, Lieutenant, do you have family back in the States?"

"There are three girls and two boys in my family. I'm the oldest. My baby sister is eleven."

"Bet your parents are still married to each other."

"Yes."

"And they're Christians."

"Yes. They homeschooled me from third grade through high school. We're very close."

"Mine divorced long ago. Dad took me and Mom took my sister. I thought families like yours didn't exist anymore." Tim sounded envious. "You're blessed." He broke a Christmas tree cookie in half. "Of course, Paul and Sandy have that kind of family." He smiled at Sandy, who had been following the conversation with interest.

"I just had a brainstorm," Sandy announced. "Tim, would you be interested in helping with children's church? Cathy is a leader, but she needs a helper. Your job would be keeping the kids in line, maybe helping with a craft."

Cathy stared at her friend's flushed face. Was Sandy now attempting to match her with Tim?

Tim's reply sounded careful. "I would like to help out somewhere at church, but Lieutenant Guillard doesn't look thrilled with the idea."

"I do need a helper," she said. Her face grew warm again. "Don't feel obligated to help in children's church. I'm sure you could be useful almost anywhere."

"But I'm sure he would rather fill a real need," Sandy persisted. "Tim, why don't you observe children's church for a few weeks, then try helping Cathy? It couldn't hurt."

"I'll look into it when I get back from Incirlik. I'm willing to try."

"You'll be gone for Christmas and New Year's Day?" Fearless Sandy asked the question Cathy was thinking. "We planned to invite you over. Our girls will be disappointed."

"I'll be back in late February."

Forgetting to be shy, Cathy looked into Tim's eyes. "We'll miss you—at church and the squadron, I mean."

His expression revealed surprise and pleasure. "I hope so. I'll miss you too. Thanks for giving me a chance to help out. I'll try to be worthy of your trust."

She sensed a meaning to his words that involved more than children's church.

"Hey, if we're going to watch that movie tonight, we'd better get started," Paul said.

Paul and Sandy shared the sofa in their tiny living room. Cathy got the armchair, and Tim sprawled on the floor near her feet. "I've never seen this movie," he admitted.

"I like it, but I usually can't stay awake for the whole thing." Paul laid his head in Sandy's lap, and she began to rub his neck.

"I can see why," Tim remarked with a grin. "You've got it rough."

To Cathy's surprise, Tim seemed to enjoy the movie. He laughed at the jokes and followed the plot without interrupting like Ken usually did. When he pushed himself up to lean his shoulder against Cathy's chair, she observed that, even during an English winter, there were natural blond streaks in his thick hair. She subtly shifted her position until her leg brushed his sleeve. He moved his head around, trying to find a comfortable position against the chair's arm.

Paul and Sandy snored a musical duet from the sofa. Tim nudged Cathy and pointed. They shared a grin. His shoulder now pressed firmly against her knee.

Oddly enough, the movie's familiar scenes affected Cathy strongly, and she cried at the ending. Tim leaned forward to snatch a tissue from a box on the side table and held it up to her. "Want me to wipe your face this time?"

She smiled, shaking her head as she dabbed at her eyes. "You weren't supposed to notice my weepiness."

Leaning one arm on the edge of her chair seat, he studied her face, his smile gradually fading. "I wish I hadn't accepted this deployment."

"You'll miss the Christmas Eve service."

"This is the first time in my life I know enough to celebrate what Christmas is really about. Did your family do Christmas up big like this?" He indicated the Volkmans' tree and gifts.

"Always. We have a lot of fun traditions. I miss everybody

the most at this time of year. Last Christmas I was stationed at San Antonio, so I could fly home for the holidays."

"And this year you'll be here alone." Tim shook his head. "You'll forget all about me by February."

Cathy could hardly believe her ears. This must be a dream. Tim scrambled to his feet and stretched until his joints crackled. "Thirsty?"

She nodded and let him pull her up. Together they sneaked to the kitchen. Cathy poured herself a glass of water. Tim took more wassail. He swirled the juice in his cup and smiled.

"What are you thinking?" she asked.

"About the movie. Funny to think that a year ago I probably wouldn't have liked it. The things George Bailey was rich in are all the things I lack—family, friends, and respect. All the things that really matter in life." He set his cup on the counter and looked into Cathy's eyes. "God has a way of changing a man's perspective. From now on I have a new goal."

"It's the chance of a lifetime." A sepulchral voice spoke from the doorway.

Sandy giggled. "Paul, why'd you have to spoil the fun? Where's the mistletoe?"

"Watch it, Woman."

Tim smiled at their antics, but Cathy caught a flash of disappointment in his eyes. While driving home that night, she decided the interruption had possibly saved her from a broken heart.

❧

"Cathy, the phone's for you!" Erica shouted across the tiny flat.

Cathy spat out toothpaste and rinsed her mouth before running to take the receiver. "Is it my mom?" she whispered.

"Not unless your mom's voice changed."

Cathy recognized the caller's voice as soon as he spoke. "Merry Christmas to the Sugarplum Fairy."

"Merry Christmas to you too. Where are you?" With Erica listening, she dared not speak his name.

"Do you know who this is?"

"Yes. Did you have a nice Christmas?"

"Getting better by the minute. So if you know who I am, tell me where I am."

"Incirlik," she said with confidence. "Did you have a special church service today?"

"Last night they had a Christmas Eve service. I enjoyed it very much, except that it made me a little homesick."

"Homesick?"

"For our church there. Did you spend the day with the pastor's family?" He sounded decidedly lonely.

"I did. It was fun watching the girls open their gifts. It brought back memories. I'm expecting my parents to call tonight."

A pause. "Guess I'd better hang up so they can get through."

"Oh, no." Cathy panicked. "I'm sure they'll keep trying. Did you have anything special you wanted to talk to me about?"

"Talking about anything with you is special. To be honest, I tried to call earlier, but you were out. Did you get my

Christmas card? I sent a few this year for the first time ever."

"I did. Did you get my card before you left?"

"I brought it along. Thank you for thinking of me. I can tell you're busy, so I won't keep you. If you ever want to write or phone, you know how to contact me."

"Thank you for calling. Have a happy New Year too."

After Cathy hung up, she stared at the telephone. Now what was that all about?

Erica zeroed in. "That wasn't Ken. It sounded like Tim Falkirk. Am I right?"

Cathy nodded.

"You're gonna get hurt bad, Honey." Erica shook her head. "That guy has more lines than a fisherman, and he's expert at every one. I would guess he's giving you the homeless puppy routine, complete with mournful brown eyes and sob story about his sad childhood."

Cathy's heart turned to stone. "Have you ever dated him, Erica?"

"Some of my friends have. Wait a minute. I've got something to show you." She hurried to her bedroom and emerged with a packet of photos. "These are from a pool party I went to with a pilot a year ago last summer." She ruffled through them and pulled out three photos. All were group shots of five men in skimpy swimsuits, posing like would-be bodybuilders.

Cathy had no trouble picking out Tim's brilliant smile and deeply tanned torso, although the reckless look in his eyes was unfamiliar. She swallowed hard.

"Of course, they were all drunk as fish at the time," Erica said bluntly. "Tim tried to pick me up, even though he knew I came with Ian. He ended up taking some other woman home. He probably couldn't tell you her name. I don't want to be cruel, Cathy; I'm showing you these and telling you this for your own good. That man would ruin your life. He's probably laughing right this minute over how naïve you are, and he's planning to reel you in as soon as he gets back to England."

Before climbing into bed that night, Cathy pulled Tim's Christmas card out of her drawer and pondered its simple inscription.

"To the Sugarplum Fairy—thanks for the other night. 'No man is a failure who has friends.' Best wishes from your new brother in God's family, Tim Falkirk."

She snapped out her lamp and let hot tears burn her cheeks.

Chapter 5

Cathy regarded the full car park with a frown. There was never enough parking at the RAF Lakenheath Base Exchange. She'd been lucky to find an empty spot. Straightening her blue skirt, she hurried along the row of cars. A few airmen saluted her, and she saluted a colonel.

"Lieutenant Guillard!" Shading her eyes against afternoon sunlight, she peered toward the speaker, who approached at a jog between parked vehicles.

"Captain Falkirk." Cathy snapped a smart salute. His eyes widened before he returned it.

"That doesn't seem right," he said as soon as her arm returned to her side.

"Why not? You're my superior officer." Regulations did have their protective value. At any rate, her embarrassing crush was a thing of the past, conquered entirely. Tim Falkirk's all-too-obvious attractions no longer held her in thrall.

"I have trouble thinking of you as an officer. Call it chauvinistic if you like; I can't help feeling that way. You're an attractive woman, not just a lieutenant."

"Thank you, Sir. Did you have something to tell me?" Avoiding eye contact helped her remain calm, but it couldn't block the effect of his voice.

"Yes. I was in children's church yesterday while the Swensons taught. I've hardly seen you since I got back from Turkey. It's been three weeks. Hope you're not avoiding me. Your roommate gave me your message, and I honored your request." The statement resembled a question.

"What did you think of children's church?" Then his last sentence sank in. "What message?"

"I see why you need help keeping order. Some of those kids run wild."

"This coming Sunday is my week to teach," she said, watching a car drive past. "I don't remember leaving you any message. Did you telephone me about children's church?"

"No, I rang you from Turkey on New Year's Day and another time. Your roommate—I don't know her name—said you didn't want me to call anymore."

"I didn't know you called." Cathy heard her voice quiver. "And I never gave any such message. How dare she!"

He cleared his throat. "Then would you join me for lunch after church?"

"A group of us singles planned to head to the Officers' Club for the Sunday brunch."

"I wanted to take you to the Riverside, but if you think it best to be among friends, I understand."

"I've heard about the Riverside Inn." Cathy's voice

squeaked. "Isn't that the place where they have live piano music in the dining room? It sounds really nice."

"Then you'll join me? Great. Are you heading inside right now? I just got my hair cut."

"I need to pick up a few things in the BX." She lifted her gaze as high as the red scarf tucked around his neck.

"Do you have time for ice cream?"

"Ice cream? In March?"

"Ice cream knows no season. It's warm inside the mall. Please?"

"All right." It wasn't as if she'd made a commitment to any other man, after all.

Seated at a table in the nearly empty ice cream shop, Cathy watched shoppers emerge from the BX. "Thank you. I didn't expect you to treat me." A pink drip landed on the table. She turned her cone and licked the melting side.

"You're welcome. I didn't expect you to join me. We're both pleasantly surprised." He wiped chocolate from his face with a napkin. Hope flooded Cathy's heart as she observed his boyishly handsome face. Arched eyebrows gave his deep-set eyes that mournful look, and gold-tipped lashes matched the blond streaks in his short hair. Bits of freshly cut hair adhered to his pink ears and his collar.

He was a believer now—not the same shameless man who had displayed his body in a scanty swimsuit, drank until he was unaware of his own rash behavior, and pursued women like a panting dog. At work he was austere and efficient, but in private he seemed vulnerable and lonely. Was this the real

Tim Falkirk, or did he put on a different act for every woman, like Erica said?

He met her gaze and grinned so joyfully that she couldn't help smiling back. "I'll be asking for an intel officer tomorrow—"

"Tim! You're back!" A woman with a British accent grabbed him by the shoulders in a quick hug from behind. His eyes went wide, and the smile vanished. "I haven't seen you in ages," she gushed on. "Someone told me you did two TDYs at Incirlik back-to-back. That's criminal. The women of England must rise up in protest." She gave Cathy an assessing glance and returned her attention to Tim. "Sorry if I interrupted business. Ring me sometime, Gorgeous." She patted his chest and rejoined a group of giggling companions.

Tim sat frozen while his ice cream melted. He looked mortified.

Cathy's emotions and thoughts spun wild. Although it was painful to be reminded that other women reacted to Tim's potent charm just as violently as she did, the warning had come at exactly the right moment and in the form most calculated to capture her attention. Tim Falkirk belonged with voluptuous redheads wearing form-fitting sweaters and miniskirts. She, Lieutenant Guillard, was "business"—not pleasure.

"You were saying?" she prompted.

He dropped the last of his cone into the bin beside their table, brushed off his hands, and cleared his throat. "We've got another air-to-air training flight in Scotland. I hope they send you over. You're competent and concise—two qualities one seldom sees nowadays."

"Thank you, Sir."

"You're also professional, one quality I often have trouble appreciating." His voice was quiet. "While we're away from work, may I call you Cathy? It would sound awkward to address you as Lieutenant Guillard at church."

"You may."

"And please call me Tim."

"I will." Curiosity finally won out. "Was that woman your girlfriend? She's stunning with that long red hair." *Even if it is dyed.*

"I think I met her at the Mildenhall O' Club sometime last year. She's a secretary at the Ministry of Defense."

"She seems to know you well. One of the pilots in the 493rd is married to an Englishwoman. It must be interesting to blend cultures into one family. What's her name?"

"I don't remember. You've got ice cream on your face." Without asking permission, he wiped her cheek with a napkin. "Such a pretty face."

Cathy jerked away. "Don't flirt with me, Tim."

"I'm not flirting." He sounded strained.

She rolled her eyes. "Maybe you don't realize when you're flirting; it comes so naturally to you. But a girl could start taking you seriously, and that would be trouble."

"You're saying 'hands off.' "

"It is the only way we can work together."

He studied her face. "Have I done something in particular

to offend you, or do you just dislike me in general?"

"I don't dislike you."

"You don't respect me."

"Your reputation as a pilot and officer is sterling—everyone respects your honesty and ability. However, a few months from now I wouldn't be surprised if you have no idea who I am."

His ears turned red. "Touché." Laying his hands flat on the table, he stared at them, frowning. "I found a new house. Some men from church will help me move this Saturday."

"That's wonderful! Isn't it good to be part of the church family?" She tried to sound cheery but felt stiff.

He blinked. "Sure."

Cathy's cone joined his in the bin. Rising, she wiped her shaking fingers with a napkin. "Thank you for the treat. It sounds as if I'll be seeing you tomorrow for a briefing. You want me to come up with an enemy threat?"

"Fine."

Tim looked so hurt that she sat back down. "What's wrong?"

He rubbed the bridge of his nose with two fingers and shook his head. "Better get to your shopping."

"Want to come along? I'm just picking up a few things." She would pick up pantyhose another time. The last thing she needed was to wander through the lingerie department with Tim Falkirk.

He gave a tight smile. "No, I won't annoy you any further today. If I head home now, I'll have time to run a few miles before it gets dark. Thanks for your time, Lieutenant Guillard." He hauled on his jacket and left her alone at the table. Cathy watched female heads turn as he passed.

❧

"Anything else you need unpacked?" Joe Hughes, a new member of the singles' group, stuck his head through the front doorway to inquire.

Tim turned around, still unwrapping his toaster. "I can handle the rest. Thanks for your help. Sure you won't stay for pizza?"

"Thanks, but I've got plans for the evening. Hope you like your new place." He waved. "Bye, Pastor."

"See you tomorrow," Paul said. "Hey, Joe, you're taking Cathy out tonight?"

Joe's dimples showed when he grinned. "There's a good movie playing on base for once."

"Have fun."

"We will. Great to meet you, Tim." Joe ducked back outside.

"Yeah. Thanks again." Tim plugged the toaster into his transformer, feeling Paul's gaze on his back.

"You've seemed depressed all day." Pastor Paul flopped into a swivel computer chair, rested his elbow on the table, and propped both feet on top of a cardboard box. "I've got time to talk before Sandy expects me home."

"It was nice of everyone to help out. I've never met some of them before today, yet they came to help me move."

"They're your church family, Tim. If you can manage to

stay in this country long enough, I'm sure you'll become a valued member of the singles' group. They're good people. Even Ken Lofty is improving since he started dating Erica Carter. She keeps him humble."

"I noticed that today. You know, he apologized to me for the Christmas party mess. Hope we can start over. I talked some with Erica too. She rooms with Cathy Guillard." He tried to sound casual. "Want a cup of coffee? It's instant."

"Fine. I'm frozen to the bone, but at least it didn't rain today."

Tim poured hot water into two mugs, then plopped several tea biscuits on a paper plate and shoved them across the table. "Milk? Sugar?"

"Black is fine." Paul accepted his coffee and studied Tim through the steam. "Cathy's been seeing Joe Hughes lately, but I guess you know that."

"I found out today." Tim didn't trust himself to say more.

"Sandy and I noticed the sparks between you and Cathy at Christmas. Your extended absence must have doused the flames. On Cathy's side, anyway."

Tim kicked an empty packing box across the small room. After a long silence, he gave Paul another glimpse of his inner turmoil. "I agreed to help Cathy teach children's church, and I've been looking forward to spending time with her away from work. Now I don't know. She cringes if I so much as touch her face or hand, and she looks at me as if I'm deformed. Since I got back, I've hardly seen her. Guess she's been busy with Joe."

Paul sipped his coffee. "I'm a poor counselor when it comes to women, Tim. If you're seriously interested in Cathy, my best advice would be to join her group of friends. Let them all see how the Lord has changed you. I can't make any guarantees, but the recommended therapy will be good for you no matter what happens between you and Cathy. Do you see her much at work?"

"Some. That's almost worse than not seeing her at all. She calls me 'Sir' and salutes."

"Isn't that what she's supposed to do?" Paul grinned. "She does intelligence work, right?"

"Yes, and she knows her stuff. She gave us a great flight plan the other day, up through Loch Linnhe. We ran into a pair of British Tornadoes on the way north."

"Did you practice fighting them?" Paul leaned forward.

"It wasn't much of a fight." Tim's eyes gleamed. Using first teaspoons, then his hands, to illustrate the engagement of jets, he explained exactly how the two-ship of Strike Eagles had annihilated the "enemy" planes. "They were dead before they even spotted us on radar, but we killed them again just to make things seem fair." Talking about flying seemed to lighten the load on his heart.

When Paul rose to head home, he carried his empty mug to the tiny sink. "This place could use a woman's touch. Sandy would be pleased to recruit Cathy's help and fix up your new home. Want me to give her the idea?"

"I doubt Cathy would be caught dead within a mile of my place. She would think I had ulterior motives."

"Don't altogether give up hope yet. Do your best with the children tomorrow; pray for patience, wisdom, and unselfish love; and you never know. Good night, Tim, and God bless."

As Tim closed his front door, he closed his eyes and immediately put Paul's advice into action, adding one significant request. *And, Lord, please let Cathy look at me again the way she did at Christmas.*

❧

Sunday morning passed quickly. Cathy told the Bible story using flannelgraph figures. Tim packed potting soil into disposable cups while Cathy counted out pinto beans. Each child took home a decorated cup with instructions for raising a bean plant. "They're easy to grow," Cathy explained afterward when asked why she chose beans.

Tim swept dirt from the tile floor. "I enjoyed hearing the Bible story and seeing those pictures you stuck on the board. There's so much in the Bible that's new to me. I've read through the Gospels, but that story about the seeds and the soil sounded different when you read it today. It made me think."

"I've been a believer for years, and I learn something new every time I read or hear Scripture. I think God teaches us new lessons from old stories as we grow and mature." She gathered up papers. "Uh-oh. Brianna left her Sunday school handout. I'll give it to her mother."

Cathy prepared to hand off the curriculum to next week's teaching team, gathered her sack of supplies, and scanned the room for anything forgotten while Tim closed and locked the back door. Then she picked up her handbag and followed him into the foyer, where she quickly found Brianna's mother and gave her the Sunday school paper.

An arm slipped around her shoulders, and Joe Hughes spoke into her ear. "Come on, Cathy. The o' club stops serving brunch at one, you know."

Cathy turned her head and nearly bumped noses with him. "But, Joe. . ." Startled by his warm breath on her mouth, she stopped.

He smiled slowly, revealing his deep dimples. "Another time and place, Honey. You're embarrassing me."

Cathy took a quick step back and cast a glance toward Tim, stunned to find him at her side.

"You want to come along, Tim? We singles have a standing date at the o' club for Sunday brunch. You're welcome to join our group." Joe, flight surgeon for a different squadron, seemed unconcerned by Tim's presence.

Cathy could not read Tim's expression. "I had plans," he said, "but maybe I'll have to change them. May I carry that sack for you, Cathy?"

"Thank you." She stepped out of Joe's casual embrace to hand it over. Was Tim really going to back out of their Riverside Inn luncheon date? He followed her to her little car, waited while she opened the door, and placed her sack on the passenger seat. Joe and the other singles chatted and laughed nearby as they packed into cars, sharing rides.

"You coming, Cath?" Joe called from his car. "I've got two open seats. Tim, come on with us."

Cathy thought fast. "We need to discuss children's church, so I'll ride with Tim this time. Thanks. See you later."

Joe looked surprised. "Okay. Are you coming to the o' club?"

"I don't know for sure. You go on without us."

Joe's pleasant expression never wavered. "Got it. See ya." With a little farewell salute, he climbed into his car.

Cathy met Tim's inquisitive gaze and asked, "Did you want to change our plans and join the others? I won't be offended."

"Exactly how serious are you and Joe? I don't want to cut in on his territory. I know you've been seeing him steadily."

"A few dates here and there do not necessarily indicate serious intentions."

"Look, Cathy, I'm not playing around here. I would like to get to know you myself but not at Joe's expense." He looked larger with his arms crossed. A fisherman's knit sweater added breadth to his shoulders, and faded blue jeans delineated his long legs.

Fear of losing something she hadn't dared to contemplate nearly choked her. She didn't want to get hurt, but what if Tim was genuinely interested? The idea seemed ludicrous. . . yet there was that certain look in his eye. . . .

"I see Joe mostly at singles' outings. Last night was the only time we've gone anywhere just the two of us, and that was to a PG movie. It wasn't even very good. Joe has asked out a few other girls besides me lately. It's not as serious as people seem to think."

Tim lifted one brow.

"I bumped noses with him on accident just now. I didn't expect him to be so close when I turned around. He even joked about it."

"I heard him."

Cathy couldn't recall exactly what Joe had said, but Tim's expression shouted jealousy. Her heart nearly exploded with excitement. "I don't go around kissing men, I hope you know. I mean, to me a kiss is for the one special man I plan to marry. I don't kiss casually." She knew she was babbling but couldn't seem to shut off the flow of words.

"I didn't imagine you did."

"Do you still want to take me to the Riverside?"

"If we take my car, you could pick up yours after the evening service."

Cathy smiled with her whole being. "All right."

During the drive into the village of Mildenhall, they discussed tourist sites. "I think I've seen more of Europe than I've seen of England," Tim confessed. "I took a ski trip to Switzerland a year ago and toured Germany and Austria last summer. I need to see some local sights."

Cathy tried not to wonder about his skiing companions, but he must have read her mind. "I traveled with Jason, Adrian, Adrian's girlfriend, and two of her friends. English-women. I wasn't a Christian then, you know."

"I know." Although Cathy knew better than to expect a godly lifestyle from a non-Christian, she still suffered pangs. "Do you have plans to travel this summer?"

"No. Have you done much touring?"

"I haven't had time for more than a few day trips to castles. My roommate, Erica, wants to set up a tour of Scotland for the church singles' group this summer. I've always wanted to see Loch Ness."

Tim pulled into the car park through a stone archway. "I wouldn't mind seeing the loch from ground level. I've flown over it many times."

"I'll tell Erica you're interested. Our group takes lots of day trips together. In June we're going to visit the Tower of London and Buckingham Palace. Would you like to come?"

"I'd be interested."

The hostess led them to a small window table overlooking the river. Tim held Cathy's chair, then settled across from her. Cathy delighted in the spray of fresh flowers on the table, a scented candle, and delicate china teacups. Romantic piano music rippled across the dining room.

"This is lovely!" she exclaimed.

Outside, daffodils bloomed beneath winter-bare trees, and willows swayed in a spring breeze. A rabbit crouched on the sweeping lawn, stuffing itself with lush grass. Puffy clouds hastened across the sky. One moment it was sunny, then it was gray, then the sun shone out again.

After the waitress took their order, Tim leaned back in his chair and rested his arm across the small table. "Talk to me, Cathy. Tell me about yourself."

"What do you want to know?"

She watched his brown eyes flicker as they studied her face. "Why are you in the air force? What do you believe

God has planned for your life? What are your goals, your dreams?"

Cathy blinked. "I'm in the air force because I didn't know what else to do after I finished college. I had a double major in humanities and geography—fascinating subjects, but not big moneymakers. I have always wanted to travel and meet new people, so the military seemed ideal for me. I applied for officer training school, and here I am."

"And now?"

He had caught the hint of irony in her voice. "It isn't what I expected. I'm not sure exactly what I did expect, but not this."

"This?"

"It's so. . .so harsh and stressful. I enjoy parts of my job, but I hate giving briefings to men who respect me neither as a woman nor as an officer. You've heard them. I thought the military would be an opportunity to reach people for the Lord—you know, to be a living witness. But nobody pays any attention."

"I do."

Cathy studied his sober face. "But you're already a believer."

"Baby Christians need good examples to follow. I admire you tremendously."

"You probably think I'm a Goody Two-shoes, just like everyone else here does." A bitter note she hadn't intended crept into her voice.

"I think you're one of the few believers I've met who is

consistent. Faithfulness like yours must please God. I know you don't tell me everything you think, Cathy, and I can't always read your expressions, but I trust you to tell me the truth."

"Thank you." She rotated her water glass.

Their food arrived. Tim entertained her with flying stories and asked questions about her childhood and family. Cathy began to relax in his presence. She couldn't help wondering if he had always been so polite and considerate. Recalling his arrogant face in Erica's photos, she doubted it.

"Do you like to walk?" he asked.

"What did you have in mind?"

"Would you like to take a stroll around Beck Row Common this afternoon?"

"Very much. I'm even wearing sensible shoes."

Tim paid the bill, and they headed toward the entryway. "Tim! Tim darling, I haven't seen you in ages!" A tall, slender woman approached them, hands outstretched in greeting. She was beautiful in an exotic fashion, her dark curls cascading over nearly bare shoulders.

Tim stiffly shook her hand. "Nice to see you, Marguerite."

The woman's amber gaze shifted to Cathy's face, regarding her as a lower life-form. "Your sister?"

"Cathy, meet Marguerite. We are just leaving. So good to see you again." When the woman showed signs of reaching for him, he turned sharply away. Linking arms with Cathy, he ushered her outside.

As soon as the door closed behind them, she heard him

release a shuddering breath. "I never did like that woman. She's a leech."

"A beautiful leech," Cathy remarked.

"She can't compare with you."

Still clutching his arm, Cathy smiled. "You're sweet to say so, but I'm not in her league. Ready to walk?"

"You're right: She's bush league; you're World-Series class. Ready to walk."

Chapter 6

"Keep the line moving," guards reminded tourists who paused to stare at glittering crowns and scepters.

Cathy savored Tim's presence at her back. Feeling her way along the velvet ropes, she followed Erica's slender form around the dark vault. Light from within the jewel cases twinkled in Tim's eyes each time Cathy looked at him.

"I can hardly believe those rubies and diamonds are real," she said.

"Believe it, Sweetheart. They wouldn't keep watch like this over glass," Tim spoke into her ear. Heat trickled down her neck and caused havoc within her nervous system.

Erica stopped. Cathy nearly collided with her friend. Tim's warm hand cupped her elbow, steadying her. For an instant Cathy leaned back against his chest.

"Keep moving!" the guard prodded, stepping forward to enforce his command. The line resumed its steady progress.

"And I thought my sister's engagement ring had a big stone! It's microscopic compared to these." Patti and Todd, two other members of the singles' group, were right behind them, marveling over the royal treasure.

Outside, shivering in a misty breeze, the group decided on their next move. "I want to see the torture chamber," Marie said.

"We know," Todd groaned.

"It's not like this is the first time you've mentioned it," Lexa said, shaking her auburn mane.

Erica gripped Ken Lofty's arm. "I'll visit the torture chamber only if I've got someone to hang on to."

Ken grinned down at Cathy's roommate. "Guess I'm elected." He covered her hand with his. Cathy thought they resembled a pair of movie stars, too beautiful to be real.

She glanced up at Tim and found him watching her again. "What do you want to do?" she asked.

"You don't want to see the torture chamber," he said.

Her face scrunched into a pained grin. "Not particularly. Things like that keep me awake at night."

"Then let's go to the armory."

Everyone else opted for the dungeons. Promising to meet the group at an appointed time and place, Tim and Cathy headed for the armory.

"My mind boggles when I try to remember England's kings," Cathy said as they strolled amid displays of weaponry and armor. "I remember Henry VIII and William the Conqueror, but those two are about the only ones I can keep straight."

"It helps if you read books about the kings," Tim said,

pausing before one case to take a closer look. "The engraving on this armor is amazing! Think of the work involved—these suits are individual works of art."

"The men were short," Cathy observed, comparing Tim's height with the suit.

"Yes, but they were immensely strong."

"Their horses were stronger."

He grinned. "True."

"Tim, are you enjoying today?" She laid her hand on his arm. His gaze rested upon it.

"England's history is fascinating."

"Have you been to the Tower of London before?"

"Once." He met her gaze.

"Then this isn't new to you."

"Don't look sad, Cathy. The first time I came, my companion lacked interest in anything historical. I had to rush through the crown jewels and the torture chamber, then hurry to a pub. I'm having a far better time today."

She studied his face. "I wish I knew what you're really thinking."

His brows lifted. "Do you?"

Her face warmed, but she did not look away.

His lips tightened. Taking her hand, he tucked it beneath his arm and strolled on, using his huge umbrella like a cane. "Think we could ditch the rest of the group?"

"You want to?"

"Guess that would be rude." His elbow squeezed her hand against his side.

Rain and rushing feet pounded on the pavement outside. Bubbled glass windows filtered the afternoon light, enhancing the pub's Old World atmosphere, but a televised golf match spoiled the ambience. Patrons perched on stools, leaning their elbows on the bar, and commented on the play while imbibing pints of golden ale.

Lexa and Marie rested their elbows atop a gnarled oak table, equally absorbed in Tim. Cathy watched her friends compete for his attention.

Lexa spoke around a mouthful of steak and kidney pie. "How's children's church been going? You two led it again last week, didn't you?" Her bright eyes shifted from Cathy to Tim and back. "I hear the kids like Tim a lot."

"They love him," Cathy said. "We work well as a team. Each month it gets better. Did you know that Tim and Joe are coaching a children's baseball team this summer? Two of our church kids are on their team."

"I would love to watch one of your games," Marie said, peeking up at Tim from beneath her lashes.

Cathy's fist clenched beneath the table. How would Marie look with shepherd's pie dripping from her dainty chin?

"Maybe you could sit with Cathy sometime," Tim said before taking another bite of Yorkshire pudding. "She comes to all our games." His left hand covered Cathy's fist and squeezed. "Did you and Cathy meet at church?"

"We met in Sunday school," Marie said. "Ken introduced

us. Speaking of Ken, it looks like Erica and Ken have something going. Hope you don't mind, Cathy. First Ken dropped you, and now Dr. Joe is dating a nurse. Don't tell anyone, though—it's a secret."

Her pitying tone swelled Cathy's chest with anger. Tim squeezed her hand again.

Deflating, she smiled. "Erica has always admired Ken. I think they suit each other well. Ken and Joe were never more than my casual friends."

Lexa licked gravy from her finger, eyes on Tim's face. "These pilots are hard to tie down. Look at Tim; he's not the marrying kind."

"On the contrary. Just waiting for the right girl to accept me." Tim dropped his napkin over the remains of his meal and leaned against the wooden booth's high back. One arm slid around Cathy's waist, and he pulled her close. Instead of pushing away, she rested her head on his shoulder.

Lexa and Marie exchanged glances. Their flirtation ceased.

❧

"Sleep well, Cathy. I'll see you at Sunday school, bright and early." Tim waited on the top step while Cathy fumbled for her house key. Her purse had never before seemed so jumbled.

"I enjoyed today, Tim. Thank you so much." One hand still lost in her purse, she looked up.

He stood with his hands jammed in his jacket pockets, feet squared. "Can't find your key?"

"It's here somewhere. Erica should be home any moment. Ken is giving her a ride."

"Good. Hope he's given up on you."

"He has. He and Erica still occasionally warn me about you, but most people now accept that your about-face in life is for real. It was always more sour grapes with Ken than anything else. He's so handsome; he's not used to having a woman scorn his attentions once he deigns to bestow them."

"You think he's handsome," he said.

"Almost too handsome."

"What about me?"

"Fishing for compliments, are we?" she asked with a smirk.

"Only way I'll catch any. Just wondered whether my looks are a handicap or a help."

"That depends upon your goal."

"Marriage. Do you find me attractive, Cathy?"

She dared not take him seriously. "As if you don't know. I'm the one with the freckles, not you."

"I adore your freckles."

"Nobody adores freckles. Endure, maybe, but not adore."

"Then I'm nobody." His finger slid down her nose and across one cheek.

Cathy's searching fingers located the key. "Here, let me." Tim took the key from her and opened the door. His arm blocked her entrance. "Yes or no?"

Instead of irritating her, his teasing intensified Cathy's desire to be kissed. "What was the question?"

In slow motion, he grasped her hand and laid it against his heart. Through the soft suede of his jacket she felt the steady beat. "Does your heart race like this when I touch you?"

She could only stare. When Tim's hand cupped her cheek, she leaned into his touch and closed her eyes, almost frightened at the intensity of her body's response. "Good night, Cathy," he whispered against her ear. His lips brushed her cheek.

Cathy watched him stride down the walkway, his shoulders squared. Her fingers lifted to her cheek. "Good night, Tim."

The telephone was ringing as she entered her flat. She caught it on the fourth ring and dropped over the arm of a plump chair, sprawling on its seat with her legs in the air. "Mom, I'm so glad you called! Remember the wonderful man I told you about? Tim. Yes, that's the one. I think I'm in love. Now please don't worry; I won't rush into anything."

Chapter 7

Y ou'll be here for our debrief, right? We should be back around two o'clock." Tim held Cathy's gaze and saw color rise in her cheeks. Could she read love in his eyes?

Jason and Adrian left the briefing room, still discussing the flight plan: a bombing run in Scotland with a bonus side trip over Loch Ness. Tim would pilot the trailing jet with Jason in his backseat. Ken Lofty would pilot the lead jet; Adrian was his wizzo.

"Have you signed up for the Scotland trip yet, Cathy?" Ken asked from the doorway. "There are ten of us going so far. Erica says you're undecided. We wish you'd join us. You too, Tim, if you're interested. August should be a great time to see the country."

Tim lifted a questioning brow at Cathy. "I'll go if Cathy goes."

Blushing even more deeply, Cathy scooped up her notebooks and moved around the table. "Hadn't you two better get out to the flight line?"

Tim followed her to the door. Although they were in uniform and in the squadron, he reached out to touch her soft cheek. "Miss me."

"Fly careful. I'll be here when you get back."

"If you're not, I'll come looking." Hoisting his flight bag under one arm, he winked and grinned.

❧

Their bombing mission completed, the pair of jets headed northeast through the Scottish Highlands. Sight-seeing in a Strike Eagle required quick eyes.

"Hey, I stayed in a cabin over there last summer," Adrian blurted over the auxiliary radio as they flashed above Loch Ness. Steep ridges lined the deep, narrow loch. The water below appeared almost black. The jets roared over a tourist boat, giving the "Nessie" watchers aboard a thrill. Tim rocked his wings to return their waves.

"There's Urquhart Castle," Tim said. The ancient ruin beside Loch Ness always sparked his interest. "Hey, Lofty, maybe soon we'll see this from ground level."

"Definitely!" Ken replied.

Just as they passed the castle, Tim saw little black dots ahead. His heart stopped. "Birds!" He hauled back on the stick and felt a thump. The jet shuddered. *Wha-boom!* A spectacular fireball blew forward out the right engine intake past the cockpit.

Tim leveled his wings and climbed slowly, pulling throttles back on both engines. Jason jabbered something incoherent over the radio, sounding as terrified as Tim felt.

"Badger two-two. Knock it off. Bird strike!" Tim told Ken and Adrian through clenched teeth, breathing hard.

In its calm female voice, the airplane said, "Warning, engine fire right. Warning, engine fire right." Up by his left TV display, Tim saw a glowing red button. Adrenaline pumped through his body. His stomach plummeted ten thousand feet.

❧

At noon Cathy packed away her books and maps and headed for the donut shop. A minivan pulled up beside her in the car park. "Cathy?"

Still climbing out of her car, Cathy looked up. "Sandy! Hi! Are you here for lunch?"

"Yes. I just dropped Hannah and April off at their friend's house. Melanie and I needed a treat. Are you here for lunch?" Sandy slid open the van's side door and unbuckled Melanie's car seat.

"Your company will be a treat for me. We've hardly talked lately."

Sandy closed the door, grabbed Melanie's hand, and grinned. "Your time has been otherwise occupied this summer. Are things as serious as they look between you and Tim Falkirk?"

Cathy took Melanie's other hand and helped her hop up the steps. "How serious do they look?"

"Wedding bells, maybe? Wait—let's talk about this over lunch. I can't listen properly while I'm walking."

Melanie was almost too large for the high chair, but she didn't protest when Sandy slid her into it. "This keeps her in one place. Here's your roll, Sweetie. Mama will share her soup." Sandy looked up. "It's just about nap time. She's sleepy."

The little girl nibbled at her roll. Her eyes struggled to remain open.

"Now, tell me all about you and Tim."

❧

Slow down, Tim. Think it through. Gotta do the memory items. Gotta do this perfect. He deliberately pulled the right throttle to idle, making sure the left engine still provided thrust. These first few seconds were crucial. *Okay, I'm doing the right thing. We're gonna live through this. Gotta get the engine to cut off.*

Ken called sharply over the radio, "Badger two-two status!"

In desperate haste, Tim and Jason jabbered orders back and forth over their internal radio. Too busy to discuss his problems, Tim snapped at Ken, "Stand by."

"Badger two-two, you've got the lead. Two-one is visual." Ken and Adrian would now follow Tim's lead, giving Tim and Jason room to do whatever they might need to do.

"Push the fire light!" Jason said, his voice nearly an octave higher than usual.

Tim repeated back, "Pushing the right fire light."

Going through his emergency procedure list, Jason barked, "Fire exten—estinguisher discharge." Frantic, scrambled thoughts made both men stutter and mispronounce words.

"H—hang on a second. Let the engine shut down."

Jason swore, threatening to climb over the seat and discharge it himself, but Tim waited. "Okay, discharging fire extinguisher."

Only heavy breathing sounded on the radio for a few seconds, then Tim said, "Climbing to five thousand and slowing to 250 knots. Jason, give me steering to Lossiemouth."

"It's near Inverness, right?" Jason fumbled for the correct book of maps and charts, looking for the Royal Air Force fighter base.

Tim snapped over the auxiliary radio, "Badger two-one, go chase. Look for signs of fire."

Ken's crisp acknowledgment, "Two," meaning number two jet in the formation, sounded like "toop" over the radio. He swung in behind the damaged plane.

Heart still pounding, Tim confirmed to Jason, "I'm seeing the fire light out." His wizzo said nothing, though Tim heard him panting. "I'm gonna test the fire light," Tim continued. Had it gone out because the fire was out or because the electrical circuit had failed? He moved the discharge switch to its test position. All fire lights should come on.

They did.

Tim gulped, sending up a quick prayer of thanksgiving. "Badger two-one flight, push three-two-two point one." Now that the immediate problem had been dealt with, Tim ordered his wingman to the Lossiemouth radio frequency. "Badger two-one flight, check."

"Toop." Ken heard and complied.

Tim called over the radio, "Lossiemouth, Badger two-

two, a flight of two F-15s, and we got an emergency."

❦

Cathy stirred her soup and watched steam rise. "At this point we are friends, Sandy."

"Is that what you want, or is that what he wants?"

"I'm not sure what he wants. I know he cares for me. He looks at me tenderly, and he treats me as if I mean everything to him. Sometimes he mentions marriage but only in passing."

Sandy swallowed a bite before asking, "Have you let him know how much you care? He might be afraid you'll drop him if he starts acting romantic. You were suspicious of him at first."

"You knew?"

Sandy smiled. "It was written all over you, Cathy. But what about now? Could you marry Tim in spite of his wild past?"

❦

"Badger two-two, Lossiemouth. Go ahead." The air traffic controller's voice held a Scots burr.

"Lossiemouth, Badger two-two. I am an F-15 just south of Inverness. We've had an engine fire, and we're heading toward Lossiemouth for a full stop landing at this time."

"Badger two-two, Lossiemouth, radar contact. Climb and maintain flight level four-zero, steer zero-three-zero, vectors runway two-three."

"Roger."

In the backseat, Jason ran through checklists, pulled out the emergency approach book, and programmed the airplane's computer to provide steering to Lossiemouth.

Lossiemouth continued, "When able, say number of souls on board, fuel remaining, and type ordnance."

Tim answered, "Badger two-two has two souls, an hour of fuel, and small practice bombs."

"Copy all. When able, say nature of emergency. Understand engine fire?" They hadn't understood his garbled explanation.

"Lossie, Badger two-two, stand by." Tim wanted vectors to the runway but was still too busy with the airplane to talk. His master caution light blinked on again, and his emergency light panel glowed like the Las Vegas skyline.

Jason said, "Getting master cautions showing uh—uh—hydraulics and e—electrics."

Tim assured him with more confidence than he felt. "It's standard stuff from shutting number two engine down."

Jason's voice cracked frequently. "I got steering for Lossiemouth in, and I got an approach plate for Lossie if you want. I can hand it to you."

"Okay, on the right side." Tim reached over his right shoulder for the map book. Jason's hands were shaking so hard that the book's pages fluttered.

The Lossiemouth controller nagged them again. "Badger two-two, Lossiemouth. Will you require an approach and arrestor cable?"

Tim answered shortly. "Lossie, Badger two-two. Negative cables this time. Planning to land straight ahead on runway, shut down on runway, then egress the airplane."

❧

Cathy sipped her soup and winced at its heat. "I'm not sure if I could marry Tim, Sandy. More than once while we've been out together a woman has approached him—one of his old flames. It makes him uncomfortable, and I feel sorry for him, yet there is anger and jealousy in me too. I want to scratch and kick—and I waver between feeling protective of him and wanting to hurt him back."

Sandy nodded, buttering her second roll. "It was like that for me too, except that my life was about as wild as Paul's before we became Christians. He had as much to forgive as I did."

Cathy blinked. "I can't imagine you being wild, Sandy."

"Good. But I was."

Melanie dozed with her head on her own shoulder. Sandy rolled up her cardigan and eased it under her daughter's head. "Cathy, it comes down to the fact that we are all sinners saved by the grace of God through faith in Jesus. Without Jesus, you would be as lost as anyone else. And without Him—who knows?—you might be as immoral as the next modern woman."

Cathy pondered her friend's words. "I'm glad I don't have a past to forget. But I can't help thinking that a man like Tim must find me childish and ignorant. I'm not beautiful like those other women he knows, and I've never even kissed a man. Not a real kiss."

Sandy looked wistful. "Be thankful—you have a wonderful gift to give your husband someday. You know what? Tim appreciates your purity more than many men would. He's never known a woman like you before. Not in all his life."

❧

Tim repeated, "Lossie, Badger two-two. Had an engine fire. It appears to be out at this time, but we're gonna need to egress the airplane after we land."

"Right, Badger two-two. Lossie copies all. Emergency vehicles have been notified and are standing by."

The other Strike Eagle slid into a trail position behind them. Tim called, "Badger two-one, two-two aux. You guys seeing any fire indications?"

Ken's voice reassured him. "Negative. We see scorch marks behind your right main gear, but no fire. We see smoke or fluids, can't tell which, coming out of number two engine."

Jason answered for his overtasked pilot: "Badger two-two copies."

"Badger two-two, you guys gonna dump any gas?" A helpful reminder. Ken and Adrian could think clearly since they were not fearing for their lives.

"Thanks." Tim reached down to the fuel dump switch in front of the throttles and flipped it up to "dump." They had just flown over Culloden Battlefield east of the Inverness airfield, and now headed out over Moray Firth.

"Lossie, Badger two-two request," Tim spoke to the ground controller again.

"Go ahead with request."

"Badger two-two has a wingman, call sign Badger two-one, who will need climb-out instructions for RTB to

Lakenheath following Badger two-two's landing."

"Understood. Stand by for climb-out instructions." Thirty seconds later: "Badger two-two; we have the climb-out instructions for Badger two-one when you're ready to copy."

"Badger two-two, go ahead."

"Badger two-one, following missed approach, maintain runway heading, climb and maintain flight level one-five-zero. Contact Lossiemouth Departure on this frequency, squawking three-five-two-one."

Adrian's voice replied, "Badger two-one copies all."

❧

"I have never known a man like Tim, Sandy. I adore him, yet I can't help being afraid. He's gorgeous and. . .and—"

"Unbelievably sexy?" Sandy supplied with a roguish grin.

Cathy blushed. "Yes, and women swarm him like bees. I don't think I could handle that. Not for the rest of my life. What if I were hugely pregnant and all these svelte women threw themselves at my husband? I would hate that!"

"So would I. I get jealous of beautiful women in the congregation sometimes—don't like to see Paul talking with them. He's around people all the time, but he's careful never to be alone with any other woman. I've had to learn to deal with my insecurities. I imagine that, in time, those women will forget Tim and go after easier prey. What does he do when they come after him?"

"He looks humiliated and tries to avoid them." Cathy grinned.

"What do you two do on your dates?"

"We go sightseeing or walking, mostly with a group of people. Tim never goes into my flat or asks me to his—he is concerned about his own reputation as well as mine."

Sandy bought a donut, but Cathy couldn't finish her soup. "I'm too nervous. Tim will be landing around two, and. . . Sandy, before he left today, he looked at me so. . .so. . .I don't know. I could have melted right there on the squadron floor!"

"The man does have phenomenal eyes," Sandy said. "And he knows how to use them. Just hope he doesn't pass them on to your kids—you'll never have the upper hand."

Cathy chuckled, then sobered. "I would love to have his children. Isn't that terrible? For a long time I thought I was just infatuated with his looks, but now we are friends and I love him more than ever." Her voice sank to a whisper.

"It's not terrible—you're normal, you numbskull! It's natural that you feel this way—God invented love and marriage and family. And I seem to recall you being immune to his looks until you got to know him."

"No, I used to dream about him even while I disliked him. I've got it bad, Sandy."

❧

"Badger two-two, Lossiemouth. Steer heading zero-five-zero. Descend and maintain flight level three-zero. Lossiemouth is reporting nil weather, visibility forty kilometers. Runway two-three approach end hook wire is down; departure end is up."

"Badger two-two."

All this time, Tim and Jason had been checking their lights and systems, working constantly to keep their plane airborne. From behind, Ken and Adrian watched for signs of trouble. Although water whizzed past beneath the jets, time seemed to drag.

"We're praying for you," Ken spoke abruptly over the auxiliary radio. Tim had no time to reply, but he appreciated the prayers.

A minute later Lossie called. "Badger two-two, entering the downwind. Report cockpit checks complete."

"Badger two-two is checks complete. Request short vectors on the final." Lossie would translate this as *I want to land now!*

They stopped dumping fuel. Jason coughed to clear his clogged throat. "Nothing particular to affect us in the single engine checklist. Just watch out for some flight control transients."

Tim's voice was shaking again. "Okay. Feels good right now. No problems." Thirty seconds later he said, "Badger two-two, gear. . .now." He lowered the landing gear and dropped his flaps.

Adrian reassured him. "Your gear is down and looks good."

"Badger two-two copies. Thanks."

But will the jet make it to the runway? Lord, are You here?

❧

"Does Tim know how you feel about him, Cathy?" Sandy dunked her donut in her coffee. It crumbled.

Cathy smiled, watching Sandy scoop out soggy crumbs with a spoon. "I don't know. I'm afraid to get serious too quickly. It's been under a year since we met, yet we already know each other well. He knows how opinionated and stubborn I am."

"And you know his faults. Guess how long Paul and I knew one another before we married."

"Not very long?"

"Six months. Not that we're the best example of wisdom to follow, but you've got to admit we're happy together. I would definitely advise the pair of you to get premarital counseling. It just so happens that I can recommend a certain wise counselor of my acquaintance."

"Can't imagine whom you could mean," Cathy teased back. "But seriously, there is also the problem of my job. What if we were to start a family right away? I still have almost a year left of my commitment. I don't want to be a working mother."

"As I recall with remarkable clarity, babies take several months to percolate before they're poured. Unless you marry and start a family tonight, I can't see why this is of concern to you. Honey, some things you have to take on faith that the Lord will provide. You can't wait until everything is perfect, or you'll never marry."

Cathy bowed her head, peeked up through her lashes, and gave Sandy a crooked smile. "You're right. I've got to pray and trust the Lord about this. But I still think I need time to know if I could handle marriage with Tim. I don't know yet if this is a lifetime love."

❧

One more time Tim heard the Scots brogue. "Badger two-two, turn right heading two-zero-zero, base to final. Contact

Lossie Talkdown on two-six-five point three."

Tim relayed the order to his wingman, then called, "Lossie Talkdown, Badger two-two with you, descending to two thousand."

A woman's softly accented voice answered him. "Lossie Talkdown, radar contact. Turn right, heading two-three-five. Slightly left of course. Eight miles from touchdown. Stand by for descent."

Somehow that gentle female voice lifted Tim's spirits. Summer sunshine radiated through the jet's canopy. Loosening his grip on the stick, Tim flexed his fingers, feeling sweat inside his glove. The rasp of his own uneven breathing filled his ears. A pulse pounded in his temples. Was that acrid odor the smell of fear?

Lossie Talkdown continued. "Badger two-two, slightly left of course, correcting nicely. Do not acknowledge further instructions."

While following heading corrections from Lossie Talkdown, Tim told Jason, "I'm gonna keep a few extra knots up. We're heavy; didn't dump much gas. Don't want to get too slow." His wingman was also too heavy to fly slowly.

Cathy, I love you. Wish I'd told you so.

"Badger two-two, circuit is clear. Cleared to land. Check gear acknowledge."

Tim replied tersely. "Gear down for the full stop. Be advised, Badger two-two will be stopping straight ahead on runway and egressing the aircraft."

"That's understood." A moment later she added,

"Badger two-two, long glide path on course. Five miles from touchdown."

Tim tried to relax his clenched jaw. "Lossie, Badger two-two taking over visually. Thanks for your help."

Jason's falsetto returned. "Okay, Tim, you got nine thousand feet of runway and a departure end cable if you need it."

Eyes intent behind his visor, Tim said, "No sweat, Man; it's lookin' sweet." *Aim, point, airspeed. Lord, I'm ready to meet You.*

❦

Melanie's head flopped against her mother's shoulder as Sandy lifted her from the high chair. The little girl's feet caught beneath the tray, and Sandy struggled to release them. Cathy hurried to assist her.

"Thank you. I'm not used to carrying her anymore. Poor baby, she's out like a light." Sandy took her purse from Cathy and headed for the entrance. "I'll be praying for you and Tim. If you ever want to talk again, I'm available."

"Give me your honest opinion: Would Tim make a good husband for me?" Cathy demanded as they stepped outside. Shivering despite the afternoon sunshine, she clutched her upper arms with her hands.

Sandy hesitated on the top step. "Cathy, I think any man can make a good husband if he's committed to the Lord and to his wife. Tim is a baby Christian, but he's maturing at a steady rate, showing every sign of sincerity, and producing a healthy harvest of spiritual fruit. He is also crazy about you. What more could a woman ask?"

Chapter 8

The injured Strike Eagle skimmed over the golf course at the approach end of the runway. Tim and Jason saw golfers looking up at them. Dozens of "bird-watchers" piled out of haphazardly parked vehicles on roadsides and focused binoculars on the jets. Word spread quickly of a wounded F-15 arriving at Lossiemouth.

The jet's rear tires touched at five hundred feet down the runway. The aircraft bobbled, then settled and landed firmly. Tim put pressure on the stick to raise the nose and aerodynamically slow the airplane. Fire trucks followed alongside the runway, lights flashing, sirens blaring.

"Coming up on five thousand feet of runway remaining; you got one hundred five knots. You're a little hot," Jason informed his pilot.

Tim kept the jet's nose up.

"Four thousand feet, ninety-five knots."

Tim said, "Okay, letting the nose down, getting on the binders."

Rapid deceleration pressed him against his harness as he applied the wheel brakes. The jet halted in the middle of the runway with one thousand feet remaining. The second Eagle roared overhead, ready to head home to Lakenheath. No time to tell them good-bye. Tim moved his left throttle to the "cutoff" position and pulled the canopy handle with his right hand. "Okay, egress, egress, egress!"

The remaining engine wound down. Tim turned off the engine master switches and all displays. Jason barked into the radio: "Lossie, Badger two-two's down, egressing the airplane."

Tim fumbled to unbuckle sundry harnesses. Free at last. He stepped over the left side of the cockpit, stuck his right foot into the first step of the built-in ladder, and pressed a button. An egress ladder dropped from its stowed position. Tim scrambled down, looking up to make sure Jason followed.

Both men hit the ground prepared to run.

Out the corner of his eye, Tim saw the nose wheel begin to turn. Startled, he spun around. Slowly the jet began to roll along the sloping runway. Tim and Jason exchanged gapes.

"Great, just what we needed!" Grabbing the ladder, Tim climbed back up into the front seat and pulled on the emergency brake steer handle. "Get some chocks!"

Jason ran off, waving his arms and shouting, "We need chocks!"

From his perch in the cockpit, Tim saw a fire truck approaching fast. Did Jason see it?

The truck blared ahead on a direct collision course with his crewmate.

"Watch out!" Tim's cry vanished amid the commotion.

The scene was a nightmare, inevitable, uncontrollable. A tortured squeal of brakes. Jason rolling on the tarmac. Firemen piling from the truck.

"Oh, God, let him be all right!" Tim's pent-up emotions burst forth in an anguished plea.

He opened his eyes. Jason stood on shaky legs amid an excited crowd.

Tim flopped back on the seat, staring wide-eyed into a pale blue sky. "Thanks."

As Cathy entered the 494th building, officers and NCOs bustled up and down hallways. Lt. Hal Redmond brushed past without acknowledging her presence. Two sergeants spoke in lowered voices, heads together as they passed. ". . .goose hit the right intake. . .fireball blew past the canopy. . .never had a chance to. . ."

Cathy's skin prickled. She hurried to the briefing room, teetering on wobbly ankles. The door was shut.

Before she could knock, the door jerked open. "Lieutenant Guillard?" Adrian's bushy eyebrows knotted, and he glanced back over his shoulder.

A boulder dropped on Cathy's stomach. "Lieutenant Hill? Is something wrong?"

Adrian thumped his hand on the doorframe and swore. "You haven't heard?"

Unable to speak, she shook her head.

"Come in." He stepped back to allow her entrance.

Ken sat at the table, sipping a soda from the can. The imprint of an oxygen mask marked his cheeks. He jumped up. "Cathy, I'm sorry. Somebody should have told you sooner."

Her face felt frozen.

Ken approached, arms reaching to hold her. "Honestly, there was nothing more we could do for them."

Reading concern in his expression, she held him off with an icy hand. "Where is Tim?"

※

Standing on the grassy verge of the runway, arms crossed, feet widespread, Jason and Tim watched the emergency crews work. Chocks against its wheels restrained the wayward Eagle.

Examining the jet's exterior made Tim's heart pound anew. He breathed countless grateful prayers. Gouges marred the leading edge of the right wing; extreme heat had removed all paint from the huge engine casing and part of the fuselage. Heat had scorched weird color patterns into the aircraft's metal frame.

A crewman remarked in passing, "Expensive bird this, having everything but a park brake, eh?"

Tim couldn't smile. At the moment, he found this lack far from amusing.

A fireman wandered over to visit. "That was some luck, landing this jet. Your right engine is shredded. Was it geese, do you think?"

Tim nodded. "Geese, or ducks, at least, to do that much damage. All I saw was black dots before they hit. I'm sure the ducks never knew what hit 'em. Good thing we have two engines."

"Think you'll be hearing from the RSPCA about your cruelty to them birds?" The fireman chortled at his own joke.

Now that he knew the jet would not blow up, Tim felt the tightness in his neck relax. Ground crews walked around the Eagle, estimating damage. Tim and Jason helped put safety pins into its weapons. "Don't know about you, but I'm not eager to fly this particular aircraft again anytime soon," Tim remarked. He patted a wing, making a hollow thump.

"This baby won't be ready to fly again for days. They'll have to dispatch a maintenance crew from Lakenheath to assess the damage and bring a new engine. Meantime, I'm ready to go home," Jason said, rubbing the back of his neck. "I've died a thousand deaths today. That always wears me out."

"They'll call a bus to take us to the train station," Tim said. "Wonder what hour of the night we'll get home."

❧

"Where is Tim?" Cathy repeated, audibly this time.

"Come sit here, and we'll tell you the whole story." Taking her arm, Ken attempted to lead her to a chair.

Cathy twisted free. "Is he alive?"

"Yes." Ken looked startled. "Oh, Cathy, I'm—"

"Injured?"

"Far as I know, he's fine. They made an emergency landing at Lossiemouth."

She collapsed into the chair. "Tell me what happened."

By the time Ken's narration ended, she felt almost normal.

Leaning back, she drew a calming breath. "When did all this happen?"

"Couple hours ago. We watched them land safely before we returned. They'll be on a train home by now."

While I lunched with Sandy, Tim might have been killed. "Who will pick them up at the station?"

"Whoever gets assigned."

Cathy picked up her purse and briefcase. "I volunteer."

Adrian grinned. "Falkirk always did have the best luck."

Cathy turned at the door. "This wasn't luck. God protected him."

Tim and Jason picked up their flight bags and waited at the train's sliding door. "Good-bye. I'll ring you soon." Jason waved to a young woman, tucking her phone number into his breast pocket. "You know, there are advantages to traveling in a flight suit," he told Tim. "Chicks dig pockets and zippers."

"Hope there's someone here to pick us up." Tim peered out into darkness.

"It might be your Cathy," Jason reminded.

Tim shook his head. "Can't get my hopes up. Not sure I'd want her waiting out here in the middle of nowhere at night anyway."

"Who do you think you're fooling?"

Tim gave him a sheepish glance. Both men gripped overhead slings when the train screeched to a halt. The doors slid open, and they stepped onto the Shippea Hill platform.

"Sure is dark out here. A guy could get mugged." Jason

dropped his flight bag with a thud.

The doors snapped shut, and the train hummed away.

"Tim?" a nervous voice inquired.

"Cathy?" He spotted her near the stairway. "Cathy! You did come."

She met him like a whirlwind, sobbing against his pockets, kissing his chest with frenzied abandon. "Oh, Tim, you might have been killed, and I never told you how much I love you!"

Her clinging embrace bolstered Tim's fragile ego. *She loves me. She really does!* He gripped her waist with both hands, feeling her quick breath, her quivering excitement.

"Cathy. Sweetheart."

Still sobbing, she pressed ever closer. "I nearly lost you."

"You're more likely to strangle him than lose him." Jason propped his fists on his hips. "A touching reunion. Lots of touching. What did I tell you, Falkirk? It's the flight suit. She's even kissing it." He waved his hand. "Hey, over here, Lieutenant. I've got one on too."

"Buzz off." Clasping Cathy to his chest, Tim turned his back on Jason and glanced back over his shoulder. "Why don't you take our bags down to the car."

Rolling his eyes, Jason obeyed. "Don't say I never did nothing for you. And keep in mind that I want to get home— sometime before midnight, preferably." He hefted both flight bags, one in each hand, and clomped down the steps.

Tim scanned the platform. Spotting a bench beneath a dim lamp, he moved in that direction, half-carrying Cathy. He pulled her onto his lap, cradling her in his arms. "Calm down, Sweetie. I'm here, and we're together. The jet didn't crash; we didn't even have to bail out. God was watching over us."

He rubbed her back with one hand. Her face pressed against the side of his neck, and her hand rested on his chest. She kept taking deep breaths and releasing them in gusty sobs. Tim smoothed her damp cheek with his fingertips. "A shame you wasted those kisses on my flight suit."

"I didn't mean to fall apart all over you," she said between gasps.

"Glad I was here to pick up the pieces." He brushed her hair back and kissed her temple.

"I hadn't cried all day."

"You were due." His lips traveled across her cheek, tasting salty tears. He felt her body grow taut.

"It—it all burst out at once." She turned her head until their noses touched.

"And now you feel better."

"I love you, Tim." Her lips brushed his as she spoke.

"You said that already." His mouth curled in a teasing smile.

Her body slumped. "Oh. Well. I'm glad you're back safely. Jason is waiting. We'd better get back to base to pick up your cars." She shoved at his shoulders, but he held her firmly.

"I love you, Cathy. I've loved you ever since you cried during *It's a Wonderful Life*. Maybe even before then, but that night I knew I wanted you for my wife. While we sat beside the Christmas tree I asked God to make me worthy of you."

Her stiff arms went limp. "Oh, Tim!"

"Today, when I wasn't certain if I would see you again here on earth, I kept wishing I'd told you how much I care. All these months I've waited to tell you, hoping you would learn to trust and love me. I almost hesitated too long."

Cathy fiddled with Tim's neck scarf. "Until today, I might not have given you the right answer. I've been afraid of my own weakness. I'm so quick to judge others—you know my sinful pride. I know how weak I am, and I expected you to be equally weak."

Tim shook his head. "I am a sinful man—but in my weakness, He is strong. Do you trust me enough. . . ? Dare I ask? Will you. . .will you marry me, Cathy?"

She gripped his face between her hands and kissed him. Her lips felt warm and moist, clinging to his even as she moved away. "I have wanted to do that for months! I would love to be your wife, more than anything."

A call came from the car park. "Are you two about done up there? Let's hit the road, people."

"Timing." Tim sighed. "You say you've wanted to kiss me for months? Why is this the first I hear about it?"

"You didn't need to know." Cathy extricated herself from his grasp. "Your legs must be numb from holding me like that. Do you want to drive?"

Knowing her dislike for driving on the left-hand side of the road, he said, "Sure, I'll drive. Maybe it will restore my confidence. I'm unlikely to hit any geese on the ground."

"You never know."

Chapter 9

The wedding party posed for one more photo, smiling with faces that felt frozen into position. Bridesmaids wore green velvet and carried poinsettias and white roses. Cathy glowed in white satin and tulle as she accompanied her husband to the reception line in the church's hallway.

"It was a beautiful Christmas wedding, my dear." A silver-haired lady kissed Cathy's cheeks and smiled at Tim. "I taught Cathy in Sunday school many years ago. You found yourself a treasure, young man."

He shook her hand. "I know it, Ma'am."

"How soon can we leave?" Tim asked between hand-shakes. His family and several friends were in attendance, but much of the crowd consisted of Cathy's Colorado church family and her throngs of friends. Tim was ready to begin his Rocky Mountain honeymoon.

"Have patience." Cathy ran her gloved fingers over the ribbons on his chest. "I love you in mess dress. I've still got photos of you from last year's Christmas party in my bureau drawer. I blew them up to eleven by seventeen and drooled over them every night."

"You're not serious."

She blushed. "I won't need them anymore—now I'll have wedding photos to stare at whenever you're deployed. A few minutes ago, one of my high school friends asked me how I ever managed to snare you. I don't think she intended to insult me—she was just amazed at my luck!"

He found a chair and sat down, pulling her onto his lap. Her bouffant skirt mounded around them like foam. "I've had people ask me the same thing. It wasn't luck. One year ago, I prayed to have you for my wife. You're my Christmas gift from God."

"Oh, Tim." She sighed.

The photographer caught sight of their ensuing kiss and snapped another photo. "Perfect," he said in satisfaction. "That one will hang on my studio wall."

"For I know the plans I have for you," declares the LORD,
"plans to prosper you and not to harm you,
plans to give you hope and a future."
JEREMIAH 29:11

JILL STENGL

After fifteen years of military life, Jill and her husband Dean built a log house beside Lake Kawaguesaga in northern Wisconsin and are happily putting down roots. Their oldest son Tom is at the Air Force Academy, hoping to become a pilot like his dad. Three other children, Anne, Jim, and Peter, are still at home. Jill's two shadows, Fritz, a miniature schnauzer, and Myles, a Siamese lap warmer, keep her company at the computer while she writes. Two more cats, Monte and Marilla, round out the busy household.

Although she was born and raised in southern California, the Midwest is now her home. "I can sit at my computer and look out the windows at bald eagles, loons, and herons, not to mention the sparkling lake and lush green trees. No writer could ask for more idyllic surroundings!" Homeschooling, scrapbooking, sewing, visiting with friends, and housekeeping keep Jill occupied, but she always finds time in her schedule to write.

Jill has six **Heartsong Presents** novels and one previous novella published with Barbour Publishing. She particularly enjoys writing about England after having lived there for seven years while Dean was stationed at RAF Lakenheath. Writing "About-Face" brought back many fun memories.

You may correspond with Jill at jpopcorn@newnorth.net.

Outranked by Love

by Tammy Shuttlesworth

Chapter 1

"I n order to register that package, you'll have to complete this form." The postmaster slid a mailing form Lacey's way. "You can use that counter over there." He pointed to a long counter beneath a row of windows filled with Louisiana sunshine.

Moments later, the form completed in neat, blocklike print, Lacey returned to the counter.

"All done," she announced, pushing the box and form across the counter.

The clerk weighed the box and punched a Chicago zip code from the address label into the computer. "Eleven dollars and eighty-five cents," he announced. "Plus, two dollars and twenty cents for the insurance."

Lacey dug in her purse for her wallet, her throat growing dry as she searched.

"Something wrong, Ma'am?" the clerk prodded.

Lacey peered inside her purse, pushing aside her makeup bag and checkbook bulging with receipts and coupons. She glanced back at the clerk. "You could say that. It appears I forgot my wallet."

The clerk gave her a tight grin. "Don't look so sad. You're the second customer today who's done that. I'll bet you're fairly new to Barksdale, aren't you?"

Lacey nodded. She chewed her lip, wondering where the conversation was headed.

The clerk glanced at two dark green stripes with a centered star that were the only decoration on her sleeves. "And you're a young airman, so you probably don't have any transportation between the dormitory and here."

"Right. I came by on my way home after work." Lacey picked up the package and tucked it under her arm. "Well, I guess I'll see you tomorrow. With my wallet," she added.

"I was a young airman once. Back then, we didn't make enough to afford a vehicle right away."

"No," she offered hesitantly. "Not enough nowadays either. I wanted to get this in the mail to my aunt today, but I guess I'll just have to wait 'til tomorrow. Thanks for your help." She gave the clerk a small smile.

"Tomorrow then, but before you go, I want you to know that you remind me of my oldest daughter." The postmaster turned a photo frame sitting on his computer tower her way. "Same long dark hair, sprightly brown eyes, and a smile from heaven."

"Sure, I see the resemblance," Lacey agreed. She was beginning to get uncomfortable. It didn't help that several faces on FBI wanted posters on the wall to her left seemed to be staring at her.

"Guess I'll see you tomorrow then. And don't worry about forgetting your wallet; it happens to everyone sooner or later."

"Yeah. I mean, yes, Sir," Lacey answered. "Tomorrow. Thanks for the help." She tried to remember her manners while thinking only of escape.

Pushing open the glass doors that led to an area filled with individual metal mailboxes, Lacey rushed down the hall. Her combat boots softly *whooshed* on the shiny off-green linoleum. She stopped to get her bearings before going out into the unusually warm December afternoon.

That clerk meant nothing other than kindness, she told herself. *I've got to quit thinking that every male over the age of fifteen is out to get me.*

She took several slow, deep breaths, hoping her heart rate and breathing would return to normal. It didn't.

One day, Lacey silently vowed, *I will put that memory behind me.*

Lacey closed her eyes and steeled herself to step outside into the heat. She leaned her weight against the mirrored doors to the outside and pushed.

"Oh, no!" Lacey flung her arms out and sought to keep from falling as her package tumbled to the concrete sidewalk.

"Whoa there." The man's firm grasp on her shoulders was accompanied by his softly spoken words. "You're not hurt, are you?"

Lacey gazed up, found she'd misjudged, and tilted her

head even farther, only to find that the eyes she sought were hidden behind polarized sunglasses. "I don't think so. I mean, I'm sorry. I wasn't watching where I was going and—"

"No problem. I know what it's like to go from inside to out in this sun. I wasn't paying attention either. Otherwise I'd have seen you coming out and wouldn't have opened the door at the same time. But I'm glad I did."

Lacey's rescuer bent down and retrieved her parcel. "If the post offices across the world didn't have military people to depend on, I wonder how much money they would lose."

"Uh, may I?" Lacey motioned to her box. "I need to—"

"Get out of the sun?" he teased as he handed her the package. "Don't think you'll have a very good chance of that here in Louisiana."

"Do you always finish people's sentences for them?"

Lacey scowled. She was tired and frustrated that she wasn't going to get this Christmas package to her aunt on its way today. She wasn't looking forward to the search for her wallet in her dormitory room either. At least she hoped it was in her room.

"Not usually. I don't think I've met you. I'm Hayden Jacobs. I just arrived here a couple of months ago." His grin revealed even, white teeth.

"Nice to meet you, Hayden. I'm Lacey White." She waited for the wisecracks some made about her name sounding like a crayon color.

"No, meeting you is my pleasure," Hayden assured her. "You look kind of pale. Are you sure that you're all right?"

"I'm fine," Lacey replied.

"If you insist." Hayden glanced at her again. "But I obviously shook you up by not paying attention. You don't happen to be on your way to your dormitory, do you?" He didn't wait for her reply. "Barksdale doesn't have a shuttle bus, so if you don't have a ride, why don't you let me take you there? I have a car."

"That isn't necessary," Lacey stated, even as she handed over the small gift to her aunt she'd wanted to mail.

❧

The tension in the car was evident. He was surprised that he'd even offered to give Lacey a lift. His past with women wasn't the greatest.

"I've never seen eyes the same color as yours," Hayden commented as they waited their turn at a four-way stop. "They remind me of one of those dark chocolates you find in a box of Valentine's Day candy."

"I used to love getting those! My grandmother always gave me one when I was young." Despite the nostalgia in her voice, Lacey turned to look out her window.

"I don't want to intrude, but I take it that she is no longer alive." Hayden glimpsed Lacey's way, wishing she would turn to face him again.

Lacey shook her head. "She passed away three years ago and—"

"You miss her," Hayden supplied.

Lacey nodded. "Yes, but that's not going to get you off the hook. You just completed my sentence—again."

Hayden frowned. "I didn't even realize that I did so. Forgive me?"

"Sure, especially since we're at my dorm." Lacey picked up her package and situated it in her arms. "Thanks for the ride. You really didn't have to."

"Yes, I did," Hayden replied. "Lacey? Can I ask you something?"

"Sure."

"Why are you carrying a package away from the post office when it has a mailing address on it that says it's headed to Illinois?"

Chapter 2

Lacey studied Hayden while she tried to figure out how to respond. His auburn hair was not quite as dark as hers. Slightly wavy, he wore it parted almost on the left side. Everything about him shouted "rich boy."

His car was an obvious indicator of wealth. He wore just as few stripes on his uniform sleeve as she, so he'd been in the air force about as long as she had. No airmen that she knew could afford to own a champagne-colored luxury car.

"Is something wrong?" Hayden quizzed.

"No. Thanks again for the ride." Lacey wondered what color his eyes were behind those sunglasses.

Hayden turned to face her across the car's front seat. "You can't go yet. You haven't answered my question."

"Right." Lacey contemplated her confession. "It probably sounds stupid, but I went to the post office after work to mail this. That's when I found I didn't have my wallet with me," she said. "No wallet, no money, no postal service."

Hayden glanced at the oversized purse slung over her right shoulder.

Lacey chuckled as she patted the huge black pouch. "You're wondering how I'd ever find a wallet in something the size of this monstrosity?"

"You guessed it."

Lacey couldn't help but grin at his cavalier response. Something about it reminded her of one of her eager young nephews. "I know what is supposed to be in there. If I feel around and don't find what I'm looking for, then I know it's not there."

Hayden looked unconvinced. "It's sure nothing like the ones my mother carries. Hers barely holds one toothpick and maybe two peppermints."

Lacey gave a small laugh. "I'd never fit everything I need in one that size. Thanks again for the ride. I really should be going."

⁂

What am I doing? Hayden asked himself. *I've never felt the need to be near a woman like this.*

True, but he sensed something different about Lacey. Her gentle name fit her sweet smile. Her eyes called to his lonely heart like none had before. And, Hayden noted, Lacey had the most beautiful hair he'd ever seen. It looked soft and silky and full of auburn highlights—not at all like the bottled kind his mother depended on to hide her gray.

"Lacey? This might sound rather forward, but would you like to go somewhere for a cool drink with me?"

"A drink? I don't think so. I don't indulge in alcoholic beverages."

Hayden drummed his fingers on the steering wheel. "I don't either. I meant something like iced tea. There's a burger joint near here. We could be there in two minutes."

"I don't think so."

"I'll pay," Hayden offered. "And I'll even wait here 'til you stow that package in your dorm room, or until you find your wallet, whichever comes first. If you happen to find your wallet before five o'clock, I'll even drive you back to the post office." Hayden gave Lacey what he hoped was his most charming smile.

"All right, but only if you take those sunglasses off so I can see your eyes first."

❧

Lacey smudged powder on her cheeks, then ran a brush through her hair. Not long before coming to northwest Louisiana, she'd considered cutting it short. Now she was glad she hadn't, because she liked the way Hayden's gaze had lingered on it. She glanced in the mirror and, using her fingers, ruffled her bangs. The misgivings she had about her abilities to choose a man hit home.

Does Hayden think I'm an easy target because I'm new on base? Maybe I should go back down and tell him that I've changed my mind?

Lacey studied her reflection. A therapist once told her that she would have to face her fear in order to get over it. If she didn't start somewhere, she'd never know. Besides, she rationalized, the military's discipline weeded out bad apples, didn't it?

I promised I'd go, and I will, despite any uncertainties. She shook her head, clearing the haunting memory. Hayden's intriguing steel blue eyes filled her mind. They seemed to pry at Lacey's heart, but they also let her know she wasn't alone in this world. Lacey wasn't sure if that was a good thing or not.

❧

They sat at a fast-food counter in the entrance to the base exchange and talked. As she listened to Hayden describe his job, Lacey marveled at how fast her heart wanted to overrule her thoughts.

"So you're from Chicago," Hayden commented. "I had an aunt who used to live there."

"That's my home of record for military purposes, but I haven't been back since I enlisted over two years ago." Lacey ran a finger around the top edge of her glass of just-right sweet tea.

Hayden impressed her with his knowledge about several sporting teams from the Chicago area.

"How do you know so much about them?" Lacey quizzed. "I grew up there and don't recognize half those names you just listed. Bears and Bulls. Why, they sound like a bunch of wild animals on the loose."

Hayden's grin broadened. "When I was young I had to find things to pass time. Sports teams were just one thing that I got interested in." He waved at a young woman across the room. "I know her," Hayden explained. "Do you mind if I ask her to sit with us?"

"Not at all."

Hayden left to greet the woman, leaving Lacey behind to squash the small stab of jealousy in her heart.

"That's ridiculous," she muttered to herself. "I just met him. How can I be jealous of another woman?"

Chapter 3

Hayden made the introductions, and Lacey was relieved to find out the woman was his sister. The trio spent the next thirty minutes marveling over how Hayden and Shelley ended up stationed at the same base at the same time. Then they all traded stories about surviving basic training and technical training in their job specialties.

"Someday I want to get assigned to Ellsworth Air Force Base," Hayden stated. "It's on the western side of South Dakota, close to Rapid City and the Black Hills. Have you ever been there, Lacey?"

Lacey shook her head. "Basic at Lackland in San Antonio, Texas; Keesler near Biloxi in Mississippi for tech school; and Eglin near Fort Walton Beach, Florida. That's the extent of my military travels. I was surprised to get reassigned to Barksdale since everyone told me I wouldn't get orders to move until after I'd reenlisted the first time."

"I guess I'm the veteran of the bunch," Shelley offered. "I've been to three other bases since tech training." She named two duty stations in California and one in Korea.

"Why do you want to go to South Dakota, Hayden?" Lacey ventured, not wanting to admit to herself that it was because she wanted to hear his deep voice again.

"Because it's so peaceful there," Hayden replied. "Mount Rushmore is only about thirty minutes from the base. The Badlands are amazing—all that sandstone carved by millions of years of rain and snow. And the one time I was there, I saw buffalo and mountain goats at Custer State Park. Shelley saw them too."

Lacey smiled as Hayden ranted about the great summer weather and often frigid winters in "So Dak," as he called the northern state.

He sounds as if he really loves it there, Lacey thought. All the memories she had of the North were definitely not good ones.

❧

"Is something wrong, Lace?"

Hayden wondered if he'd gone on too long about South Dakota. He didn't want Lacey's interest turning elsewhere. He wanted to spend the rest of the evening getting to know her.

His father once told Hayden that he would regret his assignment to Barksdale, but since he'd met Lacey, the possibilities were beginning to look better all the time.

"I was just thinking that I grew up praying I could leave the North and here you are, full of enthusiasm to go back to a place I couldn't wait to leave."

"Speaking of praying," Shelley inserted, "there's a Bible

study tonight at seven at the chapel a couple of blocks from the dorm. If you're free, will you join us, Lacey?"

"How about it?" Hayden quizzed. "Are you up for a study of Esther?"

Chapter 4

The study was friendly and spirited. Hayden enjoyed it because it was so different from those his father used to force him to sit through at home as a youngster. Of course, with Lacey beside him, he figured he would enjoy just about anything. Hard to believe he'd only met her four hours ago.

Hayden glanced Lacey's way. Her gaze followed the conversation as it bounced around the room, and she smiled politely as she listened. Hayden found himself volunteering information just so Lacey would give him one of those wonderful smiles of hers.

"May I summarize?" Hayden asked at the end of the discussion.

At the study leader's nod, Hayden said, "Esther was a Jewish princess whose part in mankind's destiny sometimes goes unnoticed. Without her, the Hebrew nation might have disappeared. And with no nation for the Messiah to descend from, we all know what that means."

Several nodded their agreement. Hayden glanced at Lacey. The look she gave him hinted of a promise of a deeper connection between them. Taken aback, he could only marvel at the peace that filled his soul when he looked at her.

You only just met her, he warned himself. *Remember what happened the last time you fell so fast?*

❧

"The evening certainly went quickly," Hayden commented as he walked Lacey to her dormitory. Shelley stayed behind to help clean up, but only after extracting a promise from Lacey that she'd meet with them again to continue the study.

"I think so too. I look forward to learning more about Esther," Lacey admitted. "Hearing her story makes me wonder where the women in the Bible got their faith from."

Reaching the patio in front of her dorm, Hayden motioned her to sit on a nearby bench. "What do you mean?"

Lacey sighed. "When I hear about the things women like Esther, Naomi, and Ruth did, I wonder if faith is something a person is born with or if it's something you have to work at."

"I think it's a little of both," Hayden replied. "Remember that even Thomas doubted Jesus rose from the dead until shown physical proof. Thomas had to work at having faith."

"Could be," Lacey answered. "Still. . ."

The turning blades of an air-conditioning unit not far away broke the silence.

"What?" Lacey joked. "You're not going to finish my sentence for me this time?"

Hayden chuckled. "I considered it, but I didn't want you to sling that big purse at me."

At Lacey's quelling look, Hayden raised his hands in mock surrender.

"I think our original topic might be safer," he said. "I do think there are some who believe more easily than others. On the other hand, I also think that those who have to work at faith sometimes have more than those who don't. Does that make sense?"

Lacey nodded and stifled a yawn. "Sorry. I'm not used to rising at dawn for twelve-hour shifts."

Hayden frowned. "You should have said something instead of sitting here and talking with me."

He watched as Lacey clasped her hands and laid them on her lap. "Can I be honest with you, Hayden?"

"I hope so," he answered. "I've met my share of women who didn't tell me the truth from the beginning."

"I needed to hear what you thought about faith. I've had my share of sour relationships. Looking back, most of them were based on nothing but the physical side of love." She paused and swallowed hard. "After something. . .that happened shortly before I enlisted, I vowed that I would never let physical attraction rule my thinking about men again."

"That's a good thing, Lacey. Why do you make it sound as if it's not?"

Lacey squirmed on the bench. "Now isn't really the best time to explain it further, Hayden. I'll see you next week at the study, okay?"

Hayden sang "What A Friend We Have In Jesus" as he walked back to his dormitory room. He couldn't wait to see Lacey again to talk more about her biblical convictions. Something about her made him think that she was the one he'd been waiting to meet forever.

The voice of reason told Hayden he was pushing things. After all, they'd just met five hours ago. If something serious developed with this newfound friendship, he would have to think ahead. Thinking ahead meant introducing Lacey to his parents, General and Mrs. Hayden Jacobs II.

While Shelley appeared to like Lacey from the start, Hayden knew his parents wouldn't react favorably once they found out Lacey was an enlisted person. They still hadn't accepted his or Shelley's enlistments.

"All things are possible with God," he stated part of Mark 10:27. "All things. . ."

Lacey sat beside Hayden at a table in the community center out of the way of the pool tables and dartboards. The tabletop was a maroon laminate with the only decoration a stainless steel napkin holder in the middle of it. Lacey turned it around and patted the edges of some napkins back in place.

"Some of my friends think I'm crazy because I couldn't wait to come to Louisiana," Lacey said. "What about you, Hayden?"

"Dad dragged us around the world, but there are still so many places I haven't seen. I joined the service so that I'd have a chance to travel, to see those countries and cultures I didn't get to while following Dad."

And without the pressure of my family trying to fit me into their idea of the perfect son, Hayden added silently.

"So your parents are military?" Lacey quizzed, looking toward the door where a group of noisy airmen entered the facility.

"My father is still on active duty. But weren't we talking about what people thought of us coming to Barksdale?"

Lacey nodded. "When I told my aunt Trini where the military was sending me, she said the only thing I'd be likely to see was swamps and sand. And maybe a few crocodiles."

Hayden grinned. "Well, unless you go to a zoo, you'll only find alligators here. Did you know that alligators can run up to thirty-five miles an hour for a very short time?"

"Seriously?"

"No kidding, Lacey. If I take you out to the base lake, maybe you'll see one."

"Real alligators? Hayden, quit kidding me." Lacey gave him a lighthearted shove.

"I'm not kidding. There are real alligators at the lake. I've seen them."

"Just remind me to wear my running shoes," Lacey said. "And make sure I get a head start if one comes after me. I may be able to pass the yearly physical fitness requirements, but I don't think I'm up to thirty-five miles an hour yet."

Lacey enjoyed the time she spent with Hayden, but in the back of her mind the thought that she'd once again make a mistake where men were concerned snapped at her much like an alligator. She wanted to trust Hayden, as a friend at first, with no pressure. Perhaps something more would eventually develop. If only she were just more sure of herself and her decision-making abilities.

Chapter 5

A small picnic bench about fifty feet from the base lake wasn't enough distance for Lacey to be comfortable. She kept a wary eye out for alligators or any other kind of critters that might try to join them.

"How do you know so much about alligators?" Lacey brushed away an annoying gnat flying around her head.

"I read a lot," Hayden replied. He shared some more facts about alligators; the one about eating habits Lacey could have skipped, but it seemed safer than thinking about the undercurrent passing between them.

"Anything else about those beasts I should know? Did the air force ever use them as cargo carriers or anything?" Lacey raised her eyebrows in challenge.

Hayden chuckled. "No. The U.S. Army once tried to use camels for that in the 1850s. They found out the railroads were faster and cheaper, so they got rid of the camels. A few escaped and lived wild in Arizona for some time."

Lacey toyed with her can of soda, wiping off some of the

condensation on the outer edge. "I wish there was a zoo near here. I haven't been to one in a long time."

"The nearest one is in Tyler, Texas," Hayden responded. "If you really want to go, we could make a day of it."

"I don't know, Hayden. I appreciate the offer, but I just don't think we should."

Lacey didn't really want to turn Hayden down. If only she trusted her ability to decide whether a man was worth pursuing a relationship with or not. Hayden seemed to be a firm Christian, which was more than most of the men she'd dated over the last few years. Still, Lacey just wasn't sure she should follow what her heart kept telling her.

❧

Hayden left the post office, pocketing the letter from his mother. He planned on reading it later. Right now he was headed to see Lacey, and he didn't want to be a bad mood when he got there. Neither of his parents understood his decision to enlist in the military instead of taking advantage of the military academy appointment he'd been offered. His mother stayed in touch, though her letters were mostly about who was getting divorced, married, or having a baby.

None of those things mattered to him, mainly because his mother used them as tools to point out Hayden's failings in those areas. No doubt there would be an identically penned letter in Shelley's mail. Hayden wondered if he or his sister would ever get far enough away from their father that rank didn't matter.

Lacey hurried to the post office to mail another package. This time she made sure she had her wallet with her. Her aunt would think Lacey was wasting money, but the small pillow with an embroidered bayou scene, complete with alligators, was something Lacey couldn't resist.

That'll teach Aunt Trini to tease me about the South and its animals! Lacey thought. She'd been tempted to keep the pillow for herself because it reminded her of Hayden and his explanation of the alligators.

Hayden. He filled her every waking thought lately. She had to figure out what she was going to do about him. It seemed no matter where she turned, there he was. Not that she was complaining, but it seemed that she had no time to herself to digest what was happening.

Things between them were moving much too fast. After many sleepless nights and lots of prayer, Lacey had decided to tell Hayden that they must slow down. Tonight, after the Bible study, she was determined that she'd let him know her decision.

How would he react? Lacey suspected that despite knowing each other for just over a month, Hayden was becoming very attached to her. Her feelings for him were growing also, but no matter how many therapy sessions she attended, she had a feeling that she would never get things right where men were concerned.

Lacey laughed while Hayden told her one joke after another

as they walked back from the chapel after the Bible study. Knowing what disclosure she was going to make and fearing his reaction, she tucked the lightheartedness of their moments in a corner of her heart.

Of all the men she'd dated, and she admitted that the number was few, no one made her relax as much as Hayden. It was as if the Lord had sent Hayden to fill the empty space in her heart.

If only she were free to—no, she wouldn't think about the possibility of them being more than friends. She would simply state that no matter what kind of attraction they held for each other, it was impossible for her to progress past friendship. Moving any further was more than she could handle right now—maybe ever. But from the way he enjoyed himself when he was with her and the way his gaze seemed to lightly caress her own, Lacey didn't think she could bring herself to say those words to Hayden anytime soon.

Maybe later, she thought.

Maybe never, her heart replied, something Lacey didn't feel led to argue with.

"Where did you learn those jokes?" Lacey turned her heart away from the dangerous direction it was headed. "Have you been collecting them for years, or what?"

Hayden grabbed her hand and swung their clasped palms back and forth between them like a pendulum as they walked to her dormitory. The temperature hovered around sixty-five degrees. A light southeast breeze flared once in a while, but the night was mostly calm.

He chuckled. "I bought a joke book at the BX last night so I could impress you today."

"You didn't!"

Hayden beamed. "I had to find some way to make you smile and convince you to see me again."

"You don't need a reason, Hayden. I like being with you. . . ." Lacey released his hand and turned her shoulders slightly away from him.

"I sense there's a 'but' I'm going to hear next. Do I get to fill in the blank for you on that one?" Hayden quipped.

Lacey shook her head. "Wait 'til we get someplace where we can sit. If I have to walk much farther, my feet will not be happy in combat boots tomorrow."

❦

Hayden led her to a patio on the side of the dormitory that was shielded by a privacy fence. In the background, tall fronds of pampas grass skittered against each other, creating a soft, swishing noise. He purchased bottled water for them both from a machine. Lacey wore a bright pink lightweight jacket, but her face was pale and drawn. Hayden worried about what she might be going to tell him.

In the past, he'd done what he could to prolong their conversations, but he sensed tonight that what Lacey wanted to say was difficult for her. Not being able to think of anything he could say to help her, he simply approached the matter head-on.

"So what is it you want to discuss?" Hayden probed, trying to keep his voice as even as possible.

Lacey's sigh sounded much like those blades of grass shifting against each other. "I'm not sure how to say this, Hayden. I mean, I've prayed a lot over the last few weeks, but I have to tell you, this isn't as easy as I thought it would be."

"Just go ahead and say it." Hayden faced her. An insane urge to tell her another joke nagged him. He sensed this wasn't the right time. Lacey's eyes were closed; though he ached to reach out and grasp her hands, he didn't.

The silence seemed almost deafening. After what felt like forever, Hayden finally spoke up. "The dormitory renovations are really nice, aren't they? Giving each of us a separate entrance to our rooms was really smart. Now we don't have to trek past everyone else's in a common hallway." Spoken aloud, it sounded silly, but he wanted to help ease Lacey's apparent anxiety.

When she didn't respond, Hayden continued. "In a way it reminds me of some of the houses I was raised in. Lots of glass and shiny steel everywhere."

Lacey's eyebrows rose as she opened her eyes. He noticed that their soft brown was now cool, as if the warmth had been snuffed out.

"You make it sound as if you resent your childhood. Do you?"

Hayden considered his response carefully. "Let's just say that my parents never settled for second best in anything. No matter where my father was assigned, Mother had to have the newest china, the most expensive floor coverings, and more famous paintings. You know, all the trappings that go with wealth. My sister and I were never allowed to be children. We had to be careful no matter where we were in the house."

"Oh." Lacey's eyes roved to a table where another couple sat talking quietly.

What is she thinking? Hayden wondered. *She seemed okay until I mentioned the type of home I grew up in.*

"You said you didn't have time to find out much about Shreveport," Hayden offered. "Well, lucky for you, I did do some studying on the town shortly after I got here. Anything specific you want to know?"

Chapter 6

Lacey's features relaxed, as if she appreciated his attempts to help her ease her way into voicing her thoughts. "Sure, but I warn you that your answers must be thorough."

"Then thorough they shall be," Hayden rejoined. He looked forward to meeting her challenge and to removing some of the worry wrinkles from her forehead.

"For starters, can you tell me why the town is called Shreveport?" Lacey asked.

Hayden winked and leaned back, placing his elbows behind him on the tabletop. "That's an easy one, Lace. Capt. Henry Shreve was commander of the U.S. Army Corps of Engineers. He was the main one behind the work that cleared almost 180 miles of the Red River of logjams and other obstructions. Shreve Town Company and eventually the village of Shreve Town were named in his honor. Shreve Town was located at the point where an overland route into the Republic of Texas and the Red River met. However, it wasn't until 1871 that the name Shreveport came about when they became a city."

"I really suspect you stay up all night not only reading jokes but entire encyclopedias in order to impress me, Hayden."

He placed his hands over his heart. "I'm hurt that you would think I'd do that. By the way, how do your feet feel?"

She gave him a suspicious glance, then stared down at her slip-on shoes. "Fine, but why do you ask that?"

"Because you told me a short time ago that you'd finish what you meant after you said you liked being with me."

"Oh. . ." Lacey's voice sounded full of dejection, or desperation; he wasn't sure which.

"I take it you're still not ready?"

❧

Lacey moved as if to stand and walk away. Hayden placed his hand on her arm.

"Don't run from me, Lace. I want you to know that you can tell me whatever you feel like sharing."

"I don't think so. Please don't be mad, Hayden, but I don't think I can tell you. Not yet."

"I respect that. So why don't I tell you more about Shreveport?"

Lacey gave a hesitant nod. Hayden spoke of the SciPort Discovery Center with its IMAX Theater, the newly established Red River Entertainment District, and a variety of other places to visit along the riverfront. Lastly, he mentioned Louisiana State University Medical Center where hundreds of doctors were trained in a variety of specialties.

He paused to wonder if there was a division specializing in healing broken hearts. If they did, he sensed he might end up as their first patient.

Their time together ended shortly thereafter. Lacey refused to talk about anything else. She said an abrupt, "Good night," and this time, successfully walked away.

As he watched Lacey head toward her room, Hayden whispered a prayer that no matter what happened, he wouldn't do anything to hurt her. Lacey had become all too special to him in such a short time, and he didn't see how he could ever stay away from her.

❧

Lacey knelt beside her bed and folded her hands beneath her chin. "Lord, I've only known Hayden for six weeks, but I feel things for him that I've never felt for a man before. Something happens when I look into his eyes, something that scares me with its intensity. But You know his background. He apparently comes from a wealthy family. I'm not good enough to associate with people of that sort. Please, Lord. Show me what You want, but don't let me get hurt where Hayden is concerned. Amen."

As Lacey lay on her bed, her gaze searched the ceiling for answers. She didn't find any—only the remnants of a conversation that she knew would stay with her forever. A memory whose power had intimidated her no matter what she did or where she went.

❧

"Your mama ain't no good," Lacey's father ranted, slamming

his fist onto the table and causing his bottle of beer to tip precariously as it rattled from side to side. "She up and left the day after you was born. Went with someone with a lot more money than I could ever make in a lifetime. She's gone, Lacey, so just quit thinking about her coming back someday. She ain't gonna do it. She didn't want me. She didn't want you. She only wanted the money."

Seven-year-old Lacey made herself as small as she could in the kitchen chair. Her fingers curled around the edges of the seat. She wished Aunt Trini were home. Aunt Trini could make anything better.

"Don't ever trust a person with a lot of money, Lacey," her dad had warned, shortly before he, too, walked out of her life.

❧

Lacey shook her head back and forth on the pillow, trying to chase away the remnants of her father's bitterness. Her alarm would go off in five hours. She closed her eyes, willing her body to relax. Her last conscious thought was that she had only sixteen hours until she would see Hayden again.

❧

Hayden detected a distance about Lacey that hadn't been there in their previous meetings. Some of it might be attributed to being tired because of her changing duty shifts, but he doubted it. He suspected something else caused the barrier between them.

"If you don't have anything else planned, why don't we go to the water park this weekend?"

"A water park? Is this something else you read about?" Lacey probed.

Hayden shook his head. "One of the guys in the dorm told me about it. Since it's February, it would be a little cold to swim. It's actually an evening put on by a local church. They've arranged to have some great local Christian groups playing."

"So Hayden Jacobs has a weak point. He doesn't learn everything he knows from books," Lacey said, her voice not quite as strong as it normally was.

"A weak point?" Hayden echoed.

Only that my heart has claimed you as its own, he thought. *Surely that can't be a weakness.*

"You listened to an airman? Was he older or younger than you?" Lacey quizzed.

"Younger, but he's been here for ten months, and he's got a fiancée."

"Being engaged doesn't mean someone is mature," Lacey cautioned.

"What's that got to do with whether or not I believe him? Lace, you're not making sense."

"Is he a Christian?"

"I didn't ask. He was in the dayroom watching television. I just inquired what types of things there were to do around town. The water park was the first thing he mentioned. Surely if he's been there, I can trust him."

Lacey sighed. "I suppose so. It's just that I don't usually rely on someone if I don't know that they're my brother or sister in Christ."

"That's a pretty heavy statement, Lace." Hayden leaned over and took her hand. She tensed but didn't pull away.

"What's bothering you? Am I pushing too fast? Do you have a significant other back in Chicago you haven't told me about?"

"There's no one else," Lacey assured him. "It's just that I can tell by the way you speak about your family that you and I were raised in totally different atmospheres. We've only known each other such a short time, but it's obvious that we don't have much in common."

"And you can't believe that we could establish something life changing in that short amount of time?"

Lacey's solemn shake of her head told Hayden everything he didn't want to know.

"You believe in Jesus, right?" he asked, bringing up the most important thread as far as he was concerned that he knew they shared.

"Yes. Why?"

"If we both believe, then what could there be that would stop us from building a friendship?"

"Is that all you're looking for?" Lacey's dark gaze bored into his.

"I won't lie to you, Lace. I think I've already progressed beyond the friendship stage, but friendship has to come first."

Chapter 7

Beyond the friendship stage, Lacey's heart reiterated. *But there's so much you don't know about me, Hayden. If I told you, it would push you away from me so fast that my heart would be shredded in the process.*

"So, are you ready for another lesson on Shreveport?" Hayden prodded.

"You mean you're not going to push and try to find out why I think you and I can never be more than friends?"

"No. I'll settle for whatever time I can have with you. And I'll pray that someday you'll trust me enough to confide in me about what bothers you. I'll be here when you change your mind, okay?"

"Sure," she said skeptically. "But I'll warn you that I've worked with experienced therapists, and they haven't been able to help me."

"Maybe they just didn't use the right approach for you despite their qualifications. I'm a patient man," Hayden said. "When I see something I want, I pray and ask God to lead my steps. With Him in control, I don't have a problem being patient until He shows me that it's the right time for something to happen in my life."

❧

"How are things there?" Hayden's mother's voice came through the receiver in her put-on Southern drawl.

Not, how are you, Son? but how are things there? Hayden noted.

"Fine, Mother. I'm having a great time. Read my Bible. Work. Eat. Sleep. Read my Bible. Work some more."

"You don't sound fine, Hayden Thomas Jacobs III. You sound tired and worried. I'd much rather you'd taken that military academy appointment. At least your sleepless nights would be worth something in the end."

Hayden ignored the sarcastic remark his mother thrust at him. "It's five in the morning here, Mother. But I wanted to wish you happy birthday first thing."

"You always were the sentimental one in the family, weren't you? Oh! Your cousin Gloria finally managed to snag Richard Gleason. You remember him, don't you? He is the most eligible bachelor in Virginia. The wedding will be in mid-August. Gloria has asked your father to escort her down the aisle. You will come, won't you?"

"We'll see, Mother. I really don't know how the leave schedule will work out for me by then."

"I'm sure your father can take care of that. Don't forget that he's a general, you know. That's got to count for something."

"No, Mother. I don't want Father messing with my

career. I've told you that before. I wish you'd understand."

❧

"Whazzup, Hayden?" Shelley used the teenage vernacular for "what's up?"

"Too much at times and not enough at others," Hayden replied, moving a stack of notes from a Bible study he'd been working on to the side.

"Ah, a cryptic statement from a man who often hides behind sunglasses. You know you can't hide from God, Hayden. He sees through those glasses right to your heart."

"I know, Shelley." Hayden glanced to where the mentioned sunglasses lay on the desk. "Believe me, I know."

"You haven't answered my question yet." Shelley drummed her fingers on the counter she leaned against.

"All right. I give. 'What's up' is that I got a letter from Mother."

"I got one too. But there is something else bothering you, isn't there?" Shelley probed.

"I've fallen for Lacey."

Shelley smirked. "I wondered how long it would take you to realize it. If that's the case, then why don't you look happier?"

"I don't know. We've known each other less than two months. The other night I tried to get an idea of how she felt about me, but I didn't get anywhere. Somehow our family came up in conversation. I mentioned how our house was always filled with expensive china and things. From that moment on, I've felt Lacey pulling away."

Shelley folded her arms in front of her. "I see. So you told her that our parents are well-off?"

Hayden frowned. "You know Father is a general. Generals make lots of money."

"Anyone can have all the money in the world and not be wealthy where eternal things are concerned."

"I know that too, Shelley. We've had this talk before. You know Father used to force us to read the Bible, but doing so never seemed to make an impression on us."

Shelley nodded. "It was only when I spent the night at a friend's house that I found out about Jesus; then I shared it with you."

"That's what I'm getting at, Shelley. I know that Father thinks history is important; after all, it was his major in college, but I'm not sure today that he—or Mother, for that matter—truly knows our Savior."

"It bothers both of us, Hay-Hay," Shelley said. "And stop giving me that 'quit-using-the-nickname-you-hate' look. I worry about Mother and Father's salvation. But we've spoken with them; we've prayed for them, and all we can do is trust God to resolve their lives."

"I guess that's what faith is all about, isn't it? That we trust God to figure out the big picture while we just paint in our own scenes."

"Sure. Each of us has a mission to fill here on earth. We are here until God's purpose for our lives is fulfilled. Only He knows why He put us here, or why He moves us from place to place."

"Or why we end up doing things completely opposite of what our family expects," Hayden offered. "Like why we both enlisted when it obviously wasn't what our parents wanted."

"While we may never know why we turned out the way we did, God knows. He also knows what He is doing where Mother and Father are concerned. So what do you say we quit worrying about them for a few minutes and let's go grab some food at the dining facility?"

Chapter 8

You're sure you don't mind, Lacey? I appreciate your volunteering, but you aren't scheduled to go until the next rotation. I can tap someone else for this TDY assignment."

Lacey smiled at her first sergeant. He outranked her, but they'd developed a quick rapport upon her assignment to his squadron. She imagined him much like an older brother, not that she had one to compare him to.

"Three days is pretty short notice for this temporary duty, but I look forward to the trip. Maybe a change of scenery will spice up my life. Or maybe I'll meet that mystery man that is destined to be the love of my life."

Sergeant Burks grinned back. "I don't know about meeting any mystery man. You'll be working mainly with others who are also stationed here at Barksdale."

"I do a lot of work with the young airmen's council, but I don't know everyone on base, Sir," Lacey pointed out. "And maybe even the ones I do know will look different in Guam."

Sergeant Burks grinned. "That's what I like about young airmen like you. You're willing to work hard and do it with a smile on your face. You always seem to have a positive outlook on life. Do you ever have a bad day?"

"There are plenty of them, Sir. But the secret is what's in my heart. I love the Lord. No matter what life throws at me, I know He'll help me survive it."

Though Lacey voiced her beliefs, she knew her faith often fell short. Sometimes her outward attitude was an attempt to convince her inner self to be the same way.

"Ah, I should have realized," the sergeant replied. "You sound like my mother. She was a good Christian woman, bless her soul. Mama sure did love the Lord. Myself, I've fallen away from going to church. I tell myself I need to get back to it, but I just never do."

"Whenever you decide to go back, God will be waiting. Now if you'll excuse me, Sir, I have some packing to do."

And I have to figure out how to tell Hayden that I'm leaving for a few weeks without hurting his feelings, she thought, her heart already aching as she realized how much she would miss him.

❦

"Aren't you too young to think about getting married?" Eric lived in the dorm room next to Hayden, and now and then the two ended up eating at the dining facility at the same time. "You should enjoy being single first."

"I'm twenty-two," Hayden responded. "Married people can enjoy life too, Eric. At least I think that is what my parents did in between the military balls and charity functions they attended."

"Didn't you tell me that your father is a general and that he didn't like the fact that you enlisted?"

Hayden shrugged, hoping he hid his innermost feelings. "He thinks I should have accepted an appointment to a military academy instead and ended up as an officer like him. My sister, Shelley, enlisted first; I simply followed her lead."

"Any chance he'll come around someday and accept what the two of you have done?" Eric asked.

"I doubt it, but I can always hope."

"Well, I've got to meet the guys at the club in a few minutes. Best of luck in your travels. If I don't see you before you leave, don't get into trouble over there. I've heard that sometimes the local girls are out to find themselves a husband. Wouldn't want you to get involved in anything that might lead to you being put in jail."

"I promise I won't be led to do something along those lines," Hayden replied, while he shivered inside. He might as well have been locked up when he was growing up. From friends to music to food, his father had controlled every aspect of his life.

"I'll be fine," Hayden continued, wincing at Eric's good-natured slap on the back. "I'll see you in three weeks. Thanks for agreeing to feed my hermit crab for me. Just remember to clean his home out more often than the day before I come back."

Eric's laughter followed him down the sidewalk.

❦

The aircraft slowly filled with groups of airmen, some talkative, some quietly reflecting on having to leave their families. Hayden took his seat toward a rear window, situating his carry-on. While he waited for takeoff from Shreveport Regional Airport, he wondered why Lacey had been abnormally quiet the last few times they'd been together.

She'd grown especially pale at his mention that he was going TDY for three weeks to Guam. Though he hadn't pushed the issue, he wished just once she'd trusted him enough to confide in him and share something more than Bible verses or jokes. Catching sight of the back of a young woman's head, Hayden almost jumped from his seat and rushed to the front to see if it was Lacey.

Don't be so stupid, he warned himself. *Why would she be on this flight?*

Chapter 9

Lacey hoped no one she knew would call out her name as she boarded the plane. When Hayden told her he was going TDY, she'd tried to figure out how she could get to the same location without him finding out. She wasn't sure she could pull it off, but that was something she didn't want to think about. She would cross that bridge if and when she came to it.

If she'd only told him that she was also going, she'd have avoided all of this aggravation. Instead, she'd chosen to be secretive about it, and now her stomach was in knots.

The only plan she'd come up with was to arrive late and hope Hayden had already boarded. She did so, just making it through the tough security check before a silky feminine voice announced the last call for Lacey's flight.

She'd asked for a seat near the front of the aircraft on purpose, hoping that Hayden would be much farther back. If he asked, Lacey couldn't explain why she hadn't told Hayden about her going on the same temporary duty assignment.

She just knew there were a lot of things she couldn't tell him, no matter how hard she tried.

As the plane's engine revved and they swung onto the runway to prepare for takeoff, Lacey's mouth grew dry. She wasn't worried about flying. She was wondering how Hayden would react when he saw her in Guam.

"Welcome to Guam, ladies and gentlemen. The present temperature is seventy-four degrees. The sunshine and blue skies couldn't be more perfect." The captain's voice droned on. Hayden barely listened as he gathered his Bible and carry-on luggage in preparation for deplaning.

It had been a long flight, saved only by a seatmate that had chatted little and slept much, leaving Hayden plenty of time to read his Bible. He'd tried to discern why Lacey kept trying to put distance between them.

Every nonverbal signal he got from her seemed to shout acceptance. Verbally was a different matter. When he was younger, he and Shelley used to work jigsaw puzzles. While Shelley got frustrated when she couldn't find pieces that matched right away, Hayden enjoyed the challenge of working to find the one piece with just the right shading and shapes to fit somewhere.

Lacey White was somewhat like a puzzle, Hayden decided. She had a variety of edges, none of which seemed to match up with any of the others. It was as if during her childhood she'd been tossed and torn between many different settings. Hayden knew she'd been trying to mail a package to her aunt in Chicago when he first met her, but he'd never asked about any other family. Lacey had never volunteered any information. So where did that leave him?

Wishing he didn't have to spend three weeks in Guam without Lacey, that's where.

❧

Lacey headed for the baggage claim area. She was eager to get the next three weeks over with. While sight-seeing appealed to her, she was more interested in using the time to figure out how to tell Hayden why she couldn't see him anymore.

She still had to give Hayden her decision about their relationship, and she had to do it soon. To leave him dangling and thinking that there was a chance for them would not be good for either of them. Looking down at her sneakers, she almost wished they were ruby slippers and that by tapping them together she could vanish to a safe world. Except that she had no safe world. Even Aunt Trini didn't act like she really wanted Lacey to live with her anymore, though they'd never really discussed the subject once Lacey had enlisted.

❧

"Lacey?" Hayden couldn't believe his eyes. Here he'd flown almost eight thousand miles, all the while wishing he'd stayed at Barksdale because he was going to miss Lacey, and she was standing in front of him.

"Uh, hi, Hayden." Lacey's voice contained no surprise, but bright splotches of red filled her cheeks. The amber flecks were missing from her soft brown eyes and had been replaced by something that he could only deduce added up to fear.

"So how long are you here for?" Hayden placed his hand along her back and guided her around other passengers headed in the opposite direction.

"The same as you," she replied, glancing around as if looking for a means of escape.

"That means that. . ." He faltered, unsure of how far to take his accusation.

"Yes, I knew I was coming on this TDY when you told me you were too. I hid it from you. Did I have a reason? It sounds lame now that I voice it; but no, I didn't, or if I did, I can't tell you what it is."

Hayden stopped their progress through the crowd and placed his hands on her shoulders. Taking a deep breath and saying a quick prayer he would say the right thing, he went on, "Lace. You don't have to explain to me. Remember I told you I'm a patient man. I'll wait for you until you work through whatever it is that is bothering you."

"I know, Hayden, but what I did wasn't right. I wouldn't blame you if you walked away from me right now and never wanted to see me again."

"Lacey, I'm not perfect, and I'm certainly not walking away. Have you ever stopped to think that God might have planned for us to share this TDY together? I can't say that I'll argue with Him about that, can you?"

❧

No, she couldn't argue with God and His reasons or methods

for keeping her and Hayden so close together. Lacey knew that. She'd unpacked but had been so baffled by Hayden's understanding that she probably wouldn't remember where she'd stowed anything. She didn't know where to turn. No one in her life had ever shown her as much patience or consistency as Hayden. Lacey wasn't sure that she knew what to do next.

❧

Hayden raised his knuckles to rap at her billet door but paused. *Lord, if my being together with Lacey is Your wish, give me words that will help her heal from whatever it is that constantly chases her.* Then Hayden knocked.

"I'm ready for some fun in the sun, as they say back in the States," he announced as she opened the entrance. "Get your things and don't give me 'no' for an answer."

"At seven o'clock in the morning?" Lacey tightened her robe and wiped the sleep from her eyes as she peered into the bright Guam sunshine.

"Okay. If you insist, I'll give you 'til seven-thirty," Hayden stated. "But I still won't take 'no' for an answer."

Lacey groaned. "Hayden. This is my first day off after eight straight days of twelve-hour shift work. I'd planned on sleeping in."

Hayden was encouraged. At least she hadn't slammed the door shut. "I planned on sleeping in too, but then I just couldn't see wasting my time off doing something so mundane."

"Big words are not going to make me reconsider." Lacey

rubbed at her eyes again.

"I could always tell you another joke if you prefer." Hayden waited for her response.

Lacey moaned. "Please don't. Look, why don't you go along on your sight-seeing mission, and we can meet up tonight for dinner or something."

Hayden didn't like it when someone pulled rank on him, especially after all the times he'd seen his father use his general's stars to gain an advantage. He didn't like insisting, and he wasn't sure how Lacey would receive it, but he spoke anyway.

"Why don't you get dressed and go along on my sight-seeing mission, as you call it, then we can still be together at dinner tonight?"

Chapter 10

Lacey and Hayden spent the morning admiring blankets, purses, and jewelry on display, but she wouldn't purchase anything despite Hayden's offers several times to buy it for her. They finally stopped to rest and enjoy a glass of chilled lemonade. The sounds of local vendors hawking their wares intermingled with bits and pieces of conversation, filling the street with a cacophony of sounds.

"Aren't you glad you decided to come along with me?" Hayden asked.

"Decided? I seem to remember that you maintained I had no choice." She gave Hayden a pointed look. "I'd like to say that it beats getting extra sleep anytime, but I don't think that would be honest."

"I think I'll ignore the hint that you'd rather sleep than be with me and concentrate on your beautiful smile instead," Hayden responded.

"So now that I'm your hostage, do you think you can fill me in on what you have planned for dinner tonight?"

"I'd never call you a hostage, Lacey. And dinner? Why, that's a good five or six hours away yet! We have a lot more to do and see before we even think about eating again. Besides, you can't tell me that you're hungry already. We just had three hot dogs apiece."

"*You* had three hot dogs, Hayden Jacobs III. I only had one, thank you."

Hayden leaned across the table to close the distance between them. "I like the way you say that."

"That what?"

"My name."

Lacey ducked her head to hide the blush she felt creeping up her cheeks. She didn't want to, but she did like the way his name rolled off her tongue. It was smooth, yet strong, and gave the impression of boldness without being too pushy.

"My mother used to call me that all the time, except when she said it, it was more the 'you're in trouble, and I'm going to tell your father about this' tone."

"If it bothers you, then I'll not say it again." Lacey stared at the tabletop. The memory of what she'd decided to tell Hayden a few weeks ago rushed to her mind.

She couldn't look at him. Why wasn't there ever a good time to break things off? Why wasn't she able to just say the words straight out? For a moment she wondered if she might find a way to stay in Guam when the temporary duty was up—Hayden would go back to the States, and that way she wouldn't have to explain a thing.

"It doesn't bother me," Hayden insisted. "I prefer the way you say it. In fact, you can call me that anytime you want."

Lacey opened her eyes and took a deep breath. She had an overwhelming need to take his hand and feel the warmth and strength he imparted whenever they touched. Her hand began to move toward his on the tabletop.

No! I can't be friends with him. And I certainly can't get to the point where I think I love him! I have to tell him that there can't be anything between us.

She withdrew her hand and hoped he hadn't noticed. The more time she spent with him, the more she learned that Hayden Jacobs III was in a league that would never allow her admittance. He'd been raised in the lap of luxury with both parents while her mother had left the day after Lacey's birth with a man who could provide her with more than love.

Unexpectedly, the perfect reason to put some distance between them occurred to her. She didn't want to say it, but she had to. She would not be controlled by another man.

"Hearing your name and all those numbers at the end is a power trip for you, isn't it?" Lacey's bitter accusation hung between them, leaving Hayden wondering where her abrupt change of attitude had come from. During their morning together, he thought they'd made progress toward understanding each other's likes and dislikes and closing some of the differences in the way they were raised.

He leaned back in his chair, then realized that put too

much space between them. He sat up and rested his elbows on the table, angling toward her. "A power trip? Absolutely not! Whatever gave you that idea?"

He watched her eyes shift from soft brown to the hardness of a coconut shell.

"Well, you are a general's son, aren't you?" she pointed out. "You were raised with all the conveniences of life that some only dream about."

Hayden was confused. This was not the Lacey White that he'd grown to care about. Something was bothering her. She'd never brought up his background with this much contempt before. Why now?

He thought back over their conversations that morning but found nothing that might identify the source of her pain.

"Lacey, I don't know how you found out about my father being a general, but doesn't the fact that my sister and I both enlisted instead of getting commissions tell you what we thought of our upbringing?"

"I did some research and found out about your father rather easily. Besides, being enlisted could mean anything, Hayden," Lacey pointed out. "Maybe your grades weren't good enough to get you into a military academy. Or you tried one for awhile and failed, and because you still felt some sense of devotion to your country, you decided to enlist."

He watched as Lacey spun her straw in the glass of lemonade around and around, studying the small whirlpool she'd created. She was evidently trying to avoid looking at him. Hayden's stomach twisted and his mouth grew dry as he realized where this conversation was headed. It felt as though he was sitting on an airplane that was already headed toward takeoff and he was powerless to make it stop.

"Lace, have you considered that mine and my sister's enlistments might mean that both of us thought it was the only way to make our own way in life without our parents directing every move?" Hayden probed quietly.

※

"Lord, I've really done it now, haven't I?" Lacey's question ricocheted around her billet room that afternoon. She got no answer from the walls or from God. She threw a pillow toward the bed, and the miniscule lamp on the night table teetered back and forth.

"I meant to be straightforward and calm when I told him that I couldn't see him anymore. Instead I sounded like a grouch. To top it off, the reason he enlisted is probably true, and I wouldn't even listen to him. What do I do now, Lord?"

Lacey sunk against the plaid-covered cushions of the recliner in her room and closed her eyes. She wished she could relive the entire day. She'd planned on letting him know they had to break it off anyway.

Maybe it's better this way, Lacey decided. Her heart gave a different response.

※

Hayden shook his head as he tried to figure out where things had gone wrong between him and Lacey. Through the last few months, he thought they were building a solid friendship, which he hoped would deepen into something more. Without warning she was implying that she wasn't good enough for him.

What did her abrupt departure mean? Would he see her again while they were in Guam—or was it over? No, he wouldn't accept the last. He replayed the morning and Lacey's parting words over and over, seeking a reason for her clear change of heart. What had he done?

He'd woken her early, adamant that she join him. Perhaps all that walking on top of eight long days of work and little sleep had made her cranky and short-tempered? Hayden didn't think that was the basis for her actions.

He headed toward the shower to wash off the remains of the sunblock he'd smeared on that morning. He might not like what had happened with Lacey, but he wasn't going to let it spoil the remainder of his trip to Guam. Clear blue skies and gorgeous sandy beaches called to him, and he was going to do something about seeing them.

Rounding up a few friends from his home squadron at Barksdale, he told them they were headed out and that he was paying for everything.

Hayden wished it were Lacey sitting beside him. The airmen that accepted his offer of a free meal and entertainment were boisterous and sometimes bordered on obnoxious. Hayden knew they were just glad to have some free time and they only wanted to make the most of it.

"Great food, isn't it, Hayden?" one of the young men shouted from the other end of their table.

He nodded in agreement, but to him the world-famous

baby-back ribs he ate might as well have been dried cardboard coated with ketchup.

Partway through the creamy rich concoction of whipped topping, strawberries, and some sort of chocolate sauce that was dessert, one of the airmen with Hayden drew him aside.

"You're not very good company tonight. When you offered to pay, I thought we were coming out to celebrate. Can you shake off whatever is bothering you for the sake of the other guys?"

"You're right," Hayden acknowledged. "Tonight is my treat, but that doesn't give me the right to sit here and ignore the rest of you."

They shared a quick laugh and though John encouraged Hayden to order a mixed drink, Hayden refused. He knew what alcohol did to people. He'd watched his uncle deteriorate over the years, and Hayden wasn't about to take that road. The Bible said to keep on the straight and narrow path, and that was what he aimed for.

From that point on, Hayden tried to enjoy the conversation and his friends, but his heart wouldn't allow it. Every beat seemed to shout, *Lacey. Come back. Lacey. Come back.*

❧

Hayden checked his hermit crab the moment he walked in his room. "I hope Eric treated you okay, Buddy," he said, reaching in and picking up the multicolored shell in order to check and see if his pet was still alive.

Eric's chuckle came through the open door. "What did you think I'd do, Hayden? Let him die?"

"I know how involved you get in your video games as soon as you get home from work." Hayden gave a small laugh to show Eric he meant no harm.

"Well, he survived. So, how was your trip? No—forget that. Tell me how great the local girls were."

"I hate to disappoint you, Eric, but other than a couple of waitresses, I didn't meet a single one."

"I knew if you and Lacey got over there together on that island you'd only have eyes for each other." Eric laughed again, but this time it grated on Hayden's nerves.

Hayden returned the crab to its plastic housing and headed to his suitcases. He tried not to sound short-tempered when he finally spoke.

"You mean you knew that Lacey was going to Guam at the same time as me? Why didn't you tell me? How could you, Eric? I thought we were friends." Hayden plopped onto the bed and glared at Eric, who still leaned against the doorframe.

"You mean you didn't know? All you had to do was check the printout on the bulletin board. Everyone who was going had his or her name on there. I'm not a general's son, and even I thought of that!"

Hayden didn't respond, but Eric was right. If he'd just read the squadron bulletin board, he'd have known ahead of time that Lacey would be going.

An unbidden question popped into his mind. He'd mentioned to Lacey that he was going on the TDY, so why hadn't she let him know that she was also? Something didn't make sense where this situation was concerned.

Chapter 11

Lacey swiped her sweaty hands on the sides of her camouflaged uniform pants, then reached up to pat her braided hair and make sure it wasn't out of place or hanging below the bottom of her shirt collar before she entered her first sergeant's office. To say that she was somewhat leery of what she was about to hear was an understatement.

Sergeant Burks looked up from his seat in his imitation leather high-backed chair. The look on his face didn't bode well and made her tongue feel as if it were made of cotton.

"Have a seat, Lacey," he said, motioning to a chair.

Was his voice gruffer than usual? She took a deep breath and settled onto the stiff padded seat in front of his desk. She let her arms hang at her sides, barely grazing the cool metal of the chair's frame.

"Don't look so worried," he said. "I called you here to tell you that I heard you did a great job in Guam."

Lacey breathed a sigh of relief that she wasn't in trouble. "Thank you for the compliment, Sir," she managed to respond, her tongue still a cottony mess even though it appeared there wasn't a reason to be worried now.

Sergeant Burks studied her face for a minute. "Did anything happen in Guam that you want to tell me about?"

"No, Sir. Nothing out of the usual." *Other than having my heart broken,* she thought.

He looked as if he was about to ask if she was sure but instead said, "The real reason you're here is so I can tell you that the squadron commander has granted everyone who returned from this TDY four days off. Take some time and relax. I know Shreveport and Bossier City isn't exactly the island of Guam, but the area does have a lot to offer."

"Some extra time off sounds great," Lacey agreed.

They discussed a few more job-related items before his ringing telephone interrupted their meeting. Lacey left the office quietly and headed down the hall toward the exit.

Do I have the power to patch my heart in four short days when I haven't been able to heal from an attack that happened almost two years ago?

❧

The first strains of "There is Power in the Blood" surrounded Hayden as he entered the chapel Sunday morning. Physically, the interior of the chapel offered a cool respite from the intense late-June humidity and heat; Hayden hoped it would provide the same soothing relief to his soul. He wondered if he'd see Lacey this morning but after a quick glance around, he realized she wasn't there.

Ever since Lacey had left him in Guam, he'd tried to

figure out exactly what went wrong between them. His efforts to get in touch with her were unsuccessful so far; it was as if she'd disappeared from the area.

Hayden sighed as he sat down in the back row. If he could soothe his troubled spirit, perhaps he might just learn to live without seeing Lacey every day. He once thought that being left behind with sitters while his parents attended one function after another every evening was lonely. Without Lacey, loneliness had a brand-new meaning. It was a definition he didn't like at all.

Hayden turned his mind to the reason he'd come to worship, hoping to ease at least some of his heartache. The fellowship auditorium had comfortable pews and a line of small chairs at the front for young children. The present minister made it a habit to preach a children's sermon at the beginning of each weekly service. Last week's message had compared God to a magnet and how His love always stuck to a person. Small magnets that said "Jesus Loves Me!" had been passed out to each child that day.

The memory of their smiles brought a smile to Hayden's face. He couldn't wait to have a child someday, a sweet little girl with long, dark hair like Lacey's. Hayden remembered what had happened between them in Guam. There would probably never be a chance that they would ever have children. The thought brought him immense pain.

Hayden glanced to a massive stained-glass depiction of Christ on the cross behind the podium. The sight, as usual, took his breath away. No matter how many times he saw the window portrait, it reminded him of the way God had revealed His power to mankind. It was that power that had given Hayden the ability to rebel against his father's forcefulness and enlist in the air force instead of seeking a commission as his father wished Hayden would.

Hayden bowed his head, letting the opening prayer flow over him. He hoped some of the words would find the open crevices in his heart, settle into them, and seal them off so that his pain over losing Lacey would lessen. The chances of that happening seemed small, though. His heart was hungry in a way it had never been before, and he knew it was because of Lacey.

❧

"It all comes down to power," Lacey said. "Power and command. He's a typical rich boy. He thinks that all he has to do is. . ." Her words trailed off. Thankfully Aunt Trini couldn't see her, Lacey thought, as she dabbed at the tears seeping down her cheeks.

"I don't understand. What is it that he's done that makes you compare him to the other destructive males in your past?" Her aunt's voice was somewhat brittle and short, as if this was not a good time for the phone call.

Lacey twirled the phone cord around her fingers as she looked around her dorm room. "It's hard to put into words, but it's a feeling that. . .I'm not in control when I'm with him."

She could hear Aunt Trini's sharp intake of breath. "And you think he makes you feel that way on purpose?"

Lacey sighed. "I guess that's not the only thing. I know

that I'm scared when I think about how I feel when I'm with him."

"And why is that, Lacey?"

As usual there were no endearments from her father's sister. Aunt Trini never called Lacey anything but her given name. Sometimes Lacey wondered how she'd ended up with her aunt when her grandparents could just have easily have taken care of her. It was a question she wanted answered someday, but today wasn't the time to ask it.

"I don't know, Aunt Trini. If I knew that, I'd know why being around Hayden scares me so much."

"Oh, before I forget, Lacey. I put the little pillow you sent on the rocking chair by the front window. That way, I see it every day and it reminds me to pray for you."

Lacey almost blurted out that she didn't want to be prayed for if the sender had to have something that reminded her to do so. She bit back her retort. Getting angry with her aunt wouldn't solve anything, at least not the anything Lacey wanted resolved.

"Thanks, Aunt Trini. I think I'm going to need all the prayers I can get in the coming months," she said.

❧

Celebratory sounds and commingled aromas of beef, potatoes, and vegetables filled the Officers' Club. Lacey spotted one of her coworkers standing in line at the buffet and moved to join her.

"Great promotion party, isn't it?" Jean Williams asked.

"Seems like it. A little too noisy for me, though." Lacey

put some meat loaf, barbecue wings, then salad on her plate as they made their way through the buffet. Finding seats across the room in a corner, the two sat down. Lacey bowed her head and offered a quick prayer of thanks for the food, knowing Jean was waiting for her to finish.

A commotion at the entrance drew their attention, but it appeared to be just a few overexcited promotees.

"Next month it will be our turn to celebrate," Jean said. "I can't wait. Not that it's much, but I have plans for the extra money I'll get every month."

"Every little bit helps." Lacey used a phrase she'd heard Aunt Trini state repeatedly throughout her childhood. Money—another reminder of the differences between her and Hayden—money and power. He had it, and she didn't.

"So it does," Jean agreed. "My money's going toward buying a new car. What about yours?"

Lacey didn't want to admit how little money she had left after she sent part of her check to her aunt. "I don't know. A car would be nice," she said without commitment.

"A car would be great!" Jean insisted. "And it would certainly make it easier to go places here."

"It would do that," Lacey granted.

With a vehicle, her time off could be spent driving around Shreveport or Bossier City and visiting some of the museums or tourist attractions. Without a car, she'd spent her four-day weekend hiding out in her dorm room, ignoring the phone—which rang every half hour from eight in the morning to nine at night. She knew it was Hayden calling, and she'd almost caved in and answered but hadn't. They were too different to find any common ground, despite her heart's desire to do so. It was just another example of her inability to choose wisely when it came to men.

❦

"All right, folks. If I could have your attention at the front of the room, please, we'll begin reading the list of promotions that take effect on August 1."

The squadron commander was a tall, lanky man, and it didn't take long for the hubbub to quiet. Lacey listened as the names were read off in alphabetical order. As each person went to the front of the room, a spouse or parent followed and helped to "pin on" the new rank.

"John Baker. Moses Disameaux. Pedro Gomez."

The list of names continued. Each promotee and their family member paused for a quick picture and a short round of applause before leaving the platform to return to their seats.

Few squadrons held such elaborate parties for their members since it was funded through money raised within the squadron and with a small contribution from each promotee. Lacey's squadron was quite successful with concession booths for lunchtime and snack breaks, so they were able to go all-out to recognize their colleagues.

Jean sat quietly, absorbing every movement involved so she would know what to do next month when it was her turn. Lacey watched also, but at the next name voiced, her gaze followed the handsome young man she'd done nothing but think of lately.

Hayden walked to the front. Accompanying him was a general in his blue, tailored service dress uniform. A stack of ribbons above a pocket on the left side of his jacket proclaimed his deeds of importance to his country; a single star on each shoulder reflected the light from the chandeliers above.

I'd rather be anywhere else other than this promotion party, Lacey thought downheartedly.

She watched as Hayden marched smartly to the front, his own glance searching the crowded room as his father prepared to hand him his new set of stripes, a not-quite smile on the rigid general's face.

Lacey knew at that moment that she'd done the right thing in Guam. Anything she and Hayden might have had between them had no chance of success. Not with a general—specifically this stiff-faced general—between them.

With no explanation, Lacey stood and rushed out the nearest door. Lacey's heart raced as she heard Hayden's voice calling to her as she ran down a carpeted hall. Along the way, pictures of past Barksdale commanders hung, the stars on their uniforms taunting her much as Hayden's father's had. *Hide,* her body demanded. *Hide now or lose whatever little control you have left.*

❧

"Hayden Jacobs III! Come back here this instant."

There was no doubt that his father was upset, and he had every right to be. Hayden running out almost as soon as his father handed him his new stripes was not appropriate military courtesy. That didn't matter. What mattered was Lacey's face as she'd left. His heart followed her out of the room, preceding his body by at least fifty feet.

"Lacey, please don't go!" Hayden felt somewhat childish as he hurried across and through the crammed room. He knew people were staring and whispering, but all of that took second place to what he needed to accomplish.

He arrived at the hallway, only to watch as Lacey disappeared into the women's rest room. Hayden seated himself on a sofa near the door to wait for her, while Gen. Hayden Jacobs II arrived and towered over him, his hands on his hips and obvious displeasure with his only son written on his face.

"We have something very serious here to discuss." General Jacobs's tone was one that said this was one battle Hayden shouldn't enter.

Hayden knew he deserved every bit of the disapproval his father voiced; however, Lacey was more important than his father. The fact filled with him with trepidation yet relief at the same time. No matter what it took, he had to get her to accept the differences in their backgrounds. His poor choices in the past with women had prepared him to understand how special Lacey was.

The only thing he could think of was that at this minute he wanted to marry her, even though his parents would object. He meant no disrespect, but his father's power over him was no longer a consideration.

Hayden might be young, but he was his own man, a man who knew that Lacey was the one he'd waited for all his life.

For now, though, his mission wasn't convincing Lacey of that; it was trying to get his father to understand his feelings.

Hayden stood, wishing he were taller than six feet so he could face his father eye-to-eye. Reaching a decision about himself and Lacey gave him a sense of peace he didn't remember ever having, except for those times when they'd been together.

"Father, before you start with your lecture, at least listen to what I have to say. What I did in there wasn't proper, and I apologize. I'll go back in tell my squadron commander also, just as soon I get done talking to Lacey."

"You will not talk to that woman, Hayden. She's just an airman. She probably owns nothing more than a portable radio and a suitcase. She is definitely not the one for you."

Hayden checked the hall to make sure no one could hear their heated conversation. "Father, may I remind you that I am also 'just an airman'? And, despite what you think, Lacey is everything to me. No impertinence intended, but I will talk to her just as soon as she comes back out here. I can't do any less."

"What you can do," his father insisted, the frustration in his voice sounding like a tank on a battlefield, "is go back in there right now and apologize to Lieutenant Colonel Murray. I will not have him thinking that I raised a son to be so. . .tactless and rude, just to mention a few things."

❧

Hayden didn't want to, but he gave up waiting for Lacey after forty-five minutes. His father, decidedly disgruntled, had long ago returned to the ballroom area, probably to assure Hayden's squadron commander that his son was not to be judged on his rash actions of the day. Hayden ran his hand through his hair.

Getting his father to understand that Hayden must make his own decisions, right or wrong, was not a job Hayden looked forward to. However, with Lacey's help maybe they could come up with a solution. If he could just get Lacey to help, that is. . . .

❧

Lacey ignored the women who came through the sitting area attached to the rest room. She'd wet down a few pieces of paper toweling and used them occasionally to pat at her eyes, forehead, and back of her neck. Thoughts of Hayden as he'd sought her out crossed her mind. She recalled the contentment she'd felt all the times they'd been together and how empty she'd felt since her TDY to Guam.

Was Hayden still sitting outside waiting for her? She checked her watch and found an hour had passed since she'd run in here to hide away. Surely he'd given up by now, hadn't he? She remembered the four-day weekend when her phone rang consistently every half hour. He hadn't given up then.

But then, she reminded herself, his father hadn't been in attendance.

Well, the only way to find out for sure was to leave the rest room. Bracing herself for what she might find, Lacey rose and walked to the door.

A prodding notion took hold in her heart. What if

Hayden was still there and waiting with his father? What would she do then?

❧

"Did our first sergeant find you, Hayden?" Eric asked as Hayden walked down the sidewalk to his dorm room door.

"No. After the promotion party, my father insisted we visit one of the riverfront casinos so he could waste a couple hundred dollars. Do you know what the first shirt wanted?" Hayden quizzed, using the well-known slang for "first sergeant."

Eric shook his head. "He's been calling everyone in the dorms that have a phone trying to find you. Sounds like it might be pretty important."

"Thanks, Eric. I'll call him right away." What could the first sergeant want? Hayden's stomach soured as he thought of how immature he'd acted that afternoon by running out after Lacey.

Hayden had taken the squadron commander aside privately and apologized for leaving so quickly without explaining why he'd done it, but the first shirt probably didn't know he had done so. That was what the phone call was about. What else could it be?

Chapter 12

"Ma'am? Airman White? You're at the base hospital. Please try not to move while we examine you. Do you remember what happened?"

Despite being warned not to do so, Lacey tried to move her head. The action caused an immediate stab of pain through her temple. Her hair felt matted and stuck to the right side of her head, so she lifted her right arm to feel what was wrong.

Another stab of pain, only this one was so severe Lacey thought she might pass out. Apparently that wouldn't be anything new as she had no idea what time it was or what had put her in the hospital.

"Airman White. I hate to be so formal while we examine you. Do you mind if we call you by your first name?"

"Sure," Lacey croaked, licking her dry lips. "It's La—Lacey."

"Yes, Ma'am. We got it from your military ID. Now you just relax, Lacey, while we finish our initial exam, and then we'll explain what needs to be done."

Lacey lay patiently on the cold, stiff examining table while the doctor and his assistants carried out some routine tasks. Just the few words she'd spoken had brought on a headache like she'd never had before. Her right arm was not only aching; it had an intense, burning pain from the shoulder to just below the elbow.

Someone patted her hand, and she moved her gaze to find a young woman in whites. "I'm Sergeant Mills, and I'll stay with you for awhile," the med tech explained. "Your body took quite a hit when that car knocked you down."

"Car?" Lacey grimaced as another wave of pain overtook her. She wished for unconsciousness simply because it would provide some relief.

"As soon as the doctor is done and knows the extent of your injuries, we can give you some pain medication." Sergeant Mills patted Lacey's left shoulder. "I probably shouldn't say this, but you might end up needing surgery on that right arm."

"Surgery?" Lacey croaked. "Not surgery."

"We'll see. I shouldn't have said anything. Now you're upset. Let's think positively and maybe it will all work out."

Lacey lapsed in and out of consciousness. In her lucid state, she asked the day, the time, and whether anyone else was injured.

"Just you," Sergeant Mills assured her more than once.

Lacey fell asleep again, relaxing as medication started to take the edge off of the most intolerable parts of the pain.

"There's a gentleman out in the waiting area who says he would like to see you when you feel up to having visitors." Sergeant Mills straightened the blanket that lay across Lacey's chest.

"Sure. Maybe a visitor will help me stay awake instead of all this sleeping I've been doing. How long did you say I've been here now?"

It hurt to think, to speak, even to breathe, but Lacey was determined to appear normal. It was probably her first shirt, and it wouldn't be polite to send him away. She was touched that he'd come to check on her.

"About five hours. We want to make sure you're stable before we move you up to the ward, which shouldn't be very long now."

"Thanks. Can you raise the bed any so I at least feel like I'm sitting up and normal?"

"Sure thing. I'll go slowly, but you let me know if it makes you hurt worse or anything." Sergeant Mills elevated the head of the bed and arranged the covers around Lacey's shoulders.

"There, you look better now." She smiled. "I'll go get the gentleman, and we'll be right back." She disappeared, her rubber-soled shoes making a soft, comforting sound on the tile floor.

❧

"I'm so sorry, Lacey," Hayden muttered from the doorway in the most even-tempered voice he could muster.

He watched as Lacey tried to move her head toward him. The rigid brace around her neck prevented her from doing so completely. The med tech had told him that the brace would stay until the neurologist reviewed the X-rays and MRI results.

Hayden ached to take her in his arms and find a way to take away her pain. However, he knew he had to tread unhurriedly. He issued a prayer that God would provide the words he needed during the next few minutes. If she asked him to leave, would he? Hayden walked a few steps toward her bed.

"Hayden? What are you doing here? Shouldn't you be at work?" Lacey's demand was somewhat weak, but he noted that there was still a touch of fire in her personality. She slid her gaze as far right as she could without moving her neck.

"By your side is the only place I belong, the only place I want to be, Lacey," Hayden began softly. "I went downtown with Father after the promotion party, or I'd have been here much earlier had I known what happened."

"You don't want to be here, Hayden. Not really. And now that you've seen me, why don't you go on and go back to your dorm room or wherever it is your all-important general father is staying. Don't worry about me; I'll be all right."

"Are you in much pain?" Hayden watched the tightening of her lips as she kept her gaze on him. Pain darkened her brown eyes and while they weren't as hard as he'd seen them in Guam after she tossed the hurtful words about power at him, he could tell her injuries were making her uncomfortable.

"The med tech said you could have another shot whenever you need it."

"I don't need pain medication, Hayden. I need to be left

alone." Lacey's tone was desolate.

Hayden moved closer. "They should be moving you upstairs shortly. Did the doctor explain what all is wrong?"

"Yes, and I'll make my own decisions where surgery is concerned, thank you very much. I don't need any help doing so."

Hayden advanced three steps to the end of her bed. He disliked seeing her normally active body and spirit so tainted by injury and pain. Something in his middle twisted cruelly. *I'd take your pain if I could, Lacey,* he said silently.

"Can I at least pray with you before you kick me out?" he asked, taking a position that allowed him to hold her left hand.

Lacey's nod was imperceptible. Her hand was slightly cold, and he rubbed his thumb across the top, noticing for the first time how beautifully smooth her skin was.

"Lord," he began, "we come before You today to ask that You provide healing for Lacey and tender souls to take care of her while she recovers. I don't understand what You have planned for our lives, but this accident is apparently part of it, and we will accept it. Thank You for allowing me to be here to assist Lacey in whatever way she needs, despite her reluctance to have me do so. In His name, amen."

Hayden opened his eyes to find Lacey sleeping. How much of his prayer had she heard?

❧

"You mean because of this injury there's a possibility that I'll be discharged from the air force?" Lacey asked, her heart sinking.

Everything she'd done to build her life better than it had

started out to be crashed down around her. Her meager savings wouldn't mean a thing if she didn't have a job. All this accident did was validate her worthlessness, as her father had pointed out often.

Her orthopedic surgeon sat in the chair across from her. Since he'd operated on her numerous times—five, to be exact—she'd developed an open and friendly relationship with him, despite his officer rank.

"A discharge isn't automatic, Lacey. They'll put you through rehab first to see how much you improve. Your right shoulder and collarbone took quite a beating, but they both seem to be healing nicely. You had quite a bit of damage to the brachial plexus area of your arm. That area contains a lot of the nerves that control your hand. Since you're right-handed—"

"Since I'm right-handed, I'll never be able to function normally again. Is that what you're saying?"

"Lacey, I can't tell you that for sure. I've seen other patients make miraculous improvements when everyone else thought all was lost as far as recovery was concerned."

"Then I guess I'm doomed to a life learning to use my left hand, because miracles in my life are few and far between."

"I know this comes as a shock," the surgeon said. "Believe me, I put all of my expertise into rebuilding your upper arm. I just wish I could tell you that things looked better at this point."

❧

Once her surgeon left, a depressing haze surrounded Lacey. She turned her back to the door and lay for awhile on her bed, tears occasionally overwhelming her. She was unaware of the aide who delivered her lunch, which sat on the push-around tray near her bed. Food was the last thing on her mind.

All she could think of was what she'd do if she were released from the military. None had any merit. Going back to live with Aunt Trini was her only choice, at least right now. She was sure her aunt wouldn't be thrilled about that. However, what else could Lacey do?

Live alone and prove that she couldn't make it? That would only confirm that her father was right; she had no business trying to succeed at anything. It was something she'd fought against since she was seven and her dad had told her about her mother leaving the day after Lacey was born.

"Lacey? Are you awake? Do you feel up to talking?" Hayden's voice interrupted.

"Yes, I'm awake." Lacey rubbed her eyes before she pushed herself up with her good left arm and swung her legs over the side of the bed.

The clothing ensemble she wore was a gift Jean had brought in hopes it would perk up Lacey's spirits. The short-sleeved blouse was dark blue and peppered with yellow suns, moons, and stars. The dark blue slacks matched the blouse. A house robe and slippers in a bright yellow that would out-shine the sun completed the outfit.

"I came to see how my favorite person is doing. Did you see your surgeon today?"

Hayden plopped into the nearest chair, a slightly over-stuffed, brown monstrosity that didn't swallow him as much as it had the surgeon earlier. His camouflaged BDU, short for battle dress uniform and the common uniform of some working airmen, was still neatly starched even after working all day. It crackled in places as he lowered into the chair.

"You don't have to call me your favorite person just to make me feel good," Lacey rejoined. "And, yes, the surgeon came by."

"So, what's the verdict?" Hayden leaned forward as much as the chair would allow.

Lacey scuffed her slippers back and forth on the cold, tile floor. "Hayden, I know you feel some sense of guilt about my injuries. You shouldn't. They're my fault."

"But it was my father being at the promotion party that sent you running away and not paying attention to where you were going when you left."

"We've covered that issue more times than I care to count. Just forget it, Hayden. What or how it happened is history."

⁂

"So what's the news?" Hayden probed, wondering why Lacey's voice had a hint of reluctance in it.

He'd watched her progress over the last few months as she recovered from surgeries to rebuild her right arm. Not once did she complain that he knew of, even though the hurt and ongoing physical rehabilitation had to be tough to get through. He admired her strength in the face of adversity and wondered if he would be as strong in similar circumstances.

"When I'm done with rehab, I have to meet a medical

review board to see if I'm still fit for military service." The reluctance was gone and she sounded relieved, as if finally saying the words helped a little.

"It's probably just a formality. I can check into it if you want me to."

"Hayden, if I'm not medically competent, the military will discharge me once they've done all the rehab they can. I don't need your help. This is my battle, not yours."

"Lacey, do you recall the verse in the Bible in which God said that gold is tested under fire in order to strengthen it?"

"Yes, but I'm certainly not gold."

"You still believe in Jesus after all that's happened, don't you?"

"Sure, the chaplain even comes by on Sundays to deliver a small sermon and talk with me awhile."

"God can do a lot of things, Lacey, including providing a way for you to take care of yourself, even if the military discharges you."

"I keep trying to remember that, but since this morning, I don't think it applies to me anymore." Lacey stood and moved to a window.

❦

From it, she could see the base exchange parking lot where families exited and entered the on-base store. A three- or four-year-old boy with sandy red hair and long legs darted ahead of his parents. Lacey watched as his mother hurried to grab his hand. Lacey cringed. Her dreams of having a family had been shot down this morning like enemy aircraft.

With her injuries, certainly no one would want her now.

She knew how Hayden felt about her before her accident. He'd been faithful in coming by every day in order to talk with her, but he did it out of a sense of duty. A sense of duty because he insisted his father was an indirect cause of her accident—if the general hadn't been at Hayden's promotion party, Lacey might never have run headlong into a car as she left the parking lot.

No matter how many times they argued and disagreed about it, Lacey couldn't get him to change his mind. At least he was honorable, which was more than the other men in her life had been. Lacey wanted to believe she could trust Hayden where her heart was concerned.

Lacey turned to look at Hayden, who still sat in the hideous brown chair. The look in his eyes captured her, and she couldn't look away. For a brief moment, her outlook changed from dreary and cold to one of hope and brightness.

She imagined him leaving that ridiculous brown chair and getting down on one knee to say, "Marry me." For just a moment she envisioned her heart at peace, not having to worry about anything.

Just as quickly, reality set in. She regretted it now, but she'd done nothing but push Hayden away since the summer. Even though he came to visit her in the hospital, she knew she gave him the idea that she was just tolerating him.

Hayden was persistent; she'd give him that. But she didn't think his persistence would win her therapy battles, nor would it overcome the memories of what had happened to her two-and-one-half years ago at technical training.

"You didn't eat your lunch," Hayden said, bringing Lacey back to the present.

"I wasn't hungry," Lacey responded, sitting back on her hospital bed.

"But you have to maintain your strength," he implored. "Getting better entails more than just exercise in a physical therapy room, you know."

"I'm tired, Hayden. Do you mind leaving so I can take a nap?"

Chapter 13

We've studied your medical records and have come to the conclusion that at the present time, you are not fit for continued military service. As soon as your surgeon agrees that you are at the maximum level of improvement, we will process your separation paperwork. You do have the right to appeal this decision. Also, we will review this case once a year for five years to ascertain your suitability for service. It is possible that you may once again serve on active duty."

Lacey sat in the rocking chair in her aunt's living room hearing the words of the medical review officer run through her head. Since she'd arrived back in Chicago, she'd done little but sit around and mope.

At first, Aunt Trini showed more compassion than Lacey had ever seen from her. But her aunt's ability to commiserate with Lacey's loss of a dream dissipated quickly after the first week.

"We've got to find you a job, young lady," her aunt now

said routinely every morning. Aunt Trini would take the morning paper and circle jobs in the want ads she thought Lacey would find appealing.

They were all secretarial positions that Lacey had no chance of performing because of the injury to her right arm. While she had some strength and dexterity back, she rated herself at about 40 percent. She didn't think a business would be willing to accept her at that level, even if she brought up the Americans with Disabilities Act.

That was really the problem, Lacey thought morosely. She refused to see herself as someone with a disability, though she was. Perhaps, just as a therapist had once explained to Lacey when dealing with her almost-rape incident, she was denying the true state of things. While denial provided protection, Lacey knew that unless she faced the truth, she would never be able to heal. . .never be able to love.

"I can drive you downtown if you set up the interviews," Aunt Trini called from the kitchen. "Just give me a couple of days' notice so I can make sure I'm free."

"Thanks," Lacey called, knowing that if she ever got as far as an interview, she would find her own transportation to it. No sense in adding Aunt Trini's stress to her own.

❧

Hayden had given Lacey a self-contained E-mail system as a parting gift. Not a full-sized computer, the product was used just to send cyber messages. He'd helped her set up the system before she left and sent her numerous E-mails each week. He continually pressed to get her phone number, and eventually she conceded. It sounded like a weak excuse, but he hadn't called her yet because he wasn't sure exactly what to say.

His work hours took away most of his free time, a fact that helped him because it kept him from thinking about and missing Lacey.

Finally, he decided he couldn't wait any longer to hear Lacey's voice. Hayden punched in the numbers that would ring in Chicago, Illinois. He drummed his fingers on the night table by his bed as he waited for someone to pick up.

"Hello?" It wasn't Lacey so he surmised that it was her aunt. He introduced himself and asked to speak to Lacey. It seemed like forever before she came on the line.

"Hello, Hayden. How are things in Louisiana?"

"Cooling off a little now that it's November. At least the daily highs aren't in the nineties anymore."

"Great. How's work?" she asked.

"It's fine. We're in the middle of an exercise, so the twelve-hour shifts are sometimes more like fourteen."

"I remember those days," Lacey said. "Life was nothing more than eat, sleep, work, and do it all over again."

"It hasn't changed any," Hayden admitted. "What I really want to know is how you're doing, Lacey. Are you still in rehab?"

"I've given up rehab for now. The consensus of the therapists was that I wasn't likely to improve much more after all this time."

The stillness on the line weighted down Hayden's heart.

He heard despair in her voice. The Lacey White he'd known as an airman was gone, replaced by one who thought she was worthless.

Hayden loved her, but a long-distance phone call wasn't the time to tell her that. Words of that magnitude should be shared face-to-face.

"I thought I'd come to Chicago to see you over Christmas," Hayden offered, knowing ahead of time she would refuse.

"That's not necessary. I'm fine," Lacey said in short, clipped words.

"Fine or not, it's something I want to do. I haven't seen Christmas lights on snow-covered houses for quite a few years. I'm looking forward to the trip and to seeing you."

"We don't have any extra room here," Lacey stated. "You'd have to stay at a hotel."

"I'll see you on the twenty-third."

❧

Lacey counted the days 'til Hayden's arrival. She wouldn't admit it to Aunt Trini, but her pulse raced at the thought of seeing him again. It had only been a few months since she had left Barksdale, but they had been long, lonely weeks, filled with sitting in a rocking chair and looking out a window as traffic passed by.

"At least with Hayden here, I might find some joy in this Christmas," Lacey said to the frosted pattern on the front window.

She was disappointed in the small amount of disability

pay she received from the military and it barely made ends meet, even though she didn't contribute anything to her aunt as she'd once done. Her Christmas present to Aunt Trini was a small pillow, much like the one she'd sent from Louisiana not long ago. She'd bought this one before her discharge. The back was a dark green and the front a tweedy brown with the saying "Home is where the heart is" on it.

Aunt Trini's house was a house and not a home, but it was the only home Lacey knew. Her father lived in New York and didn't keep in touch with her. Lacey was ashamed to admit that she hadn't sought him out over the last few years either. Through therapy, she'd grown smart enough to realize that if he wanted to get in touch with her, he would ask Aunt Trini where she was. It hurt but that was the way it was. Maybe someday she'd find the courage to look him up and contact him.

Lacey had tried to pin Aunt Trini down several times about why and how Lacey had ended up living with her, but her aunt said it was Lacey's father's place to divulge that answer. It was just another example of the power men had over her, but at least now, Lacey accepted that she might never have that answer.

Chapter 14

Once he got his luggage, a rental car, and checked into the hotel nearest Lacey's house, Hayden felt better. Lacey hadn't offered to meet him at the airport and he hadn't pushed, sensing that it was her way of saying there was still nothing romantic between them.

His parents were against his trip North, especially at Christmas, but he politely told them that it was his life and that he would make the decisions, not them. While they didn't respond, Hayden hoped they were learning to accept that he didn't need their constant guidance and interference.

After a quick shower and a phone call to let Lacey know he'd arrived safely, Hayden set up a time to come see her. He picked up a dozen roses for her and a box of chocolates for her aunt from a small convenience store near his hotel. *A little convincing can't hurt*, he thought.

The closer he got to Lacey's neighborhood, the smaller the houses became. He began to get a sense of her upbringing and how deprived of material things she must have been.

The gap between them turned into a chasm as he drove down a roughly paved street with rusted cars parked off the sides of most driveways.

The house Lacey lived in was covered with a dingy white aluminum siding. A single strand of icicle lights hung across the front porch light and a wreath of undecorated pine boughs adorned the door. Hayden sat in the car for a moment, bolstering his spirit and figuring out how he would approach Lacey when he finally saw her.

He was relieved of that duty when Lacey herself hustled out of the house and headed toward his car. She opened the car door and slid into the front seat, rubbing her gloved hands rapidly together.

"I'm glad you made it safely." Her eyes were filled with laughter, something Hayden hadn't seen in them for over six months.

"Me too. I was just about to come to the door, but I guess I don't have to now."

"Aunt Trini isn't sure of your motives. I tried to assure her that you only wanted to visit me because, as a friend, you helped me through some rough times. She isn't convinced."

Hayden unbuckled his seat belt and turned to face Lacey. He took her left hand in his, feeling her tremble even through the glove. Staring at her didn't seem appropriate, but it was all he could do. She didn't know how beautiful she was.

Tendrils had escaped a girlish ponytail and now framed her flushed face. Glittery eye shadow of some color he couldn't make out in the twilight accented her expressive eyebrows.

"Is that all I am to you?" Hayden queried. "Just a friend?"

"Hayden," Lacey said warningly, "this isn't the time or place for that discussion."

"You're beautiful, Lacey."

"Right," she replied. "Despite the dark circles under my eyes from lack of sleep and the weight I've lost from not eating right."

"Those are physical things," Hayden answered. "Your spirit is still in one piece. I can see it shining in your eyes. It's what made me fall in love with you from the beginning."

Lacey abruptly pulled her hand from Hayden's. "Love? What do you mean, love?"

"What does love mean?" Hayden took her left hand again, covering it with his own.

"I guess, well, I never really. . . I know the Bible says that love is patient and kind. That it bears all things and endures all things."

"You've never really known that type of feeling in your life, have you, Lacey?"

"Not until. . ." She stared off through the windshield.

"You found me," Hayden inserted.

"There you go, completing my sentences as you did when I first met you."

"You got me there. I'm sorry."

"No, you're right. I haven't ever known love like what I feel when I think of you, Hayden. But look at me. I can't make decisions and I'm disabled. I can't even use my right arm to hold a cup of coffee."

"I don't care about your right arm, Lacey. I care about you and your heart. Do you love me? It's the only decision I need to hear you make." He linked his fingers with hers. "Well?"

"Yes, I do love you. But—"

"No buts, Lacey. I want you to be my wife, no matter what."

"Won't your parents think I'm not good enough for your family?" Lacey prodded.

"I think you're good enough for me. That's all that counts. Besides, I've informed the general and my mother that this is my life. The decisions I make are mine alone and not available for family discussions anymore."

"You did?"

"It will take time, but they'll accept my pronouncement sooner or later. Shelley, however, is ecstatic because I've now opened the door for her to become the artist she's always wanted to be."

"What do we do now?" Lacey asked breathlessly.

"Just as soon as we can find out what the Illinois laws say regarding marriage licenses, we get married," Hayden said.

Epilogue

S o, Mrs. Hayden Jacobs III, what do you think of our honeymoon suite?"

Lacey glanced around the huge, open area. A king-sized bed, overly plump sofa, and a big-screen television barely dented the available space. Heavy drapes blocked the sound of the raging blizzard outside.

"It's wonderful," Lacey answered as she snuggled against Hayden's chest, the sound of his heart beating beneath her ear a comforting change from the noisy Chicago traffic.

She let the room's quiet fill the space around them. There had been a few surprises on this, their wedding day. Lacey felt compelled to voice her thoughts, knowing that Hayden would accept her no matter what or how she said them.

"Not to change the subject, but I didn't expect to see your parents at our wedding," she began. "And the way your mother and Aunt Trini got along so well—it seemed as if they were sisters."

"Yes, Mother and Father sure gave us all some shocking

moments today. From showing up, to lighting the unity candle for us, to Father wearing a suit and tie instead of his air force uniform, I think perhaps they're beginning to accept what I've been trying to tell them about you all along."

"And that is?"

"That despite our different upbringings, love outranks us all. We had no choice but to follow God's plan for our lives, knowing that He would never steer us wrong. I only wish we'd had time to get your father here also."

Lacey kissed Hayden's cheek. "Someday I'll be ready to face him and begin that part of my healing, and I'll have you beside me when that happens. Right now, I only want to cuddle in your arms and begin our life together. Christmas will always have a more special meaning to me now."

"Whatever you say, my dear." Hayden swept her into his arms, and the kiss that followed surpassed any other they'd shared since their wedding ceremony earlier that afternoon.

TAMMY SHUTTLESWORTH

Tammy is in her eighth year of teaching Junior ROTC after retiring from the United States Air Force. She is an Ohio native who has been transplanted to Louisiana. Her husband, Rick, two daughters—Caryn and Taryn, a son-in-law, a grandson, a cat, and a mini dachshund puppy bring lots of joy and love to her life. Writing took a backseat while she completed her bachelor's degree and spoiled her only grandchild, Kaleb, for a few years. She hopes her stories show that God loves each and every one of us no matter who we are or where we come from.

Seeking Shade

by Paige Winship Dooly

Dedication

To my loving family:
Troy, Josh, J T, Dalton, Tessa, Cassidy,
and our newest blessing, Jetty.
Thank you so much for your constant support!
I love you.

Chapter 1

"All right, boys. Let's get this party on the road and head on home." Nick smiled as his words were met with high fives and cheers from the men on the team. They were riding high on adrenaline and ready to return to the States.

Hunter called out over the noise. "I'm going to buy us all the biggest, juiciest steaks that I can find, and Nick-o can smoke 'em off in his cooker."

Nick grinned. "Make sure you also buy some potatoes. I'll eat mine slathered with butter and sour cream."

"Ah, and then top the feast off with some of Clara's home-made apple cobbler, hot from the oven and covered with a scoop of melting vanilla cinnamon ice cream." Hunter paused. "We are going to the colonel's for debrief, aren't we?"

"Yes. Debrief will be at the colonel's," Nick confirmed, watching as the men all settled back into their seats with visions of Clara's cobbler dancing in their heads. The colonel's housekeeper loved to pamper the men after they'd been out in the field.

Turbulence rocked the jet as they quieted, but Special Ops Agent Nick McLeod barely noticed as he sank farther into the buttery-soft leather of his seat. After weeks of sleeping on hard-packed dirt, the comfort of the luxury jet was beyond description.

Nick looked around and noticed that the interior of the aircraft was decorated in a classy blend of mauve and blue. The tables, chairs, and accents were a snowy white. The color tone definitely rang of Shade's touch—they were her favorite combinations. Not wanting to dwell on her, Nick abruptly forced his thoughts to take another direction.

Concentrate on the colonel and debrief, Nick-o, he chided himself, forcing the scowl from his face. *Time enough to think about Shade later.*

The colonel—Col. Sean Matthews, whom they'd served under when in the military—had pulled out all the stops for this homecoming, probably to personally show his appreciation for their success this time around.

Nick loved his job and thrived on each mission. But on this trip. . . For the first time, he'd found himself counting the days until it was time to go home.

"Hey, McLeod! You look awfully content over there for a man who has to go home and face the fact that he's lost his best friend."

Nick winced, then shook his head at Billy—the one man who was a constant thorn in his side. He was the best when it came to his special ops skills, and his wavy black hair and dark brown eyes made him a hit with women. But he had an unfortunate knack for knowing just the right thing to say to each of his team members in order to make them cringe. They usually overlooked the bad trait, as they knew he had come from a rough home life and the jeering was a survival skill he'd developed years ago. Nick just kept hoping Billy would move beyond it someday.

"I haven't lost anyone unless you want me to start the list with you as missing person number one. If you're referring to Shade, I just need to come up with a way to convince her that she still loves me. Just a little glitch in the plans, my buddy."

"Yeah, the plans for a Christmas wedding," Billy scoffed. Hunter sent Billy a warning glare, and Billy turned to the window.

A lavish Christmas wedding awaited Nick as soon as he overcame one minor obstacle—to get his fiancée—well, at present ex-fiancée—to agree to marry him and put the wedding back on the calendar.

Shade Matthews, the only daughter of the colonel's, had kept a piece of his heart when she gave him the ultimatum that ended their relationship. He remembered her words with heart-piercing clarity.

"If you go on this mission so close to our wedding, you won't have a wedding to worry about returning for!" She'd yelled, totally out of character for her. "Daddy's already away, and who knows if he'll return in time. I've lived with this my whole life. Missed birthdays, missed graduations, and missed holidays. I won't go through it for the rest of my life. Either you quit the team. . .or you quit our relationship."

The words hurt, but Nick had no choice.

He hadn't worried too much about the situation, knowing that when he returned and explained why he needed to take the mission she'd forgive him.

Nick's best friend, Hunter, plopped down into the seat next to Nick with a moan of contentment. "Hey, Nick. Did you even get a chance to explain to Shade why you had to go on the mission? Does she know about her father?"

Nick appreciated the fact that his friend lowered his voice so no one else could hear. Hunter was Billy's complete opposite: blond, blue-eyed, and as gentle-natured as they came. He was the one who had led Nick to Christ years ago and had kept his spirits up throughout their missions. He'd also led Beau to Christ, and they were making progress on the others—well, except for Billy. Then again, Billy had started asking some questions in the past few months. Still in his jeering way, but it was obvious he was searching.

"No. I didn't have a chance to explain anything to Shade. Besides, the colonel made me promise not to say anything. Shade would have been on the next plane to the island, or worse yet, would have hidden in the luggage compartment or something in order to be a part of the operation personally." He shook his head. "No way could we let her find out that her daddy had been kidnapped and that we were going in to get him back out."

Their last fight was one that Nick couldn't forget. He knew he was breaking her heart by refusing to quit the team. He also knew he was jeopardizing the wedding by leaving so close to the date. But he didn't have a choice. So instead he had stood his ground, his jaw clenched as she rightfully lashed out at him, then watched regretfully as she pulled the diamond engagement ring from her slender finger.

Blue eyes flashing with hurt and anger, Shade carefully placed the ring on Nick's palm, then closed his fingers around it. She held his closed fist a moment longer than necessary and, with tears in her eyes, turned and walked away, never once looking back. He'd watched her long black hair sway as she went, before realizing despondently that he hadn't even been able to kiss her good-bye.

Nick had called her the day they flew out, and her voice cooled to the temperature of frostbite when she realized it was him.

"We've said all we need to say," she'd stated with all the passion one would use when talking to a telemarketing solicitor. "I have nothing more to say to you. You made your choice. Now live with it."

"Come on, Shade. You know I love you. Why can't you understand that this mission is special?"

Shade interrupted. "They are all special. I've heard it my whole life. Let's not drag this out, please!"

Nick heard the pain in her voice but had to try one more time. "Shade, please give me a chance. Trust me, and I'll explain when I get home—"

Again Shade interrupted. "No. No more chances. No more good-byes. I knew better than to fall in love with you, but I couldn't help it. Now I'm paying for that foolish mistake. I won't live the life my mom lived. She was always alone, raising me as if she were a single mother, even though she was married. I'd rather stay single for the rest of my life than live like that." Her voice broke and she hurried on. "I'm sorry it has to be this way, but you made the choice. Now let it go."

Nick tried to speak, but the phone line went dead. The team was waiting, and Nick had to leave without making things right. In all honesty, there was no way to make things right. When they last spoke, Colonel Matthews had been adamant that Shade not be aware of what was going on.

Now they were heading back, and Nick had no idea how to approach Shade. If the truth were known, he was scared. What if she wouldn't see him? What if she wouldn't talk to him? They'd been in love, had planned to marry. Surely she would at least hear him out, and by now the colonel had explained the situation, and things would be set right, wouldn't they? He longed to hold her in his arms and hear her whisper that all was well and that she understood. Until then, his world was tilted on its axis. Nothing felt quite right. He couldn't imagine life without Shade.

Nick sighed and picked up the phone to place the long-distance call. He'd ask the colonel how things stood, even though the colonel hadn't known about the problem—that the wedding was off—while they were out on mission. They were too busy to talk at the time. The colonel was weak, abused, and malnourished, and Nick's only thought was to get him back to the States for treatment. By now the colonel would be home at the estate and would know about Shade's reaction to the mission. They had a very close relationship. It had only been the two of them since Shade's mother had passed away when she was a young girl. Clara had joined them and acted as a surrogate mother to Shade, but Nick knew it wasn't the same as having her mother. Anyway, surely by now Clara and the colonel had worked things out with Shade and the wedding was still on.

The phone rang a long time before a breathless Clara answered. Nick identified himself and asked to be put through to the colonel. Clara paused, then cleared her throat, her voice coming through in a raspy whisper of devastation.

"Oh, Nick. I'm so glad you called. Something awful has happened." She stopped, a sob coming across the miles of air as she apparently tried to pull herself together. The silver-haired woman was usually in complete control, not given to theatrics, so Nick knew something was seriously wrong.

Nick's heart dropped, and he fought off the urge to snap at her, wanting her to get to the point. Instead he reminded himself he wasn't dealing with one of his men; this was Clara and he needed to be gentle. "It's okay, Clara. Calm down. Tell me what happened."

Nick could hear her struggling to calm down on the other end, the connection full of static. "Oh, Nick—some guys br–broke in last night and shot the colonel. They sh–shot the colonel and—" Static interrupted her next few words. After interminable moments, her words came back through. "They ki—" More static and then, "Sh–Shade. She's gone. Nick. . . Shade i–is gone."

She broke down completely, and Nick's blood pounded in his ears as he tried to decipher and comprehend what Clara had just said. The other men were suddenly quiet, concern evident on their faces as their respected leader deftly barked out the order for Clara to slowly repeat once again what she'd just told him.

"Not Shade. No." Nick's voice choked up momentarily, and he fought the panic that threatened to overtake him.

Hunter clasped Nick on the shoulder in a show of support, and Nick tried to relax as he realized he was clutching the phone in a death grip. The static grew worse, and Nick lost the connection before he could get any more information. He punched the numbers again, only to get a busy signal. After several more attempts, Nick gave up and turned to face his men.

"We're back on mission." He slammed his fist into the table, welcoming the dull flash of pain that briefly distracted him from his anguish. He knew exactly who had taken Shade. His and the colonel's one disagreement on this mission was on how to handle cleanup.

Nick wanted to permanently take the enemy out—especially after seeing the colonel's condition by the time the team arrived to rescue him—while the colonel, a strong Christian, had insisted they turn the kidnapping, drug smugglers over to the authorities. While Nick considered himself a Christian too, he thought there were certain ways to handle protocol in these situations. Of course he had bowed to the colonel's orders, but now he was sorry. Obviously someone had slipped through their net. And that someone was going to be mighty sorry when they faced the wrath of Nick McLeod. This time no loose end would go untied.

Filled with blind rage, he tried to piece together what Clara had been trying to say about Shade. At the moment, only two words came to mind that started with that sound. Had Shade been killed or had she been kidnapped? Nick thought nothing could compare with the pain of losing Shade a few weeks earlier. Now, with the thought that his precious Shade could possibly be dead or in the hands of his enemies, Nick began to pray. Two emotions battled within Nick: the need to pull close to God and the need to lash out at Him for letting this happen. He could only sit back and wait to find out more as the jet drew them closer to the colonel's estate. Nick's personal mission—to win Shade back—would be put on hold. If she was even alive.

Chapter 2

Shade struggled to open her eyes, panicking against the complete darkness that surrounded her. She lay still for a moment, trying to place where she was. A small cry filled the air as she remembered the attack on the estate and the gunfire as her father was shot down before her eyes. She'd tried to rush to his side, only to be grabbed by one of the militiamen who had invaded their private home. As a gun barrel swung into focus, she'd heard a crack and felt a blinding pain on the side of her head. The last thing she remembered as she went down was an angry voice shouting in Spanish, something about violence not being necessary with her. She sank into blissful darkness, whispering a prayer for her father as she welcomed the relief from the explosive ache in her head. Her last thoughts were of the incongruity of the gunshots and acrid stench of gunpowder mixed in with Christmas music pouring from the speaker system and the smell of cookies baking in the oven.

Shade knew she wasn't home anymore and wondered as she lay in pitch-darkness if she was now blind from the blow to her temple. She dropped her hand to her side, feeling a rough, strawlike mat beneath her. The air was dank, and she moved her hand farther, coming into contact with damp earth. She was in a primitive place, maybe a cave? Had she been abandoned, blind and alone? She tried to sit, but the shooting pain between her eyes quickly changed that idea. She fell back on the mat and felt her stomach churn in protest—a not-so-subtle warning that she was about to be sick. She turned to the far side, hitting her head against a plank wall as she retched. As she lay slowly back on the mat, she felt herself slipping once more into the protective sleep and gave in to it.

When she awoke again, Shade knew she needed to stay calm, and she needed to regroup before trying to move. She whispered a brief prayer for patience and a level head, then slowly eased up into a sitting position. Her head swam, but at least she didn't become nauseous this time. Again she tried to see something—anything—but was rewarded only with darkness. Remembering the plank wall to her left, she felt her way along it, earning herself a splinter for the effort. The wall was primitive but solid. She scooted along the mat slowly, feeling her way as she went. No door, no window. . . Maybe she was brought in by a trapdoor in the roof?

Shade knew she'd have to feel her way around the whole room first, then worry about how to reach the roof. Raising slowly to her knees, she moved back down the wall from the corner. Nothing. She slowly stood, dizziness overtaking her. Clutching the wall for support, she tentatively stepped off the mat and moved on to the second wall. Claustrophobia was threatening to overwhelm her. She whispered her need for peace, "Jesus, please keep me calm," and momentarily felt stronger again.

A large bug crawled from her hair to her face, and she brushed it off with a shriek. Tears fell from her eyes, and she mumbled her irritation that her tear ducts apparently worked even if she was blind. Shade hated to cry. She hated feeling out of control even more, and right now she was about as out of control as she could possibly get.

Shade could blame this whole situation on one person. Nick McLeod. If he hadn't left her for another one of his all-important missions, he'd have been there to protect her father from being shot and could have prevented her from being kidnapped. Instead he was off saving the world as her world fell apart. Her white-hot anger at Nick overrode her anger at her kidnappers. She knew that didn't make sense—at least Nick hadn't shot her father—but if he'd been at the estate no one else would have shot her father either, so indirectly it actually was his fault.

Determined to break out of her earthy prison, Shade began walking along the second wall, past the corner, and on to the next. She'd explore each wall in depth if she had to later, but for now she needed to figure out if there was a door in one of the other two sides.

On the fourth wall, she felt a crack, and followed it down to the floor. She couldn't reach the top, but found a similar crack about thirty inches over from the first. It had to be a door! She slowly inched her hands up to waist level, mindful of the splinters that pierced her sensitive palms. A leatherlike strap stopped her exploration and she hesitated, wondering if she really wanted to know what lay on the other side. Deciding anything was better than this suffocating prison, she grabbed the strap and tugged hard, falling backward as the door gave way and she landed on her backside on the hard-packed ground.

Blinding light caused her to close her eyes, and it took a moment for her to realize that her eyes worked fine. At least they would when she could open them again against the brightness. Another wave of nausea rushed over her, and she fought it off. Covering her eyes with one hand to her forehead, Shade slowly lifted her face to the doorway and, wincing, peered out into a deserted street. Her eyes adjusted, and she crawled weakly to the frame, pulling herself up and leaning against the wood for support. The blast of heat from outside took her breath away.

Apparently no one was there to guard her or to prevent her escape. She turned to look at her prison—nothing but a dirt floor, the rough mat, a crate, and four plank walls. Large palmetto bugs scuttled into the darker corners, and Shade shuddered, the sight making her more than ready to face what lay on the other side of the doorway.

Seeing a clean dress lying on the crate, she washed herself as best she could with the tepid water that waited in a bowl beside it. After slipping into the dress, she scrubbed her soiled clothes and laid them out to dry, wanting to put them back on as soon as possible.

Stepping outside, she immediately noticed other buildings like the one she had exited. She stood in the roadway, cautiously optimistic that she'd been left in a deserted town and would be able to find her way to help if she kept her wits about her.

Her anger at Nick notwithstanding, Shade considered herself to be a strong Christian. God would lead her out of this mess. She felt a twinge of guilt that she expected Him to be there for her, when she was holding on to such anger at Nick, but the man had left her at the altar for a mission! Well, he hadn't quite left her at the altar; the wedding was still a few weeks away—but it was virtually the same thing. Anyway, she didn't have time to get into all that right now. She needed to find a way home. At this point she was so angry that if Nick rode in on his white horse, she'd be tempted to knock him off of it.

A sharp shout behind her and the blast of gunfire had Shade pressing flat against the building, her breath knocked out of her. Footsteps pounded and a small boy rushed past, an apple clutched in his little hand. A squatty man yelling in Spanish chased him and shot the gun into the air again. Shade translated the Spanish and heard the man reprimand the small boy for stealing the apple. The gunman wasn't after her at all. He ran past without much more than a glance at Shade, then disappeared around the corner. Shade sank to the ground as her knees gave out.

Several doors had opened and women peered out, shaking their heads as they watched the scene take place. Though a few stared blatantly at Shade before going back inside, only one lone woman hesitantly approached her.

"You are ill?" she asked in broken English.

When Shade shook her head in denial, the woman tenderly took Shade's hand and raised it up to her head, causing her to wince in pain as she contacted a huge gash and dried blood. Ah, her souvenirs from the gun barrel.

Shade allowed the woman to lead her to another shanty, this one only slightly more settled than the one she'd left, but at least it had basic furniture. Sinking gratefully into a chair, she accepted the plate of rice and beans placed before her. A bottle of water appeared next to the plate, and she realized she was famished as she used a tortilla to scoop up the food. Since she'd spent a lot of her life in South America, she was familiar with the casual cuisine.

Shade ate as the woman cleaned and doctored her wound.

"What is the date?" Shade had no idea how long she'd been captive. She was shocked to find she'd already been away from the estate for two days. No wonder she'd felt so grubby.

"Do you know who I am?" she inquired next.

The woman shrugged, as if finding an injured American was a common, everyday occurrence. "That is not for me to ask."

"So I can just walk out of here if I want to? I'm not being held here against my will?" Shade felt a glimmer of hope. Maybe she'd just been set aside so she didn't interfere with whatever the militiamen wanted at the estate.

"Only if you can get past the armed guards that protect the compound. It is also surrounded by fencing." The woman made it sound quite matter-of-fact, like living this way was normal. Apparently for her it was.

"Are you being held prisoner here?" Maybe they could

break out together. It would be easier if she had an ally.

"No. I have been here my whole life. This is home to me. I love this island."

"And does this island have a name?"

The woman rattled off a name that meant nothing to Shade. Her heart sank. She couldn't exactly swim from an island to the mainland, even if she knew which way to go. And in this case she didn't even know that much. There were hundreds of islands out there.

"Caribbean."

The woman apparently saw Shade's confusion and wanted to help. Okay, so now Shade knew she was in the Caribbean, but that tiny piece of information still was not a lot of help.

Her only hope seemed to be a rescue, but with her father dead and No-Help Nick out saving the world, who was left to save her? A rescue wasn't going to happen. Tears formed again, and Shade quickly pushed them away. She'd have time to grieve later. For now she'd just have to gather her wits and save herself. Shade thanked the woman—who finally identified herself as Nina—for her hospitality and headed out the door, wanting to see the layout of her bigger, but just as confining, prison.

She now noticed a high, barbed-wire fence at the far end of the dirt road. Walking toward it, she was finally forced to turn to the left. She followed the fence around, peering up several more streets that looked like the one she'd just left, and reached the far end again, once more turning to the left. It was a repeat of her exploration of the hut, but on a larger scale and with daylight guiding her. Dense jungle surrounded the outside of the fence, and Shade couldn't see any sign of a path or road through the foliage.

She startled when a small, scraggly girl about four years old ran up and smiled shyly, her brown eyes warm and welcoming, yet at the same time wary. Long, dark curls cascaded down her back in disarray, and her eyes glinted with curiosity. The child clutched an old, ragged stuffed bunny in one hand. Shade smiled and the young girl reached out her other hand to Shade. Shade looked around, trying to figure out where the child was from, but the little girl just kept smiling, not understanding or wanting to talk. Shade shrugged and took the outstretched hand in her own, welcoming the comfort of the tiny clutch.

They walked on. Ahead, about midway along this side of the compound was a huge gate, protected by armed guards with menacing weapons. Shade hesitated, wondering if she should turn back or continue her explorations. One guard turned to look at her, his eyes showing faint interest, but no challenge, at her approach. He seemed bored. She decided to feign confidence and continue on, praying her legs wouldn't give out from fright. She didn't look the guard in the eyes, but turned down the main street leading from the gates, afraid continuing her walk along the outer fence would draw attention to any escape plans.

The man called out to the little girl in Spanish. "Angel, does your papa know where you are?"

The little girl nodded and continued on.

The main street was only a bit wider than the others, but at least it wasn't deserted. People sat outside the few storefronts, talking as if it were small-town America. Shade couldn't imagine living like this, but then again, if it was all they knew, maybe they felt secure with the guards at the gate and the protection from whatever the jungle held.

She continued down a block, then doubled back toward the fence. She made it completely around to the spot where she'd begun, finding no escape route and only the one gate. Forlornly, wanting to settle in for the night and figure out her game plan, Shade walked back in the direction from which she'd come. She cringed at the thought of spending another night in that dark, lonely shack but didn't know what else to do. To stay outside would be even scarier.

She'd picked up a few more children as she and Angel walked, and while the child still didn't open up to her, the other children chatted away. Apparently Angel lived with only her father. Shade listened as the others scampered along behind her, happy to tag along and spout out information on their families. As she reached her street, she bade them good-bye and said she'd see them in the morning. Angel reluctantly headed toward the main street with the others, looking back sadly and waving before disappearing into the dusk.

A tiny older woman walked down the road toward Shade, limping as she carried a huge basket against one hip. Out of habit, Shade hurried to her and took the basket just as the woman stumbled. Shade asked where the woman was headed, and she was rewarded with a hesitant but surprised smile. They entered another run-down shanty where an armed guard was just exiting the door. The woman explained that Shade had helped her, and he grudgingly approved his wife's request that Shade stay for dinner.

Shade was relieved not to have to enter her lonely prison of a shack just yet, and the woman directed her to be seated at the table. She was feeling weak again and knew she'd overdone it. The day had been well spent, though, as she'd met two potential friends and had been able to freely observe her surroundings. As she ate, her eyes began to droop and she was only vaguely aware as the elderly woman helped her to a much softer, bug-free pallet along one wall and eased her down, freeing her to give in to a welcome sleep.

Chapter 3

Nick's worst fears were confirmed when he arrived at the estate. Shade was definitely in the hands of the man they'd let go on the last mission. Nick made a promise to himself that this time, no matter what, he'd take the man responsible out.

With the colonel down, Nick was in charge and there was no one to change his mind with their Christian convictions. While Nick lived by his Christian convictions, he also felt that war was war, and in this case, if he'd taken care of the situation like he'd wanted, the colonel wouldn't be in intensive care and Shade would be by his side, sipping eggnog and preparing for their wedding.

He stopped by the hospital long enough to be assured the colonel would recover; then the team left for the island.

Nick felt the trip had taken way too long, but they couldn't just fly in and grab Shade. They had to drop in quietly, then move across the island on foot so Ferdinand's soldiers wouldn't warn him of their approach. They were at a different location from where the colonel had first been taken, so they had to analyze the layout and specifics before they could proceed. They'd wasted precious time returning to the original rescue spot before an informant directed them to the proper island.

Nick had prowled like a caged lion as he waited for his men to report on the setup so he could continue on.

It had been seven days since Shade had been captured, and Nick couldn't imagine the abuse and trauma she might have suffered during this time. Now Nick and his men were back on the move according to their radio contact, and they were finally approaching the compound.

Nick located the scout, Beau, and slipped into a crouch beside him. "What do we have?"

"They're cocky, Chief, which works in our favor. An armed guard at the front gate, but no one seems to patrol the fence. It's a small village inside; everyone seems to come and go within as they please." Beau had to have been sitting in this position for hours, but he looked as fresh as if he'd just stepped out of bed. His green eyes were sharp, and only his tousled brown hair gave away his nerves at being so close to Shade and having to wait for the team before rescuing her. The men all loved Shade, having grown up with her under the colonel's tutelage.

"Do they patrol the perimeter? On the outside?"

"Not that I've seen. It's completely overgrown, and there aren't any paths. They come and go once or twice a day from the front gate, but that's the extent of their outside activity."

"Excellent." Nick's tension level dropped considerably hearing that. Fighting his way through armed guards with

Shade's safety at risk wasn't something he'd relished. "And Shade?"

"Chief, she's like the Pied Piper. Everywhere she goes she's followed by a passel of children!"

"You've seen her? She's been out and can walk around?" Nick was grinning now. This was better than he'd hoped for. First of all, it meant she was healthy. Secondly, if they could get her away from the children, they might not even put her in an unsafe situation as they rescued her. The men quickly got to work on putting the rescue plan in motion.

❧

Shade awakened on her seventh morning in captivity, wondering how she was ever going to make her escape. She was treated well but wanted away from the people who'd hurt her father. She would miss silent Angel and their walks, but she was ready to go home.

The little girl tugged at her heart; she was so sweet and she seemed so alone. Shade had yet to meet her father or any other family members that might be out there. A couple of nights Shade had heard a noise at the door and opened it to find Angel lying on the threshold sound asleep. Not knowing where she lived, Shade brought her inside and snuggled with her. They spent a lot of time together, with Shade sharing stories about Jesus. Angel was especially taken with the story of baby Jesus. Shade's heart was taken with Angel.

Nina openly showed her distaste for the little girl, only saying she was the daughter of an evil man and that she was bad news. Shade had no idea how such a tiny girl could be bad news to anybody and felt more drawn to the child than ever. She knew what it was like to live a lonely childhood with no mother to draw comfort from. Clara had been a great nanny, but she hadn't filled the void left when Shade lost her mother when she was a bit older than Angel.

The other children from the compound also kept their distance from Angel, and Shade dreaded leaving her behind. Angel would never know how much Shade cared for her. She prayed that someone else would step in and fill the void the little girl had. She also prayed for her captors, which was weird since she couldn't even pray for Nick at this point. She had no clue if he even knew what had happened yet. He was probably still on his other mission.

Shade bowed her head in prayer, asking God to guide her so she'd know when and how to make her move. Feeling the urge to get outside, she left the hut and began her morning walk. It was earlier than usual, but she felt the need to get some fresh air while having the silence of the sleeping village to help her think things through.

As she approached the back fence, Shade paused as something in the foliage caught her eye. She couldn't place what it was, so she walked closer and studied the trees.

Hooking her thumbs into the belt loops at her waist, she had a humorous thought. *It's my seventh day of walking around this compound. If I go around six times today, would the fence mysteriously come tumbling down?*

With a grin, she turned to walk on when suddenly a huge section of fencing fell to the ground. Gasping, Shade stumbled backward as she raised her eyes heavenward. "God?"

"No, it's me," Nick whispered as he darted through the

opening to grab her. He had her on the other side and into the trees in moments, and the fence popped back into place, the tiny wires holding it there barely able to be seen by the eye. It appeared to be supported by a small-scale pulley system. Nick pulled her deeper into the foliage.

"How. . . ? When. . . ?" Shade wasn't able to keep up with all that had just happened, but she was more than happy at the moment to bury her face in Nick's shirtfront, holding on for dear life, forgetting her vow to knock him off his white horse if he appeared. She pulled back slightly, peeled his hat off and ran her fingers through his wayward soft brown hair, wanting to make sure he was real.

His hair stuck out in all directions, and she could picture him pushing it back with his familiar act of frustration before slapping the cap back in place, as she'd seen him do many times before when stressed. Nick's hazel eyes met hers; happiness, wariness, and exhaustion each battling for a place in his expression. He pulled her close and she could feel his breath against her temple as his lips caressed her forehead. She heard him mutter a prayer of thanks for her safety before he answered her questions.

"Beau had it all in place. We barely had time to prepare before you showed up. We didn't expect you until later."

Shade remembered her prayer and the intuition that she needed to go outside and begin her walk right then.

For the first time since her capture, she gave in to her tears. "Oh, Nick, my father. . .he was shot. He was already frail from his illness while on that business trip. He'd just been released from the hospital."

Nick wrapped his arms around Shade and closed his eyes in frustration. If she still thought her father had been ill, she hadn't been told of his capture and Nick's rescue mission. The colonel hadn't had a chance to explain what had happened, and Nick must still be in the doghouse, despite Shade's warm greeting. "I've seen him. He's going to be fine. I'll tell you more in a bit, but for now we need to get you away from here. Even though you've been able to move freely, I can imagine if you suddenly disappear they'll start looking and be on our heels."

He signaled for the team to move out. He watched the emotions pass across Shade's face as her initial relief at seeing Nick quickly moved to anger.

"Nothing has changed."

Nick winced as Shade hissed the angry words. "It's still all about the mission when it comes to you. If you'd been at the estate for me, my father wouldn't be shot, and I wouldn't be crawling through the jungle hoping I don't end up like him. Or worse. This is entirely your fault! You owe this rescue to me!"

Nick didn't have time to explain, so he tossed Shade a black jumpsuit, and she shrugged into it, her displeasure obvious over having to wear the bulky suit in this humid jungle. Her hot pink T-shirt wasn't exactly appropriate for camouflage, though, so she didn't have much choice. He watched as she pulled her hair up into a dark hat so the shine wouldn't be seen.

Nick tenderly grasped her chin and smeared dark makeup

over her face, not mistaking her glare for determination. She was one angry lady.

"We'll get you out of here and back to your father; don't worry."

❧

Shade pulled away.

"Yes, Nick. See that you do. I'd like to see him as soon as possible," she snapped, turning her head and moving forward, leaving him behind. She grabbed at the pack Billy handed her and dragged it with her. Shoving past Nick's best friend, Hunter, Shade moved to the front of the line of men and continued forward, not knowing where she was going. She wouldn't go far, not wanting to get lost and cause unnecessary trouble, but she knew she had to get away from Nick to regroup her emotions.

She felt adrift being out of Nick's embrace, and that only made her angrier. Even her body betrayed her when it came to Nick. She didn't need his hugs to feel safe and protected. His kisses wouldn't keep her from being shot at.

She didn't stop until she heard the urgent whisper from Beau back at the fence line. "Chief, we've been compromised."

Shade swung around in fear, expecting to be facing the gun barrel again. Instead, Beau sat on the ground, Angel on his lap, the ever-present bunny clutched to her chest, her terrified eyes huge over the burly hand that clenched her tiny mouth.

"Angel! It's okay, Baby," Shade crooned in a soft whisper as she quickly headed back to the terrified little girl. Beau pulled the child away, not releasing her. "Beau, she doesn't talk. She had some type of trauma that left her speechless a few months ago. Let her go."

Beau looked at Nick. "Chief?"

Shade swung around to Nick. His eyes met hers, the tortured look in the hazel depths all she needed to see before she realized with sickening clarity that Angel couldn't be released. There was too much of a chance she'd give them away. The all-important mission couldn't be compromised. "Nick. Let her go. I'll go back with her before I allow this precious child to be hurt."

Nick shook his head. "Shade, you don't understand. These people are killers. You can't go back, and we can't send her back either. She's a loose end we can't afford."

Shade walked to squat at Angel's side and caressed away the tears that ran silently down her soft face and over Beau's rough hand. "She comes with us, or I don't go. It's that simple. Nick, she kept me sane the past week. She sat outside my hut each day and only went home when it was dark and she had to. I can't abandon her."

She watched as Nick looked at his men. He was measuring his options. She almost smiled at his indecision. There wasn't really a decision to be made. They couldn't send the child back. . .and they couldn't leave her there. War or not, Nick could never hurt a child. The little girl would have to go along with them. Though worried, Shade was ecstatic at her chance to spend more time with her little Angel. Hunter placed a supportive hand on Nick's shoulder and gave him a squeeze, his typical show of support.

Nick closed his eyes in exasperation, nodded at Beau; and

Beau slowly removed his hand. Shade shot Nick a glance of thanks when he looked her way. Angel sat silent, then reached for Shade with a wary look in the agents' direction. She'd probably never seen men in jungle paint before, and it obviously unsettled her, but she made no noise. She snuggled into Shade's embrace and touched her makeup.

"You want some? We need to play a hiding game for a bit." Shade spoke in Spanish and the little girl nodded. Shade was aware of the agents' nervous shuffling as she applied the camouflage paint to Angel's tiny features. They needed to move out. She pulled a dark T-shirt over the little girl's head and took her hand, finally ready to follow the men. "These men are our friends. They're going to take care of us, okay?"

Angel nodded again, looking at Nick out of the corner of her eye as he walked close.

"I'll carry her. We can move quicker that way. We've already wasted too much time, and we've got to get out of here. For future reference, don't be so predictable with your routines if you ever get captured again. When you don't show for your morning walk, they'll be looking for you. Now, let me take the girl."

Shade made a face at him, then turned to explain his words to Angel and was surprised to see the little girl already lifting her arms toward the huge man. Nick swung her up, and she laid her head on his shoulder, snuggling into his embrace. Nick's surprised glance met Shade's, and she raised her eyebrows, shrugging in disbelief.

He held the child so gently, as if she were a feather, but after carrying his hundred-pound-plus pack she probably was pretty weightless to him. Shade shrugged her pack onto her back and fell into line.

Hunter took the lead, and Beau fell in to watch their backs as the others found a place in between.

Chapter 4

S hade wiped at her forehead with the back of her hand. December was obviously just a name down here, not a season. Sweat poured down her spine, and she was ready for a break. The sun had already passed overhead and now the dense trees hid it from sight.

The place would have been beautiful if it hadn't been her prison. Eden must have been something like this with all the fragrant flowers and brilliant pinks, blues, greens, and yellows of the different plants and foliage. But Eden's occupants didn't have armed drug smugglers chasing around after them.

Shade had seen a few snakes and other reptiles, and she wasn't nearly as friendly to the serpents as Eve had been. She kept her distance, while not letting the men see her repulsion. Her nerves were taut, and she was getting tired. The group had only stopped once so far, for a quick lunch, and Shade was ready to drop.

"Nick," she whispered, tripping on roots while trying to catch up with him. "Shouldn't we be at the beach by now? I could see it from the compound."

Nick didn't break pace. "We aren't going that way. It's too obvious. We came in on the far side of the island and will leave that way. The first area they would have patrolled when they found you missing would've been the beach."

Shade sighed with disappointment. The philosophy made sense, but she was so ready to be away from this place. She had fantasies of taking Angel away from here—spoils of war—and dolling her up back at the estate. No one here would miss her anyway.

Nick glanced back at Shade. "I know you're tired. We'll stop soon and have dinner, maybe go a bit farther before we stop for the night. We'll be here a couple days at most, and then you'll be home."

Shade didn't have a reply for that, so she trudged along in Nick's trail. Angel was awake but clutched Nick's neck in silence, staring over his shoulder at Shade for reassurance.

Shade winked at her, and Angel gave her a quick grin. The little girl was a good distraction when Shade's traitorous thoughts dwelled on Nick too long. The past few months when they were together they were always touching in some way—holding hands, arms around each other's waists, sitting with Shade's head on Nick's shoulder—as they talked and dreamed. Shade was having a hard time being this close without touching the man she loved. *Used to love,* she quickly corrected herself, again focusing on Angel.

In less than an hour they found a small clearing, and Nick declared it time to eat. The agents dropped their packs. Shade dug out MREs for each, and the men took their rations and weapons, silently disappearing into the foliage to sit watch while Nick, Shade, and Angel had their dinner.

Angel looked at her meal in distaste.

"It isn't so bad," Shade laughed, speaking in Spanish as she opened a bottle of water and Angel's container of stew. "Just take a bite and wash it down with the rest of this water. At least you get candy when you're finished."

Angel began nibbling at her dinner, and Shade leaned back against a tree. She wanted to take her shoes off but figured her feet were so swollen she'd never get the shoes back on.

Nick settled down next to Shade, where they could talk without being overheard.

"What will we do with Angel, Nick? We can't take her off the island, can we?"

She waited breathlessly for him to correct her, to say they could and would take her with them.

Nick looked off into the trees opposite him, not answering right away. Shade knew by the way he worked his jaw that he was choosing his words carefully, knowing she wouldn't like what he was about to say.

"We won't take her off the island. As soon as we get you a safe distance away, I'll take Billy and Angel and head back to the compound's main gate. We have a few other men who will be there for backup—they should be there already holding off anyone that comes too close in our direction—and Beau and Hunter will take you on to the boat. I—"

Shade's blood began to boil. "No way. I absolutely won't abandon Angel that way!"

Nick motioned for Shade to keep her voice down. Shade

did as he asked, her angry whisper probably carrying just as far. "I go where she goes. Until I know she's safe, I'm not leaving her." She picked at the moss on the ground beside her.

"Angel won't be hurt, Shade. We'll take care of her. She needs to go home, but we need to get you home safely too. The only way to be sure we've done that is to get you far enough away so that I won't have to worry about you."

Shade found a small twig and snapped it, wishing she could break Nick's stubborn attitude as easily. She saw Angel looking at them with apprehension and closed her eyes, leaning her head back against the tree, trying to get control of her emotions.

She knew angry words weren't going to get her anywhere, and she felt a check in her spirit, gently reminding her that God didn't approve of her bitterness. She needed to be more forgiving of Nick—after all, he'd come all this way to rescue her—but she also knew he'd do it for anyone. She was just another mission.

"Nick. I want to go with you. I want to see Angel home safely." She held her hand up as Nick started to argue. "I know I'm not a trained agent, not in the way you all have been trained. But you know I can do this, that my father prepared me for survival and taught me the skills I'd need in this situation. I won't be a burden to you."

Nick was also leaning back against the tree, and he now turned to look into her eyes. His were the familiar hazel, but Shade had never seen him look so cold, and she shivered involuntarily as he analyzed her. She wanted to rub away the lines etched on his weary face and see him change once again into the gentle man she loved. Had loved. Maybe this was the real Nick. She'd never seen him on the field. She knew he was highly respected and had many medals of honor, but so did her dad and he was a pussycat with her too. She had never stopped to think of what they were like when on duty.

"Shade. You won't be going with us. You will go back to the boat with Hunter and Beau, and I'll keep Angel safe. I don't want you there when this all goes down."

Nick's words and attitude scared Shade. It took her a minute to understand, and when she did, her blood boiled again.

Jumping to her feet, she hissed, "You're using Angel as bait, aren't you? You aren't expecting a peaceful ending to this. . .you intend to go in with both guns firing. I won't let you do it!"

Nick was on his feet in a flash, covering Shade's mouth with his hand and leaning so close she could feel his breath against her face. "I'm going in to do what has to be done. If I'd done it right on the last mission, we wouldn't even be here right now—*ow!* "

Nick's hand dropped from Shade's face, and she looked around to see him rubbing his leg where Angel had just bit him through his field pants.

Shade didn't know if she should laugh or cry. Angel was guarding her and obviously didn't like the way Nick was acting. The bite wouldn't have done much damage through the thick fabric, but Angel had sure made her feelings known. Shade had never seen Nick so angry, and it wasn't a pretty sight. She didn't want her own bitterness to make her that way.

She turned to Angel. "It's okay, Sweetie. Don't be scared. Nick's upset, but he wouldn't hurt me. He won't hurt you either."

Shade sank back down against the tree, and Angel curled up on her lap, twirling her hair with her hand and eyeing Nick warily. Nick sat back down too.

After several minutes of silence, he sighed. "I'm sorry. I didn't mean to lose my temper that way."

He looked away, and when he turned back around, Shade saw pain in his eyes. She wanted to wipe it away, to make it better, but instead she sat silently, waiting for him to continue. She didn't have to wait long.

"The last mission—the one that caused you to cancel our wedding—was called to save your father from these same men. They're the reason he was so sick when he returned. You didn't see how bad he was when we found him. You didn't see how they treated him as a prisoner. He was beaten and half starved. When I realized they had you, you can't imagine the images that went through my mind—or the anger that flew through me. I didn't know if you were dead or alive. If they had hurt you. . ."

His voice broke, and Shade was surprised to find herself reaching for his hand. "But they didn't treat me bad. They pretty much ignored me—"

"I know," Nick interrupted, "and I'm thankful for that, but they did hurt the colonel again. He was already weak and the gunshot almost killed him. If I'd taken care of the situation the first time, it never would have happened again."

"Taken care of?" It took Shade a moment before the

meaning of his words became clear to her. "You mean, you wanted to kill them?"

"Yeah," Nick said bitterly. "That's exactly when I mean."

"Nick, you're a Christian. You have to have compassion." Shade was shocked at the depth of his anger.

"That's what your father said, and look at where it got us. Yes, Shade, I'm a Christian, but I'm also a soldier, and this is war. Sometimes these things happen. There's no other way."

Shade stared at this man who now seemed a stranger. "Yes, there's always another way. The authorities can take care of these men. You can't just go out and kill them in cold-blooded anger! Not like this. This isn't a battlefield."

"Watch me." Nick's voice was cold as he stood, turned his back on her, and stalked into the brush.

Tears streamed down Shade's face as she caressed Angel's hair, trying to reassure her that everything was okay. She was so glad the little girl didn't know English.

Everything wasn't okay, and Shade had no idea how to stop Nick. She knew now why Nick had broken his word and gone on that final mission. She knew her father well enough to know he would have sworn Nick to secrecy and forbidden him to tell Shade why he was going.

What she didn't know was what had driven Nick to this point of bitterness. It was a new side of him, and she didn't like it. Maybe it was her fault, the fact that she hadn't trusted him enough to know he wouldn't have gone on the mission without good reason. Maybe the fact that she had broken off their engagement and subsequent wedding had broken something in his spirit to cause this white-hot anger.

Her conscience prickled as she realized she still hadn't said she forgave him, and if she were honest with herself, she didn't know if she was ready to. Now Nick was gone, and she didn't even know if she'd ever have the chance.

She glanced around the small camp and realized he hadn't taken his pack and obviously hadn't taken Angel, so he most probably would return. Did she have it in her to forgive him this soon?

She wanted to do the right thing, but she was still angry and confused. How could she expect Nick to let his anger go when she couldn't even do the same herself? Sighing, feeling a million miles away from God, Shade bowed her head in prayer.

❧

Just out of sight, hidden in the trees, Nick grappled with his own faith and emotions. He'd handled the situation with Shade horribly, and now that he'd found her again, he'd probably just lost her for good.

He had two battles to win—one for Shade's freedom and one for her heart. The first one seemed easy; if he took the enemy out, he wouldn't have to worry about them getting to her again. But Shade had grown to love the people who she was with the past week and wanted this to end peacefully. If he could swing a peaceful ending, Nick would win battle number two, Shade's heart. He had to seek his way back into her heart. He was torn.

The reign of terror from the drug smugglers had to end. Nick knew of only one way to make sure that happened.

He knew she was right about the compassion. But all was fair in love and war, right? And this was war. The colonel had been shot. He'd been abused. If Nick didn't stop Ferdinand this time, it would only happen again, and next time the colonel, Shade, or one of the team's other men might be killed.

Nick couldn't—or wouldn't—take that chance again. He ignored the voice that told him he could take the chance. He had friends in the government here that knew about the case and were ready to step in as soon as Nick called them. They'd make sure justice was served.

But Nick was extremely angry and wanted to personally see Ferdinand suffer. He wanted to be sure this never happened again.

The thoughts ran haphazardly through Nick's head, and he knew this would be an ideal time to pray. He chose not to. Nick didn't have anything to say to God right now, and he knew God didn't approve of where he was headed. His conscience prickled, but at this point, he chose to focus on letting the bitterness rule. He'd clean up his spiritual life later.

Nick grabbed for his weapon as a twig snapped ahead of him. He was on his knee and ready to shoot as Hunter stepped into view.

"We heard the raised voices. Everything all right?" he asked, sinking to a squat beside his buddy.

"No," Nick snapped, "but the sooner we get going, the sooner it will be. Shade isn't happy about being shut out, so you'll really have to watch her. In the meantime, we have a mission to fulfill, whether she likes it or not."

"Are you sure, Nick? Maybe we should all discuss this before we proceed. I know you're in charge, but I think in this case you're too close to everyone involved. I've never seen you like this."

"I'm fine. We proceed as we discussed earlier." Nick's clipped tone barred any further comments.

Unfortunately, Hunter ignored the command. "Can we pray?"

"Not enough time. We need to move out."

From the concern on Hunter's face, Nick knew without a doubt he didn't agree with Nick's attitude any more than Shade did. Fortunately for Nick, Nick was in charge, and he headed back to the camp before Hunter could protest any further. The twinge in his conscience became an aching pain.

Chapter 5

Nick rose silently from where he'd rested and gently disentangled the still-sleeping Angel from Shade's tight embrace. Neither female woke up, a small miracle that showed their point of exhaustion.

Signaling Billy, the trio moved out. Nick did take time to pray for Shade's situation and for Beau and Hunter as they led her out. He knew she was going to be roaring mad, and the two men would have their hands full keeping her on track. Carrying the sleeping child slowed him down, but he cradled her in his arms rather than placing her over his shoulder so she'd sleep as long as possible. He had no idea what her reaction would be when she realized she'd been separated from Shade, but today wouldn't be the time for her to decide to get her voice working again. Yesterday she'd been complacent and stayed in any position he carried her in. He hoped today would be the same. His ankle still throbbed where she'd bit him through all his layers of clothing, and when she discovered she'd been taken from Shade, Nick had no doubt she'd become the wildcat Shade could be when angry. He knew better than to provoke a female, even a four-year-old beginner model.

He planned to call a meeting from the front gate with Ferdinand in the ruse of trading Angel back to them, and then he would have Billy take Ferdinand out. He'd tuck Angel safely out of harm's way before it all went down, and with the other agents that were meeting them, they should be able to capture the few other kingpins that weren't as dangerous. Without their leader, he didn't expect them to be quite as macho.

Nick's friend on the island promised him the drug cartel would face stiff punishment if Nick could bring them in. Nick promised he'd do just that, but he left out the fact that Ferdinand would not be joining his goons in prison. Nick would see to his fate.

He didn't fail to see the irony of his acts, cradling a precious sleeping child in his arms while plotting another man's murder.

꿎

Shade awakened to find her arms empty and knew immediately she'd been had. The night before was strained, and Shade didn't bother to apologize to Nick, but she really had thought he'd take to heart her opinions and she'd have at least one more chance to try and talk him out of the violent ending he was planning.

She felt tears of anger prick her eyelids, mixed with guilt over not making amends with Nick as he walked into a hostile situation. Now she might never have the chance to say she was sorry, all due to her stupid, stubborn pride.

The morning was cool, but humidity already hung in the

air, promising another hot day. Shade's neck was sore where it pressed on her pack, but it was the only pillow she'd had—way better than the alternative of sleeping with her head on the ground. She shuddered at the memory of all the bugs she had brushed off in the dark as it was. As she moved to a sitting position, she realized more than just her neck was sore. She didn't know how these guys did this night after night for weeks on end. Even her pallet at the compound had been comfortable compared to the jungle floor.

She irritably scratched at some of the myriad of bug bites that now covered her body, glad the jumpsuit covered as much as it did. Only her face, neck, and hands were exposed, but that was enough to provide an apparent smorgasbord for the dreaded insects and entry to the other areas.

Shade needed to get going if she was going to sneak off to stop Nick. She glanced around. Beau was sleeping less than two feet away from her, and Hunter wasn't in sight. If she rose quietly, she just might be able to track Nick and catch up. What she'd do then was anybody's guess, but she'd figure that out when the time came.

Slipping soundlessly to her feet, she turned and came face-to-face with a smirking Hunter.

"Going somewhere, Shade? You weren't moving so quietly out of concern for Beau's beauty sleep, were you?"

"I hope not," Beau's voice answered softly from behind Shade. "I wake up when someone's breathing changes in their sleep."

Shade glared. "It figures Nick had to leave me with the eyes and ears of the team." Nick was nobody's fool. "I'm going after Angel. And Nick. He has to be stopped. You both have to realize that."

Beau looked wary at her determined expression, but Hunter didn't back down. His blue eyes narrowed menacingly. "No way. You aren't to be anywhere near that area. You've made this hard enough on Nick as it is."

He hesitated and appeared to be rethinking his approach. "Shade, you don't know what you put Nick through the past month. He adores you, and you broke his heart. You owe him this—to be able to complete this mission without worrying about you."

Shade wrestled with her thoughts. "That's a whole 'nother can of worms. Now that you bring it up, I didn't ever say I was sorry for that after he told me about the mission. I know I should have, but I thought I'd have this morning. If Nick gets hurt, I'll never get to say I'm sorry. Another good reason you need to take me to him."

Hunter looked sympathetic. "After it's all said and done, you can worry about your relationship—or not. That's up to you." His face took on a gentler expression. "This is why you aren't supposed to let the sun go down on your anger. You never know what tomorrow will bring, so you should take the moment when it's there."

He grasped Shade's arm in support. She knew she wore her feelings on her sleeve. She sighed. "I know that, but I didn't take the moment, and now I need to say I'm sorry. I can't let him go without clearing all this up. Then he can focus on the mission, and we can all move on with our lives. I have to tell him how I feel!"

"Nick is good. He'll come back to you. You keep praying and keep out of his way. . .and we'll do the same."

Shade knew further argument was useless and remembered Nick's words. "This is war." Well, that meant she could do what she needed to, right?

She knew that wasn't true either, but for now she had to give the guys the slip. It was obvious they weren't going to help her, so she'd have to do this on her own. She just hoped her acting skills would convince them of her compliance.

"I guess you're right. I don't want to cause Nick any more problems." She swung her pack around her waist, and then hesitated. "I'll do what you guys ask, but first let me use the. . . um. . .facilities."

The guys looked relieved that she'd come around and turned to make sure their packs were ready so they could move out when she returned. They'd stayed at the drop point the night before and had gear stashed there waiting for them. Now they had to make sure the gear was covered before starting today's trek. Shade hoped the process would distract the two men long enough to not notice she was gone longer than necessary for a trip to the latrine, in this case, a hole behind the trees.

Shade made a show of slinging her pack carelessly over her shoulder and disappeared into the trees. She could tell where Nick had gone by looking at the crushed foliage. From the looks of it he was more concerned with a quick getaway than he was on not being tracked. And since he was going back to the compound, he probably wasn't worried about Ferdinand following him, so that made sense.

In his defense, most people wouldn't have noticed the slight signs of recent visitors to the area, but she'd been trained by the best—her daddy—and knew how to track Nick even without most of the signs.

With a smirk, she quietly thanked God for Nick's carelessness as she moved quickly through the trees.

Nick's guilt at sneaking out on Shade increased with each step he took. Angel had slept the first hour into the hike, but when she awoke and couldn't see Shade over his shoulder, silent tears fell down her cheek, and Nick felt like a complete heel.

He consoled her in Spanish, but he couldn't forget the fact that in all probability she'd never see Shade again, nor had Shade been able to say good-bye to the little girl she'd grown to love so much.

Shade would have a hard time forgiving him for that, so their future didn't look very hopeful no matter how he handled the rest of this journey.

He tried to keep his focus on plans for the mission, but the little niggling twitch of his conscience kept interfering. He knew what God was trying to tell him, and he didn't want to hear it or deal with it right now.

Shade's voice joined in to make his thoughts into a chorus. "Compassion," Shade's voice seemed to whisper. "There are other ways to handle this situation."

He remembered storming off after telling her to watch him go take out the enemy. Not meaning it literally, of course—that was something he'd never want her to see—but was he doing the right thing? Was Hunter right about the fact that Nick was so close to this situation that he wasn't seeing it straight and might be making poor decisions? Worst of all, he kept thinking that in this case, if he shot Ferdinand outright like he wanted to do, he'd be sending the man straight to hell and would have that on his conscience forever. There were times in war when you had to shoot, but was this one of them?

Nick knew the answer to that too but pushed it aside, focusing only on his anger. He had to protect Shade and the colonel at all costs. This couldn't happen again. He wanted to yell out his frustration.

Nick had never second-guessed his instinct until now. Was that because in this case he was wrong? If only he could go to the Lord and pray, but he'd shut Him out for so long he felt he couldn't approach Him now.

Billy slowed his steps and looked back as Nick dropped behind, concern evident on his face. "What's up, Nick?"

Angel lifted her tear-streaked face and looked warily at the two men.

"We're getting close and I'm trying to cover all the bases. We need to make sure Angel stays safe no matter what goes down. I'm not sure how to do that without one of us stepping out of the loop, and I'm not sure we can afford to lose any of the members to baby-sitting, with Hunter and Beau escorting Shade."

He lowered Angel to the ground. Opening his pack, he pulled another meal out and prepared it for her. They settled down for a brief rest and tossed around their best ideas. Angel ate silently as the men decided to proceed as planned, though Nick still felt sick to his stomach at the thought. Finally, hesitantly, he prayed for intervention if God didn't like the way he was handling this situation. For the first time in a month, a small sense of peace settled in his heart.

~

Shade was getting tired, having pushed herself nonstop since leaving the base camp. She couldn't afford to stop and have the guys catch up, and she knew they were getting close as it was.

The signs of Nick up ahead were getting fresher too, and she didn't know if she should make her presence known—forcing him to take her with him since he couldn't lose the time to take her back—or if she could somehow stay to the side of his trail and follow them on in. If she did that, there was a good chance Hunter and Beau would catch up to her, or to Nick, giving her away.

She sighed over not having thought this part through better. Her worst fear was that Nick wouldn't have enough manpower to hold the drug cartel back with two of his most talented teammates baby-sitting her, and the team worked at its best with all the members in place.

She froze as she heard a noise in the brush to her left. The area was dense, and she couldn't see a thing. Dropping to her knees, she crawled toward the sound, praying she didn't give herself away.

There was no way Nick had doubled back beside her, and with his trail still ahead of her, she knew she wasn't off track in following him.

Hunter and Beau wouldn't be careless enough to make

the noise she heard, so it had to be someone else.

Her third guess of who it could be was her captors. She didn't relish the thought of recapture.

Her mind reeled with sudden possibilities as that thought crossed her mind. If she were captured again, Hunter and Beau would soon catch up with Nick and Billy, and the team would be complete once more. They would be much more proficient together, ensuring Nick's safety, and she could use herself as bargaining power in a trade for Angel, keeping the girl safe in the process.

Of course, Nick would then want to personally kill Shade, blowing all future plans they had together, but it was probably a moot point anyway. She'd messed things up so badly by now that her only choice was to do what she could to keep Angel, Nick, and the team safe. Then again, voluntarily throwing herself at the wolves didn't feel real practical, so she was back to square one.

Shade decided this would again be an excellent time to pray.

Lord, You know the outcome of all this and the fact that Nick is going into battle out of anger instead of protocol. I want to help but not if I'll make matters worse. If I'm in the skirmish, I know Nick will have to proceed with caution on using force, but he'll also be distracted and infuriated with me. I don't want to mess up the mission by making the wrong choice. Please guide me and let me know in no uncertain terms what I need to do.

Shade hoped God would hear her prayer and provide a speedy reply.

Quickly hiding her pack and slipping out of the jumpsuit, Shade discarded all signs that the team had rescued her. Placing both just out of sight near the path, she hoped the team would find it quickly when they met up and realized she hadn't made it to Nick.

She jotted a quick note that explained if they found the pack, she'd been captured again and that she was keeping their existence a secret. She noted that she hoped it would buy them some time and the surprise factor. She also jotted down that she loved Nick, and she was sorry for messing things up so badly—on both missions.

The pink shirt was a dead giveaway to her location, but it was worth the effort if she was captured again and the drug cartel decided she'd escaped on her own. That would give the team some valuable time to set up their operation.

She crept forward cautiously, gasping as she came face-to-face with a small snake. In the moment it took for her to place it and remember it was a harmless variety, she felt the cold steel of a gun press into her back.

Slowly lifting her eyes, she stared into the cold face of Ferdinand himself, his dark eyes glittering menacingly as he smiled, white teeth perfect; the combination sending shivers of fear down Shade's spine.

"Well, look who we have here. I suppose you broke out on your own and decided to crawl through the jungle for fun?"

Though she'd only seen him from a distance, the man looked familiar. Charismatic and handsome, she thought it sad that he chose to waste his life in such a lifestyle. Knowing he didn't expect her to answer, she kept still, glaring defiantly back into his eyes.

She was near enough to her men that a scream would bring either team running, but in that moment she chose to believe this was God's answer to her prayer and instead clamped her mouth shut. Her knees felt weak as she wondered if God had indeed acted or if she'd foolishly set herself and the men up for further danger. She could only hope it was not the latter as she was roughly placed into handcuffs and shoved back in the direction of the compound.

Chapter 6

Shade was dragged roughly behind Ferdinand as he walked carelessly through the jungle. He didn't seem concerned at all about being detected, a fact Shade didn't miss that caused her great concern. Had he already captured Nick? Or was he just so cocky that he didn't care who heard him?

If Nick had been captured, then she'd made things worse by getting caught herself. How would she warn Beau and Hunter or call in further backup if that was the case? Hopefully the two men would figure it out and make it all work. Maybe it was still a good thing they were headed back to the compound chasing her instead of sitting on the beach babysitting while Nick faced this without them.

She began praying and didn't realize her desperate words could be heard until Ferdinand swung around to look at her. He moved close, and Shade shuddered at his nearness. His evil was palpable. Shade noticed up close that he didn't appear as calm and collected, so maybe he wasn't as cocky as she'd thought. Though he obviously wanted Nick to show, he apparently wasn't at peace with the way it was all about to go down. That fact should have scared Shade, but it actually encouraged her to see the chink in his armor.

"What is this you are saying? You follow me muttering and whispering, and I warned you to stay silent or I'd put a gag on you. If your hero comes running, I have men who will take out your—how do you say. . .white knight?—before you can make another sound. It will be in your best interest to stay silent. . .though perhaps it would serve my purpose even better if you want to alert your rescuer that I have you. Distraction is always to the victor's advantage."

Shade guessed she should be relieved to know that it didn't sound like he had Nick in his custody, but so much for their sneak attack. It was apparent that Ferdinand knew exactly how she'd escaped and also who had rescued her.

"I wasn't muttering; I was praying," Shade snapped. "I didn't realize I was doing so out loud. I'm sorry and won't do it again." *That you can hear anyway,* she silently added. She wasn't about to stop praying at a time like this.

Ferdinand laughed softly. "Ah, you think your God can get you out of this? How amusing. Such an old-fashioned habit for a modern woman. Why would a smart woman buy into such foolishness?"

Shade bristled at his words. "You'd do well to 'buy into it' too. It's true. Christ is real. I've been taught about Jesus my whole life, from His birth in a manger to His death on the cross. You can't hurt us because the worst thing you could intend to do—to kill us—would send us straight to paradise and to our Lord."

"Ah, yes. The belief that a child can save the world. How quaint that people really believe such a thing. It must give you great peace at a time like this."

Ferdinand's sarcasm and condescending tone sickened Shade. If he only knew what he was saying. If he only knew that his death was also imminent, if Nick had his way, and that he was living his final moments making fun of the one true way he could avoid eternal damnation. . . .

Her eyes filled with tears at the thought of the eternity he faced that day and how he'd possibly rue his words very shortly. She felt it was critical that she warn him.

"You seem so sure of yourself, but what if things don't go as you plan? What if you are the one to die today? Are you so cocky that you're right and I'm wrong that you can take that chance? You make fun of my beliefs, but if I'm right—and I am—do you realize where you'll be when Nick comes after you? If you are the one to die?"

Words spoken from Shade's mouth had never felt so important. She prayed frantically for the perfect thing to say to reach this man's heart—if he even had one. He was smiling again with that menacing, cocky expression, and Shade felt the full burden of her opportunity and the fact that she'd apparently failed to reach him.

Ferdinand's face reddened in anger but his tone remained the same.

"Well, much as it entertains me to hear of your simple faith, we need to continue on. Please keep your prayers to yourself—and perhaps they will be better spent on your hero—or I will place the gag over your mouth. I'm a gentle man and don't want to use undue roughness on you unless you force me to."

Shade begged to differ in opinion on his "gentle" technique, as she'd personally seen the violence the man could inflict, starting with her father's poor treatment while in Ferdinand's care and subsequently being shot by his men. She would keep her prayers to herself, but not only about herself and Nick. Instead she pleaded for God to reach Ferdinand's cold, unbelieving heart before it was too late.

⤳

Nick heard a slight sound behind him and quickly passed Angel off to Billy. He was in a kneeling position with his rifle aimed before he heard the signal that Hunter was approaching. He signaled back and willed his adrenaline to slow down as his thoughts went in sixty different directions as to why his team would defy him and be approaching. They were supposed to have Shade safely on the other side of the island.

He knew the moment he saw Hunter's face that his friend wasn't there with good news. Beau slipped in behind Hunter, and Shade was nowhere in sight.

Nick glanced at Angel in time to see her excited expression crumple when Shade didn't appear. He could relate.

"She slipped away, Chief. We thought—hoped—she'd be here with you." Hunter's despair was palpable. "I don't know how we missed her. She had to have gone off trail at some point, and we missed the signs."

Nick wanted to yell, to let his anger explode, to do something to let loose these bitter feelings that consumed him. Instead, he suggested they backtrack slightly and see if there were any clues as to where she might have gone off track. The whole situation was getting to him, and he knew Hunter felt bad enough without Nick vocalizing his feelings.

They were losing valuable time, and Nick felt more out of control than he'd ever felt in his life. He wished he could go back in time and make the past two missions disappear. He and Shade should be making final plans for their wedding instead of traipsing through a jungle playing seek and find. Seek and find with deadly drug runners who only had evil on their minds.

Within thirty minutes, the men found Shade's pack where she'd placed it, and Nick's heart sank as he read her note.

"According to this, Shade's been captured again. It sounds like she might have planned it, but I can't imagine what she was thinking if that was the case. Ferdinand is going to be more angry than ever, and I didn't want him provoked until we pulled him out." Nick sighed as he looked over at Angel, who still clutched the dirty stuffed bunny. He hoped she didn't know English. The child looked exhausted.

"Okay, I guess we head on to the compound, continuing with our plan. If Shade's plan worked, they won't be expecting us. We'll proceed as if they are, just in case. Billy, now that we have the team back together, you'll keep Angel with you. With your scope on, she shouldn't be able to see what is happening. I don't want her hurt—physically or emotionally—by what we're about to do."

The men fell into line and moved to the clearing around the compound. Billy found a strategic viewpoint and placed Angel behind him. Nick was relieved to see her curl up against the man and close her eyes in exhaustion. The other men scattered to various points in order to cover Nick as he moved out into the clearing. It was game time.

※

Shade sat at the guard's shack just inside the gates, her stomach in knots over what was about to happen. Though she watched for any sign of movement in the trees, she saw nothing. The team was good, so it was doubtful she'd note their arrival anyway, but still she peered into the endless shadows.

Belatedly, she saw the wisdom in being across the island. She didn't want to be here, didn't want to witness the violence about to erupt. There didn't seem to be an easy ending no matter which stubborn man she approached.

Nick and Ferdinand, though opposites in their beliefs, were each as impossible as the other. She didn't even know how Nick planned to play this out. She was worried about Angel, and though she knew Nick would take care of her, she knew the day had been hard on the small girl who'd already seen so many bad things in her life.

She wanted to hold Angel in her arms, and if she admitted the truth, she wanted to be held in Nick's arms. Their fight and her anger seemed ridiculous now that she looked back, and she might never have a chance to know if he'd received her note and if he'd accepted her apology. She continued to pray earnestly that God would give them a second chance to show what they meant to each other. Shade knew she'd do everything in her power to earn Nick's forgiveness if they survived.

A sudden noise distracted her from her prayers, and she

watched as Nick walked boldly from the brush, Angel's stuffed bunny held out like a surrender flag. Shade had expected more of a sneak attack, but Nick obviously wanted to get on with things.

❧

By holding out the bunny, Nick hoped to prove they had Angel. Though Ferdinand had shown disinterest in Shade and had treated her well, he hoped the man cared at least a little bit about tiny girls, too, and wouldn't laugh in their faces at their desire to keep her safe. He knew the man could be ruthless and might not care at all about the child's fate.

Instead of starting subtly, Nick was angry enough now that he'd decided to go boldly forward. "Send me Ferdinand."

Ferdinand stepped from the shack, an amused expression on his face. Armed guards surrounded him, weapons aimed at Nick as he continued to move forward. "I've been waiting for you, Nick. I had hoped borrowing your fiancée would flush you out. Don't do anything foolish, and she won't be hurt."

"You're a coward, Ferdinand. You sent your goons to flush me out while you hid here in your fortress. Why don't you move on out here and face me like a man." Nick waved the bunny again.

"What do we have here, Nick? Did you bring your lucky charm to keep you safe?" The man smirked at his own humor.

Nick grinned. "I don't need a lucky charm. No, this would belong to Angel, the small child from your village. Or didn't anyone even realize she was missing? According to Shade, the child was all but abandoned and ignored."

Ferdinand blanched visibly, not the reaction Nick had

expected from a cold-blooded killer. "You would use a small child as a pawn in such a situation? You are even more evil than I."

"No," Nick stated. "She's safe for now. And I intend to keep her that way, but we will use her to negotiate Shade's release. This is no different than what you did to Shade and her family. They were innocent. You used them. I want to see her."

Ferdinand's reaction to the news that they would use Angel threw Nick. Did the man have a heart after all? He'd use it to their advantage. Ferdinand hesitated, lost in thought.

As he waited, Nick saw movement from the corner of his eye as an armed guard raised his rifle and took aim in his direction. He heard Shade scream and saw her run from the guard shack toward the man, then watched helplessly as she placed herself between Nick and the shooter. One of Nick's men took out the guard before he could complete his shot, and Ferdinand swung his weapon toward Shade in shock as another scream issued from the brush.

"No, Papa! No! Not my Shade!" Angel screamed as her tiny figure shot out from the trees. Her voice was loud and clear as she flung herself into the circle of Shade's arms, just as a bullet fired from a second guard's rifle.

❧

Time seemed to slow down as Shade cradled the little girl close to her heart, trying to shield her from the oncoming bullet. Another guard's weapon fired, and Shade felt their bodies fly through the air as this shot connected with its target. The pain was beyond intense as Shade slammed into the ground, the bullet burning through her body.

As darkness settled over her, Shade heard Ferdinand's pained voice yell harsh words at his guard as more shots rang out, even as he ran closer to the spot where Shade lay with a limp Angel in her clutch. His voice was full of heartache. "It is as you said. A tiny child can change the world. My little Angel has tried. I must find out more about this Jesus you spoke of. Maybe He will save my daughter and you, her protector."

Shade fought for each whispered word. "No, she tried to be *my* protector."

Shade now knew why he'd looked familiar. He was her guardian Angel's father. She would have smiled at his words if the pain hadn't been so bad. God was already working in this bad situation, making it into good. She felt Angel being removed from her arms and didn't have the strength to fight to hold onto her. For a moment she felt empty; then she sensed Nick's presence as he leaned over her, pulling her up into his arms while yelling for a medic to see to Shade and Angel.

The gunfire had ceased, and Shade could hear commotion in the background as men were rounded up and arrested. The images around her sounded fragmented as Shade fought for consciousness.

Nick's tears fell onto her cheek as he pulled her close and pushed her hair away from her face with gentle fingers. "Don't leave me now, Shade. We have a wedding to plan and a lifetime to spend together. Christmas is just around the corner. Hang in there, Baby."

He kissed her forehead, then covered her face with desperate kisses as Shade felt herself begin to drift away. She heard his choked words as he began to pray. "Lord, I've been so pigheaded. . .please don't let Shade pay the price because I rushed in here with the wrong attitude. We'll close the mission out properly, but please give me a second chance. Please let Shade live."

"I love you, Nicky," Shade whispered, hoping he heard her heartfelt declaration.

"I love you too, Shade. Don't leave me." His tear-filled voice continued to speak loving words as Shade succumbed to the welcome pain-numbing darkness.

Chapter 7

Shade looked over at the man slumbering on the pillow beside her. Nick looked boyish in his sleep—hair tousled, his features peaceful, and his mouth turned up in a slight smile, not even remotely resembling the tough jungle soldier of a few weeks earlier. On this, the third morning of their marriage, her heart still jumped at the sight. This was a view she'd never tire of.

Not wanting to wake him, Shade carefully slid out of bed. She crossed the room to pull her soft pink robe off the white rack near the door and wrapped it around her matching silk gown as she tiptoed out of the room and headed to the small kitchenette off the living room.

The coffee machine had been preset to make a pot of hot water, and not wanting to miss the sunrise, she hurried to make a cup of mint tea before walking out onto the balcony of their condo. Squinting as the bright morning sun peeked up over the horizon, she sank onto a wicker chaise lounge, mesmerized by the beauty as she watched the Florida sun play off the emerald waters of the Gulf of Mexico. This was another view she'd never tire of.

Nick had planned the whole honeymoon, surprising Shade daily with his thoughtfulness and the time he'd put into planning each detail. Since he'd only had a couple weeks from the time he rescued her—and during her time recuperating in the hospital—he'd done a remarkable job putting it all together before the wedding. Shade had healed nicely and tried to help, but Nick insisted she rest and let him handle all plans. Since she'd pretty much planned out the wedding—and at the time was still sore and tired—she'd left the honeymoon planning to him.

Now that she had time to reflect, she looked back at how blessed they'd been the past week as all the details came together. The wedding was fairy-tale perfect, held the weekend before Christmas, with all their friends and family in attendance. Her bridesmaids were breathtaking in their green satin dresses, and the groomsmen were handsome in their black tuxedos with red cummerbunds. Ivy and poinsettias filled the sanctuary of their church while tiny white lights covered all the greenery to finish out the Christmas theme.

Of course, all that was a blur in Shade's memory compared to the smile on Nick's face as she walked down the aisle toward him on her father's arm. They'd both cried during the ceremony and had floated down the aisle on the way to their reception, which was held on the first level of the condominium building they were now staying in.

Today was Christmas Eve, and Nick had planned more surprises. Shade couldn't imagine how he could top all the moments they'd shared so far, but he insisted this would be the best day yet. Shade smiled in anticipation.

"Ah, from that smile I'd guess you're thinking happy thoughts this morning?" Nick sank down onto the chair beside Shade, startling her with his quiet entrance onto the balcony. Apparently some of his jungle habits had followed him to their honeymoon.

Shade took the hand he offered, caressing his palm with her thumb. "I'm just reliving our wedding and wondering how you think you can top the past three days."

Nick grinned cockily. "I don't think; I know I'll top it all. This will be the best day you've had in a long time." He gazed into her eyes for a moment before continuing. "I know I said this before, but I'm so sorry for my bitterness and for what I put you through out there on the island."

Shade was already shaking her head as he finished. "I'm the one who was bitter from being so angry when you left. You were just doing what my father ordered. I'm sorry I didn't have more faith in you and caused you more worry and stress in the field."

Nick tugged her to her feet and pulled her into his embrace. "Okay, then. It's all over and behind us. We only have the future to think about, and if you want it to begin, we'd better get going on our day. We have a lot to do."

They ate a leisurely brunch on the balcony, and Shade was surprised to realize it was already almost noon. They packed and said their farewells to the beautiful condo, knowing they'd be back for special occasions in the future, and left their suitcases at the front entry ready to be moved to the next stop on Nick's agenda. He wouldn't say where they were headed, only that they were moving to another place for Christmas Eve.

They took a long walk up the beach before Nick said it was time to head to their next stop.

The temperature was dropping along with the sun, and Shade was glad she'd grabbed her jacket out of the car before they began to walk. Nick said the car wasn't necessary for this part of the journey. Shade loved the small beach community of Destin. Cars passed them as they strolled, and they walked up the main strip before heading north on a side road. With one hand clutched in Nick's grasp and the other tucked into her pocket, Shade was content to follow him wherever he led.

Nick stopped, turned to face the gulf, and pulled Shade back against him. Winding his arm around her stomach, he put his chin on her head and pointed toward the horizon to the west.

"Look at the sunset. I've never seen such colors before!" His tone was teasing, lovingly mocking the comment she'd made in delight every one of the past three evenings.

Shade grinned as she took in the breathtaking view of oranges, pinks, lavenders, and blues. "Aha! I'm already training you in the important things in life! Here I was enjoying the walk and the feel of my hand in yours—and you noticed the sunset even before I did."

She snuggled back against him and watched the sun sink out of sight, thanking God for the millionth time for such a thoughtful, loving, and goofy husband.

Nick pulled away, heading back up the road. "We

need to hurry so you can still see when we arrive at the next destination."

They walked another quarter mile, turning into a residential neighborhood, and Nick stopped in front of a charming cottage with its perimeter defined by a white picket fence. Christmas lights decorated the outline of the home. "Welcome to your next and final honeymoon location."

Shade choked up as she took in the pretty, white-trimmed, sea-foam green cottage. She'd always dreamed of a home such as this after all her travels and moves with her father and was touched that Nick had found it and rented it for the remainder of their honeymoon.

"It's just perfect," she whispered, the words getting stuck in her throat. "It's the house from my dreams. I can't think of a place I'd rather spend the rest of our honeymoon."

Nick touched Shade's chin, tilting her head back so she could look at him, his crooked grin making her heart all aflutter.

"How about the rest of our life? The cottage is ours. I bought it before I left for the mission."

Shade looked at Nick in disbelief, turned toward the house where Nick pointed out the sold sign, then gazed back at Nick's handsome face.

Squealing, she threw herself into Nick's arms, smothering his face with kisses. "Ours? It's really ours?" she kept asking as he twirled her around.

"It's really ours," Nick said, his laughter showing his pleasure in her reaction as he pulled her into his embrace. "And there's more."

Just as he said the words, the front door of the cottage flung open and a sarcastic voice called out. "Hey, Saint Nick! Why don't you stop spreading all that Christmas cheer out there and get in here and help decorate this place for your bride!"

Shade spun around to see Billy standing in the doorway, flanked by Beau and Hunter.

She grinned as she and Nick walked through the gate and up the walkway to the motley group, "Ah, the three wise men. Now all we're missing is the Christmas child."

"Oh, you'd be surprised," Beau piped in, looking exhausted and giving Billy a pointed look. "We have wise guys, and then we have a Christmas child here."

Hunter punched Beau's arm, then pushed the men out of the doorway and waved the couple in. "We just got in with your luggage. The way these two are whining, you'd think we had two Christmas children here. Tired and ready to open their presents."

Beau rubbed his arm dramatically while feigning hurt. "I resemble that comment."

Shade laughed. "Don't you mean resent?"

Beau grinned back. "No, I have to admit I resemble it. Billy does too. It's been a long three days while you two were hiding out at the beach."

"How about the grand tour?" Nick suggested, leading Shade into the cozy living room, complete with a Christmas tree in the corner, gifts piled high beneath it. Christmas music played on the stereo, and the aroma of hot cider filled the air.

Shade peeked beneath the tree. "I hope these three are

staying through tomorrow, because otherwise there's a lot of gifts under that tree for just two of us."

"They'll be here, along with your father."

They headed on through the kitchen and eating area, which was filled with the mouthwatering aroma of food cooking on the stove. A buffet was laid out on the counter, and Shade suddenly realized they hadn't eaten since late morning and she was ravenous.

Nick pulled her to the patio door and flicked on the light. Shade was delighted to see a pool in the backyard. The yard was dark, but she could tell it was spacious beyond where the porch light shone. They headed down the hall, passing a bathroom, spare bedroom, and then entered the master suite. The room was decorated just as she'd always planned.

Shade was shocked. "How did you know? The house can't have come this way, just as I would have decorated it."

It was as if Nick had been looking at her dream house notebook, but she hadn't ever shown it to him. It was where she kept pictures, drawings, and plans for her future home. She hadn't planned to show him until after they were married.

Nick pointed to the notebook on the white wicker dresser. "Your dad gave me that while you were in the hospital. These three and your father have worked hard to put it all together."

Shade was speechless. It was as if she'd walked into a dream. Not only did she now have her dream cottage, but it was also decorated just as she'd always wanted. Mouth open, but with no words coming out, she turned to the men.

"Uh, uh, uh! Before you tear up again. . .we have one more surprise to show you," Nick said.

Nick led the way into the hall, and Shade saw that the last door was wrapped in Christmas paper and ribbon, looking like a giant present. He nodded. "Go ahead, open it. See what's inside."

Shade laughed nervously, not knowing what to expect. "Is it an office? A place for me to write?" That was also in her dream book.

Four deep voices replied, "Just open the door already!"

Shade did as she was told and entered a pink room that would be any little girl's fantasy. It wasn't in her book. "I don't understand."

Her brain tried to put it all together, but it didn't make any sense until a squeal of delight filled the room.

In the far corner, where she'd been kneeling just out of Shade's sight, Angel popped to her feet, abandoning the manger scene she'd been playing with. "Shade!"

Shade's knees buckled and she dropped to the floor even as Nick grabbed for her. "I don't believe it," she sobbed. "My little guardian Angel."

She pulled the tiny girl into her embrace, shaking with the convulsive tears that racked her body. The little girl clutched her with both arms while cradling the small figures of Mary, Joseph, and baby Jesus in her fists. Nick dropped to his knees and enveloped both females into his arms.

She and Angel clung to each other and cried for several minutes before Shade could calm herself enough to glance up at the men who towered over them. All three had tears streaming down their faces and were self-consciously wiping at them.

"Whew, it's those onions you used, Hunter. I told you they were too strong," Beau accused.

"Isn't that the truth," Billy agreed, sniffling while turning to Hunter with a glare.

Hunter raised an eyebrow. "My onions? No way, it's the jalapeños you put in the salsa. It's infiltrating the whole house."

Shade glanced at Nick, who just shook his head, grinning at his macho team of men who were melting into puddles over the tears of a petite woman and tiny girl.

Shade lifted Angel away so she could look at her. Angel's unruly curls had been brushed into shiny ringlets, and her skin glowed pink. She looked precious, dolled up in a pink dress, white tights, and shiny black patent leather shoes.

"Did you all do this?" she asked the three men, hiccups still racking her body. She couldn't comprehend what the last three days must have been like.

They nodded and then hurried off with excuses that the kitchen needed their attention.

"Oh, Nicky. How'd you pull this one off?" Shade asked, leaning back against his chest as she and Angel studied each other, hands clutched tightly together as if they'd lose each other again if they let go. "The room. . .she's staying awhile?"

"She's ours, Shade. Her father will be in prison for a long time, and he requested we take her and give her the life she deserves. He's a changed man, and he wants the best for his little girl. My friend down there pulled some strings, and here she is." He caressed her cheek and softly said, "Merry Christmas, my lovely wife. You're a mother."

Shade's tears were falling again.

Angel's eyes lit up at Nick's words. She held up the dolls in her hand, one at a time. After gazing at Joseph, she pointed from him to Nick.

"The daddy," she stated in careful English.

She then shuffled Mary into her clutch and held her up. She looked at Mary, then at Shade. "The mommy." Again the word was pronounced in careful English, with the child pointing from the doll to Shade. "Angel's mommy."

Shade bit her lip as the tears flowed down her face. She watched as Angel looked at baby Jesus with reverence. "Baby Jesus."

She laid Mary and Joseph down and lovingly placed baby Jesus between them. She then turned to Nick and Shade, sliding onto their laps. She pointed to herself, her voice full of awe.

"Angel. Mommy and Daddy's baby," she whispered, snuggling into their embrace.

"My Christmas child," Shade whispered back in a choked voice, holding the little girl tight. "Let Mommy and Daddy tell you the story about Baby Jesus. . . ."

⁓

Nick wiped the happy tears from his face. Never had he felt so choked up and blessed. He had sought Shade and found her but had also found so much more. He'd found forgiveness, compassion, and a closer walk with God. He listened to his wife as she told the Christmas story, and never had the meaning of Christmas meant more than it did on this Christmas Eve.

PAIGE WINSHIP DOOLY

Paige enjoys living in the warm panhandle of Florida with her family, after having grown up in the sometimes extremely cold Midwest. She is happily married to her high school sweetheart, Troy, and they have six, homeschooled children. Their oldest son Josh now lives in Colorado, while their newest blessing, Jetty, rounds out the family in a wonderful way. The whole family is active in Village Baptist Church.

Paige has always loved to write; she first tried poetry in grade school—*not* for her, though she was published in the school paper!—and then writing short stories all through her youth. She feels her love of writing is a blessing from God, and she hopes that readers will walk away with a spiritual impact on their lives and smiles on their faces.

A Distant Love

by Janelle Burnham Schneider

Dedication

To the memories of the many Canadian soldiers
who have given their lives in peacekeeping
missions around the world.

Acknowledgments

The authenticity of this story wouldn't have been possible
without the help of several men who patiently answered my
many questions. Heartfelt thanks to MWO Dan Debrie and
MWO Dave Wylde of the Canadian Military Engineers,
and Capt. Kevin Rowcliffe and Capt. Greg Losier of the
Canadian Military Police. Any errors are my own.

Most of all, thanks to my very own military hero, Capt.
Mark Schneider, Military Engineer. The descriptions of
Katrina's duties and environment are based on Mark's year as
Contingent Engineering Officer in Camp Ziouanni.

Chapter 1

The Christmas decorations adorning the mess hall seemed at odds with the balmy weather outside. Capt. Katrina Falkirk stood just outside the kitchen area, watching 150 soldiers find their seats. Today's annual Men's Dinner would be served in sit-down meal fashion rather than the buffet style usually used here in Camp Ziouanni in the Golan Heights area between Israel and Syria. The officers would act as servers for the meal which was in honor of the noncommissioned members.

She shifted from one foot to the other, wishing herself back in her office in the engineering section. Social events just weren't her thing. Before she'd even learned her multiplication tables, she'd perceived that her perspective of life wasn't the same as most people's, and "different" just didn't work in social settings. Her uniqueness no longer bothered her, but she doubted she'd ever get over her discomfort with social interactions.

The deputy commanding officer, Major Davis, rapped the gavel on the table. The contingent commanding officer,

Lieutenant Colonel Kelly, had gone home to Canada for his Christmas leave, so the DCO would preside at official functions until his return. "In keeping with the tradition of the Men's Dinners," he said in the pompous tone of voice he reserved for such occasions, "I will now exchange my epaulets with the youngest private here." He turned to the petite young woman seated at one end of the head table. "Private Boyer, you are now invested with the rank and authority of 'major' for the duration of this dinner." He accepted the private's epaulets in return, affixed them to his shoulders, then joined the line of officers waiting to serve.

Private Boyer rapped the gavel once timidly, then again more firmly. When she spoke, her voice rang with the authority of assumed command. "Thank you, Major Davis. I'm just glad we're not in Canada where we'd be swapping tunics." Laughter filled the room—the petite private would be lost in the tunic designed for the six-foot major. "Now I believe it's time for the regimental sergeant major to bestow his powers on Master Corporal Kane."

Again, laughter echoed through the room. The RSM was a small man, not much taller than five-and-one-half feet, and twig-thin. Master Corporal Kane, one of the refrigeration technicians who worked under Katrina's command, was one of the larger men present. The RSM's epaulet fit much better on his shoulders than a tunic would have. As it was, the master corporal went down on one knee to exaggerate the differences in their sizes.

"With that settled," the acting DCO said, "I'd like to ask the chaplain to say grace."

The twenty officers serving, pouring drinks, and removing dirty dishes each had to move quickly. Katrina knew most of her fellow officers well, having lived in Camp Ziouanni for six months. The exception was Capt. Brian Smith, the United Nations force provost marshal. Though he was also part of the Canadian contingent and had his quarters in Camp Ziouanni, he spent most of his time away from camp. Between his absences and her reluctance to participate in social events, this was the first time she'd seen him in other than an official capacity. He apparently thrived in group settings, judging from the laughter that followed in his wake.

Once the appetizer course had been served and all drink glasses were filled, the participants began passing notes to the acting DCO, requesting special "performances" by the various officers, in the form of Christmas carols. Katrina noticed how often Captain Smith was called on, which told her of the affection his soldiers had for him. As she leaned over to remove a salad plate from in front of Corporal Ainsworth, one of her electricians, he commented sotto voce, "Wouldn't you like to sing for us, Captain?"

She grinned while answering just as quietly. "Sure, if you'd like to be my official ratcatcher."

He laughed and she moved back toward the kitchen, confident she wouldn't be asked to "perform." She'd let it be known among all twenty of the soldiers who worked under her command that she would exact retribution, albeit in a friendly fashion, if they got her name called.

But she hadn't accounted for everyone else—specifically, Captain Smith. The fifth time he was asked to sing, he responded with, "Only if Captain Falkirk joins me, since she hasn't had this honor yet."

If Katrina could have found a hole big enough to crawl into, she would have done so. However, the point of this dinner was to provide a morale boost to the soldiers who were unable to return to Canada to be with their families for Christmas. It would be nothing less than churlish of her to refuse, despite her deep embarrassment.

So she sang with Captain Smith, pleasantly surprised at how well he carried a tune, making it easy for her to slip into a high soprano harmony. Though she disliked performing, singing itself had been one of her few pleasures as a child. She took all the music extras she could while in school, then continued her studies throughout her four years of military college. As they reached the end of the carol, she couldn't help the sense of nostalgia she felt for those years in which music formed part of her everyday life. Since leaving military college, she'd done little music, instead putting all her energies into her job as an engineer, wanting to stay on track for her promotions. Now a twinge from deep within hinted that maybe she'd let something precious slide out of her life.

She and the captain took their bows at the end of the song, then scurried back to the kitchen to help serve dessert. However, she ended up doing little serving. She got called back for two solos, and Captain Smith requested her assistance in one more duet. By the time the dinner ended, her already minimal Christmas cheer had completely evaporated.

She ended up working beside the provost marshal during cleanup, stacking dishes in the industrial-sized dishwashers.

"You can really sing," he declared. "I'm glad I roped you into helping me out."

"I'm not," she returned. The only thing worse than being forced to perform was having to discuss it later.

"You don't like singing in public?" He sounded incredulous. "With a voice like yours I would think performing would be old hat."

"Just because a person can carry a tune doesn't mean she enjoys parading the ability," she informed him.

"But when a person can't carry a tune, that's when it's really painful to have to sing in public," he returned, his dark brown eyes shining with humor.

She couldn't think of a neutral reply, much less a pleasant one, so she said nothing. He seemed unfazed and continued chatting about a variety of topics, none of which seemed to need her input. As soon as she could, she slipped out of the mess hall and made her way back to her office at the construction engineering section. The ever-present wind pulled at the ends of her hair not firmly held in place by the pale blue UN beret. Her tan desert boots crunched on the gravel pathway. Though the sleeves of her uniform were rolled up in accordance with the Canadian military "warm weather dress," the wind gave her no chill as it would have at this time in her hometown. She had a hard time convincing herself that the calendar really read December. She'd heard that snow could come to the Golan Heights, but at present, she couldn't believe it.

Camp Ziouanni was the name of the Canadian camp, which formed part of the United Nations Disengagement

Observer Force, or UNDOF, which supervised the uneasy cease-fire between Israel and Syria. Since the Six-Day War in 1967, Israel had occupied the Golan Heights along its northeastern border. In 1973, Syria unsuccessfully attempted to reclaim the area, and the UN was called in by both sides to establish a peace agreement. Part of that agreement included this narrow division, much more obvious than a mere line on a map, clearly marking the borders of the two countries. Though the Golan Heights lay on the Israeli side of the Area of Separation, Syrians and the United Nations still referred to it as "Israeli-occupied Syria." Regardless of the name used for it, the area could only be described as semiarid.

Katrina reveled in the warmth as she walked. She'd spent too much of her childhood shivering against winter weather. From the time her parents separated just before her fifth birthday, she and her mother had lived precariously. The breakup had severely threatened her mother's mental health, making it necessary for Katrina to care for her mother almost as often as her mother cared for Katrina. At first her mom was able to find minimum-wage jobs, which kept a roof of sorts over their heads and food, though often meager, on the table. Then a serious depressive episode hit, rendering Mrs. Falkirk incapable of holding a job. Welfare was their next step, and looking back, Katrina still felt grateful the safety net had been there. How they would have survived the ensuing years otherwise, she didn't know. At times, her mother had been able to contribute to their support, but it never lasted long. The divorce seemed to have drained her of any emotional stamina she might ever have had.

So Katrina had learned young how to ignore uncertainty. She found tasks in the moment on which to focus her full attention, and she learned to shut her emotions away through work. This mind-set got her through high school with honors, despite the stress of holding a part-time job and caring for her mother in addition to her studies. She applied to the Canadian forces, and then to Royal Military College, simply because she knew the military was her only hope of obtaining the engineering degree she needed in order to give herself and her mother the life she wanted for them both. As soon as she graduated from RMC, she began accepting any peacekeeping opportunity offered her. Not only did she want the experience, but in being part of various missions, she felt she was doing what she was meant to do. She reveled in the opportunity to be part of making a significant difference in war-ravaged countries.

So now she found herself as the contingent construction engineering officer, which meant she supervised the maintenance of infrastructure throughout the two-hundred-person Camp Ziouanni, as well as in over twenty UN observer posts. The work could have consumed twenty hours out of every twenty-four if she'd let it. Still, it felt more like maintaining a bit of Canada in a desert, rather than doing something which made a real difference. Nevertheless, she enjoyed the work and knew it was necessary to the peacekeeping force.

The ten-minute walk back to her office worked out the emotional maelstrom caused by the public performance. By the time she entered the CE office area, she was able to respond to Master Corporal Little's teasing remarks with a grin. "No, I won't hold you responsible for my having to sing," she assured him. "Not this time anyway."

"You have a wonderful voice, Ma'am," he responded. Uncertain how to handle the compliment, she ducked into her office. Moments later, her phone rang.

"Wonderful singing, Captain," the DCO's officious tones greeted her. "I didn't know you had it in you."

"Thank you, Sir," she responded, squelching the urge to snarl at him. She wished everybody wouldn't make such a big deal out of it. From this man, in particular, she didn't want to hear compliments. It seemed every month he came up with a new complaint he wanted the CE section to investigate, a matter that usually ranked far lower on their list of priorities than he would like.

Today was no exception. "I had to go to the gym around 2100 hours last night, and the smell just about knocked me out," he explained in the rational tone he always used when wanting her to understand the urgency of his request. "We expect our soldiers to do all they can to maintain a high level of fitness, but it's not right they should have to do it in that environment. How soon can you look into it?"

Katrina rubbed her forehead where her beret had left a faint indentation. She knew ventilation in the gym should be improved, but it wasn't urgent. Getting the camp's boilers serviced and ready to produce heat in the colder months coming up was a priority. Upgrading the walk-in refrigerators in the kitchen was a priority. But she couldn't explain those matters to the DCO. She'd tried in the past and found it useless. "Sir, I can't promise we'll get to it before the New

Year, but as soon as I have everyone back from Christmas leave, I'll make sure your request gets attended to."

"Thank you, Ma'am. It's just an issue of troop morale, which is why I feel it's so urgent. I'm sure you understand."

"Yes, Sir, I do," she informed him, her attention already taken from his call by the pile of paperwork in front of her. To her relief, he hung up and she continued sorting through the many pieces of paper it required to do even the simplest job under UN authority. It certainly wasn't the most inspiring work, but it would keep her busy until the opportunity to make a difference came along.

Chapter 2

Brian hurried up the walkway toward the Officers' Club. The officers' Christmas party was supposed to begin at 1900 hours, and here he was just showing up at 2000 hours. Ever since arriving at UNDOF six months ago, he'd felt like he was running in three directions at once. With his second in command now in Canada for his Christmas leave, Brian felt doubly handicapped. He'd spent the day on the Syrian side in Camp Faouar at a meeting of all the top brass in UNDOF, giving his opinions as to necessary guidelines to ensure the safety of UNDOF personnel. He'd made it to Bravo gate, the Syrian checkpoint, only half an hour before closing, then made the mistake of stopping at the Military Police Headquarters situated between the Syrian checkpoint and the Israeli checkpoint, referred to as "Alpha gate." The MP headquarters had been dubbed "Charlie gate." The three points lay less than a hundred meters apart. Alpha gate marked the Israeli border of the Area of Separation, and Bravo gate the Syrian border. The central location of Charlie gate helped the UN military police keep a watchful eye on all

Rolling Stone

POSTAGE WILL BE PAID BY ADDRESSEE

PO BOX 62230
TAMPA FL 33663-2301

BUSINESS REPLY MAIL

FIRST-CLASS MAIL   PERMIT NO. 22   TAMPA FL

NO POSTAGE
NECESSARY
IF MAILED
IN THE
UNITED STATES

traffic making its way across this area.

What he'd intended to be just a quick stop at his head-quarters turned into something significantly more lengthy due to a ten-page fax from an Israeli army major with whom he'd been discussing security issues. Then one of Brian's corporals needed to brief him on a conversation he'd had with one of the shopkeepers in nearby Tiberias. The result was that Brian barely made it to Alpha gate before closing. Had he been two minutes later, he would have been stuck at Charlie gate until the morning. From a physical comfort standpoint, that wouldn't have been too onerous. Charlie gate had complete accommodations, including cooking facilities, since a number of MPs lived there. But Brian had few opportunities for purely social interaction with the other UNDOF officers. With less than a week left before Christmas, he'd found himself thinking a lot lately about what his brother and sister and their families would be doing. His brother had already invited their mother to spend the holiday with him and his family, so she would be well cared for during this time. Brian found himself missing them more than he'd anticipated. He loved them all deeply, but usually work kept him too busy to be lonely. But this time of year seemed designed to induce loneliness.

Especially in military personnel, he continued musing half an hour later as he finished the dinner he'd managed to claim from the kitchen staff before they started cleaning up. Not another person was present in the officers' dining room, leaving his thoughts free to return to the family he hadn't seen in almost a year. His sister, Jillian, lived in British Columbia with her computer programmer husband and their two sons.

His brother, Kevin, and his wife, Tammi, lived in Chicago with their three children. His mother resided in a seniors' complex in Ottawa, the town in which he'd been born and raised. Her health hadn't been good since the death of her husband two years previously. Thankfully, Brian had been living in Ottawa at the time of his father's death, and so he had been able to give her emotional support. This was his first deployment since then, and he worried about how she was managing without any family nearby. He checked the date indicator on his watch—December 20. If all had gone according to plan, she should be at Kevin's now, enjoying the grandchildren. He'd make a point of giving Kevin a phone call tomorrow, if at all possible. Just before bedtime, his time, would be early afternoon Chicago time.

Even his quarters felt lonely tonight. His position as force provost marshal entitled him to private quarters, consisting of a small trailer set off to one side of the building which housed the rest of the officers. Most of the time, he enjoyed retreating to the solitude of his personal living space. Even in Canada, he usually lived in single officers' quarters on whatever base he was posted to. When he wanted social interaction, there was always the gym or the Officers' Club.

He received a fair bit of ribbing about his single state. Though he'd dated occasionally since the demise of his engagement eight years ago, he'd felt little inclination to pursue a serious relationship since then. The experience had shown him that no woman in her right mind would want to tie herself to a man who jumped at every chance to go overseas. He loved peacekeeping work, whether the mission was a few weeks or a year in duration, like this one. This job had been particularly fulfilling so far as he interacted almost daily with both Israeli and Syrian personnel. He felt the UN had made a significant difference in this troubled area, and he relished being part of it.

But tonight, the fulfillment he felt in his job couldn't overshadow his loneliness, and he knew casual socializing wouldn't meet his need. In fact, the thought of making small talk with people he barely knew made him more homesick than ever. However, even a phone call was out of the question at this time of night. He knew neither of his siblings nor his mother would fault him for waking them in the wee hours of the morning, but he couldn't bring himself to do it. Besides, he was already late for the Christmas party.

He grabbed the loosely wrapped package he'd prepared a week ago and hurried over to the Officers' Club. Hopefully the gift exchange hadn't taken place yet. He'd found the perfect gag gift during an excursion through the Syrian souk.

Everyone was milling around as he entered. The TV, for once, was sitting ignored in its separate room. An array of platters of finger food lined the bar, and the volunteer bartender for the night, the operations officer, seemed to be pouring drinks without a pause to catch his breath. "What can I get for you, Captain?" he asked as Brian approached.

"Cola, please," Brian responded, laying the appropriate number of coins on the bar.

Captain Dunham poured the soft drink without comment or even surprise at Brian's nonalcoholic choice. Brian had been pleasantly surprised at one of the first gatherings he attended here to find that fully a third of the group didn't drink alcohol. Those who did seemed to respect the choice of those who didn't, and there was never a discussion of each individual's reasons. With ice-laden drink in hand, Brian made his way to the Christmas tree in one corner of the room and added his package to the pile.

The maintenance officer sat at a nearby table, a pile of small papers in front of him. He scrawled a six on one and handed it to Brian with a piece of tape attached. "Stick this on the package, please," he requested. "We'll distribute the packages by number a little later."

Brian had wondered how the gifts would be assigned to their recipients. He grinned to himself, thinking of the DCO's reaction should he open Brian's gift. He felt like he had as a boy, waiting for his sister to discover the beetles he'd turned loose in her room.

Conversation swirled around him. Usually at such gatherings, he quickly found a conversational group he could join. Tonight, perhaps because of his late arrival, he felt more like being a silent observer. There were plenty of stories being told and lots of laughter. Several of the officers who lived at Camp Ziouanni had returned to Canada for the holidays. Of those remaining, only six were present at the moment.

In eighteen years of military service and five deployments, he'd found Christmas to be one of the hardest times of year to be deployed. It seemed this gathering was no different from other Christmas parties he'd attended overseas. Everyone tried their best to forget they were separated from their families during the holiday season. Some people hid their loneliness behind a "life of the party" facade. Others tried to drown it in alcohol. Still others focused on their work to the exclusion of everything else, including the "working friendships," which he found kept him sane so far from home.

The *squeak-thump* of the outer door attracted his attention, and his spirits lifted as Capt. Katrina Falkirk strode into the room. She'd been often in his thoughts since the Men's Dinner last week, like a puzzle which refused to be solved. All at once, socializing seemed like the ideal activity.

He watched the tall, blond captain, waiting for her to pause in one place so he could casually make his way in her direction. She looked like she'd had a long, frustrating day and wanted to be anywhere but here. At the bar, she obtained a glass of some clear, carbonated beverage with a slice of lemon perched on the rim of the glass. Then she turned toward the Christmas tree, apparently with the intent of depositing the artistically wrapped package she held. When her gaze encountered his, annoyance flashed in her eyes, then was quickly replaced by a bland expression. He noticed that she didn't hurry toward the tree immediately behind him. He glanced over his shoulder to see if he could discern the cause of her reaction. Was she still irritated at him for putting her on the spot at the Men's Dinner? For her sake, he was sorry he'd done so, but for his own sake and that of the other soldiers, he didn't regret it for a moment. It had lifted his spirits to hear a trained voice singing the Christmas carols. It almost made the dinner feel like a real Christmas function rather than something cobbled together out in the desert to help everyone cope with being here rather than in Canada. He wished there were some way to get her to sing again. In the meantime, though, he'd better keep his distance. Tonight was obviously not the night to try to make amends.

The maintenance officer stood to his feet and raised his voice to be heard above the chatter. "Now that everyone is here. . ." He gave the CE officer a pointed look. "We can commence with the gift exchange. Captain Falkirk, if you'll bring your gift over here, I'll label it and add it to the stack."

Brian noticed the narrowing of Captain Falkirk's eyes as she moved around people to get to Captain Galenza. If he wasn't mistaken, animosity crackled between these two, as well. He wouldn't have expected Captain Falkirk to be the kind of person to carry a chip on her shoulder, but maybe he was wrong. Maybe she hated being at Camp Ziouanni, and thus, just disliked everyone associated with it.

Captain Galenza stirred a number of small papers around in a bowl. "I'll pass this bowl around, and each of you can take a number. That number corresponds to the number on the package which is your gift for this evening. Feel free to open the gifts right away, and remember that we're hosting the Japanese officers at 2100 hours."

The bowl was passed with much teasing as each person selected his or her number. Surprisingly, no one drew the number of the package they'd brought. Brian stood closest to the tree, so he retrieved his gift first.

He noticed Captain Falkirk seemed in no hurry to claim her gift. The other officers swarmed in, and with a sinking sensation he saw the only one unclaimed was the gift he brought. She must have drawn the six. In a moment of panic, he almost swapped the present under the tree with the one he held, but he knew that would make the situation worse.

Unwilling to watch her embarrassment as she opened the "surprise," he turned his attention to his own gift. It bore the DCO's name on the wrapper and turned out to be a set of four coasters with the Canadian flag embossed on them.

He heard the tinny sound of a cheap noisemaker and knew the captain had opened his gift. She looked at what she held as though she couldn't decide how to feel about it. In her hand lay a small plastic box from which had bobbed a plastic figurine of a bald man singing some Syrian song. Would she connect it with their singing adventure? He hadn't intended it to be a reminder; he had, in fact, expected one of the other officers to receive it. It was the kind of silly toy that often made people laugh, simply because it did something unexpected and was totally useless.

She met his gaze across the room and nodded in acknowledgment, still not betraying her feelings. Had he inadvertently just torpedoed any chance of getting to know her better?

Suddenly tired of asking himself questions about her feelings and reactions, he started toward her, an explanation forming in his mind. Just then the front door thumped open again, and the ten Japanese officers filed in, right on schedule. His attempt at personal peacemaking would have to wait.

Chapter 3

A cold wind seemed determined to bar Brian's access to the camp services office. He yanked on the handle one more time, and the door slammed open against the outside wall of the building. He stepped through the hard-won opening, and the wind banged the door closed behind him. A master corporal watched his awkward entrance with a hint of a grin. "Blustery day, eh, Sir?"

Brian dropped his beret into a nearby chair. "Almost makes me think I'm on the Canadian prairies instead of in the Middle East," he responded. "I'm here to make a deposit on the Cairo trip for Corporal Wilson."

The welfare section was the heart of Camp Ziouanni's recreation. Staffed by the master corporal at the front desk, and a warrant officer and a civilian in the back room, the section not only kept the various recreation clubs running; but they also planned and arranged various "welfare trips" into nearby areas which were still open for travel. Each soldier in the camp was entitled to one sixty-hour leave and one two-week leave every three months. Most took the short leaves in a group setting, enjoying trips to nearby Syria, Egypt, or in more peaceful times, one of the many tourist haunts throughout Israel. Welfare also handled all out-of-country travel arrangements for those on the two-week leaves, which usually took the soldiers either back to Canada or to some other vacation spot such as Greece or Germany. A trip to Cairo was the next event coming up, and one of Brian's corporals was ecstatic over the opportunity. She'd made arrangements by phone to sign up for the trip but now needed to get a financial deposit made to secure her place. Since Brian had to come to Camp Ziouanni this morning anyway, he'd offered to deliver the young woman's money.

"Okay," Master Corporal Thomas said while riffling through a pile of paper. Extracting one, he handed it to Brian. "If you'll just initial beside her name on this list, that will confirm the money has been delivered and confirm her place on the bus."

Brian held his pen ready to scribble his initials, then stopped. Higher on the list, a name caught his attention. Katrina Falkirk. He'd never been particularly interested in seeing Egypt, but all at once, the trip appealed to him. Since the Christmas party, he'd tried several times to melt the captain's reserve. It seemed their jobs conspired to keep them from attending social events at the same time. On the rare occasions they did meet at the Officers' Club, she maintained an air of remoteness. Perhaps in a more casual setting he'd be able to get to know her better, maybe even strike up a friendship.

He checked the price given at the bottom of the poster. Easily affordable, as were most trips arranged by welfare.

Because the UN soldiers were known for having plenty of disposable income and for spending it on expensive souvenirs, the welfare section was often able to get outstanding bargains for travel and accommodation. "Are you still taking names for the trip?"

"Registration closes today," the clerk replied. "Are you interested?"

"I think so," he answered.

The clerk's face held a questioning expression, and Brian realized his reply had sounded uncertain. "Yes, I am," he told him more firmly. He pulled several Israeli banknotes from his wallet. "In fact, here's my deposit, and I'll be back a little later with the rest of my payment."

He walked out of the camp services building, stunned at his own rapid decision. He couldn't remember the last time he'd planned a recreational activity based on someone else's plans. Still, this felt right. A short walk took him to the boardwalk in front of the financial office, where he'd be able to withdraw cash from his pay account to put the deposit on his trip.

A light dusting of snow covered everything around him, transforming the dull brown into something vaguely reminiscent of the northern winters he was used to. Behind him, Mount Hermon stood completely shrouded in snow, though he knew the town of Tiberias, at a lower elevation, would still feel like summer.

The financial office and the camp headquarters occupied opposite halves of the same building. He climbed the steps onto the boardwalk that ran the length of the entire building. Just as he passed in front of the door to the headquarters offices, it swung open, knocking him sideways. Captain Falkirk glared at him for a moment; then her expression melted into a combination of embarrassment and apology. "I'm so sorry, Captain. Are you all right?"

Brian felt tempted to fake more serious injury, just to tease her. Just as quickly, he realized this wasn't the time for mischief. "I'm fine and actually glad we met, though I wasn't counting on it being quite so. . .so. . ." He pretended to search for the right word.

Confusion clouded her face; then a self-conscious smile broke through. "I get it. You wanted to meet me, not be flattened by me."

"Something like that." He risked a chuckle, and when her smile broadened a bit, decided to say what had been on his mind for three weeks. "I've been wanting to apologize for the gift you received at the Christmas party. I meant nothing personal by it, I assure you."

She shrugged and laughter now twinkled in her eyes. "I didn't take it personally. It's actually kind of cute, in an ugly sort of way."

"That's what I thought, but I wasn't sure how you'd feel about it after my part in the musical portion of the Men's Dinner. I didn't know it would make you so uncomfortable or that my actions would snowball like that."

She met his gaze. "Please don't give it another thought. I must apologize for being so prickly that day. It had been a rough day at the CE section, and I'm afraid social gatherings bring out the worst in me. I had no right to take my feelings out on you."

"Forgiven and forgotten," he assured her, offering a handshake that she returned firmly. "I hope your day today gets better."

The hesitant smile appeared again. "I think it has. Thank you, Captain." She retrieved a bicycle leaning against the railing and pedaled off down the road toward the CE section.

Brian conducted his business at the financial office and returned to the welfare office, more convinced than ever he'd made the right decision in planning to spend some casual time with the increasingly interesting engineering officer. The first thing he did upon returning to Charlie gate was fill out a leave pass for the dates of the trip to Cairo. He was due for a holiday since he hadn't taken any time off in December. Since his second in command had just returned from leave, the MP headquarters would be well managed in his absence.

Though Brian saw Katrina several times over the next three weeks, he didn't mention the trip. He didn't want her to guess she was his reason for going, nor did he want to give her time to back out. Still, knowing her extensive responsibilities, he didn't feel totally certain she'd actually make the trip until he saw her boarding the bus at 0445 hours on the morning of their departure day. He breathed a deep sigh of relief as he added his suitcase to the tidy row lengthening in the luggage compartment.

He chose a bus seat behind hers and across the aisle. Any closer, and she might suspect his intentions. He couldn't explain the sense he had that he'd have to be subtle in his part in building their friendship, but he knew any overt moves on his part would likely make her withdraw completely.

Hopefully this five-day trip, being constantly in one another's company and yet part of a larger group, would help form the basis for a solid friendship when they returned.

For the first hours of the trip, no one said much. Several, like Katrina, had brought pillows and light blankets, taking advantage of the darkness around them to catch up on sleep. Since the seat ahead of him was empty, he thought about moving so he could watch her sleep, but the thought that she might catch him doing so made him stay put. Instead, he prayed silently and watched out the window as they traveled.

Some of his mother's words about prayer came to mind. "Prayer is not only telling God what we want Him to do. He wants us to express our hearts to Him, and if that includes telling Him how we think He should answer our prayers, that's okay. But Jesus taught us in His prayer to ask that His will be done." She'd always pause at this point and look directly into his eyes. "You don't have to know details about a person in order to pray for them. All you need do is mention that person's name to God and ask for His will in his or her life. Then listen. He might want to make you part of the answer."

Thus, he prayed for the people of Israel, both Arabs and Jews. He prayed for the UN peacekeepers and military observers. He prayed for his family at home and for each of the soldiers under his command. Then he began praying for Katrina. He didn't know her spiritual state or anything about her life before arriving here in the Middle East. So he simply prayed, *Father God, please make Your presence real to Katrina.* He couldn't explain his attraction to her, but neither could he dismiss it. His brief encounters with her had stirred something long dormant in him.

As he continued praying for her, the rumble of the bus and the gradually lightening sky faded to background, and he felt his senses become attuned to what he called his "inner landscape," the part of himself—his soul, really—that was thoughts and feelings and that communicated with God. Having learned the importance of "listening prayer" from his mother, these moments of inner clarity were not unusual for him. As if he'd been given a divine order, he realized he was meant to befriend Capt. Katrina Falkirk. This was more than simply enjoying her company or acting on an emotional attraction, though both of those reactions hovered around the edges. No, it seemed God had a purpose in their becoming friends, and He wanted Brian to put effort into making the friendship happen.

Brian's environment took over his awareness again, leaving him with nothing more than a certainty, somewhat like the fragrance of fresh-baked bread that lingers long after the loaf has been baked. He felt shaken by what had occurred within, so his prayer took on words again. *Show me how to be her friend. Guide us in Your will.* Then he let his mind go silent. He watched dawn begin to color the sky, and he soaked in the awareness of being one of God's children, loved and guided by Him. He couldn't predict the outcome of what God had put in his heart, but at least for the moment, he didn't need to.

As daylight claimed more of the sky, the sleepers began stirring. It was a slow awakening, and conversation remained muted. But by the time they arrived in Tel Aviv, three hours from their departure point, everyone had awakened and begun chatting.

Almost everyone, that is. Katrina still slept. The bus pulled into the parking lot of an American fast-food restaurant. "We have an hour stop here," the driver announced. "We have boxed meals if anyone is interested, or you can buy breakfast here or at one of the shops across the street. I'm going to fill up with gas and be back. We'll load up again in forty-five minutes."

Since Katrina didn't stir, Brian stayed seated as well. She didn't wake when their twenty traveling companions reboarded amid chatter and jokes. After another hour of travel, they reached the Israeli-Egyptian border, and Brian knew someone would have to wake her up. They would all have to pass through Egyptian customs individually. He moved to the empty seat and leaned across the aisle. "Captain!" he called in a conversational voice.

No response.

A bit louder this time. "Captain Falkirk!"

Still no response.

He had two choices. He could yell, which would draw attention to her deep sleep and thus make her the focus of jokes for the rest of the trip. Or he could reach over and shake her shoulder. He felt reasonably certain she wouldn't appreciate the physical contact, but better that than embarrassment.

Chapter 4

Katrina wanted to bat away the insistent voice calling her name, but there it was again, accompanied by the feeling of being shaken. "Captain Falkirk!" She opened one eye partway; then both eyes snapped open. Where was she? The bus. Right. The trip to Cairo. It seemed only moments before that they'd boarded the bus, but the sun was now high overhead. She looked up into Captain Smith's face as he leaned over her. "I must have been really out of it," she mumbled, feeling the heat of embarrassment work its way up her neck and into her cheeks.

His smile held no mockery. "You seem to have the enviable gift of dropping into a deep sleep when you have the opportunity."

She tried to force a laugh past the lump of vulnerability in her throat. "My mom told me that as an infant, absolutely nothing would wake me up until I decided to wake up on my own. Guess I haven't lost the knack. Where are we?"

"We're almost at the Egyptian border, which is why I had to wake you up. We're all going to have to unload and take our own luggage through customs."

The bus groaned to a stop; then the trip director stepped outside to talk with a guard. In short order she returned and announced, "This is the Israeli checkpoint and they've waived us through. Just ahead is the Egyptian checkpoint, and we'll all need to get off there and take our luggage inside. When we finish there, we'll be driving several hours through the desert, so I'd recommend using the facilities now. I would not, however, recommend drinking the water. There is also an exchange booth for obtaining Egyptian money. As we mentioned in the memo you received a few days ago, you'll want to exchange American money, rather than Israeli, into Egyptian money. You'll also want to keep a stock of American dollars on hand as they're quite popular among street merchants."

Katrina retrieved her single suitcase from beneath the bus and carried it inside the frame building, which looked as though it had been braving desert winds for at least a decade. The wood had faded to the same grayish brown as the scenery around them. A number of people milled around inside, adding the odors of sweat and garlic breath to the stale-air smell. Dust covered everything. She looked around for anything that might indicate where the customs line might be. The money exchange booth was doing a brisk business, and beside it were two windowed cubicles with the shades drawn and doors closed.

"Looks like we'll be waiting awhile," a familiar deep voice said near her ear.

She didn't have to turn her head to know the provost marshal stood right behind her. She felt a thrill of awareness, rendering her instantly uncomfortable. "Then I might as well see how bad the facilities are," she said, looking down at her suitcase, then over her shoulder at him. "Would you mind watching my luggage?"

"No problem."

He seemed pleased that she'd asked, and that weird ripple went through her again. She'd avoided romantic interactions ever since she was old enough to be aware of them. In high school, she'd been too studious and too poorly dressed to attract much attention from the boys. In military college, she'd had several male friends. There had been two guys who had each expressed romantic interest in her, but she'd quickly let them know she wasn't interested. One of them had reacted badly, and she'd had to endure some unflattering epithets, but it wasn't an issue she was willing to compromise on. She'd seen what a broken romance had done to her mother. She had no intention of letting herself be similarly victimized.

By the time she returned to the main room, one of the customs booths had opened and a long line now extended from it to the opposite side of the room and along the length of the back wall. She saw Brian standing near the middle, both their suitcases at his feet. "Thank you," she mumbled, grasping the handle of her suitcase.

His hand covered hers, warm and gently restraining. "Where are you going?"

"To the back of the line, where I belong. I wasn't here to claim a place when it began forming, so I have to take my place at the back."

"I saved a place for you, if anybody cares enough to notice."

That was exactly what she didn't want anyone to notice. She didn't want to begin this trip with people thinking of the two of them as a couple. They just happened to be in the same group.

But that didn't seem to be the way he felt. Though he let her go to the back of the line for Egyptian customs, for the rest of the trip he always seemed less than an arm's length from her. His droll comments enlivened the tour through the Egyptian Historical Museum. As they climbed the hill leading to the entrance to one of the pyramids, his presence beside her helped her get through the throng of child-merchants, frantically waving postcards and other souvenirs.

On the third night of the trip, they had dinner on a Nile riverboat. Katrina didn't feel at all surprised when he offered his arm to escort her into the glass-walled dining room. She'd become comfortable enough with his presence that she smiled at his invitation and laid her hand in the crook of his elbow, though mentally she dared him to comment on her appearance.

They'd been told before they left this would be a semi-formal dinner, so Katrina had come prepared. She wore a yellow, ankle-length dress with cap sleeves and straw-colored sandals. Made from a soft polyester fabric, the dress hadn't even required ironing before she put it on. Dangly pearl earrings and a pearl necklace she'd purchased in Syria for a fraction of their North American value completed her ensemble.

He seemed to understand her unspoken dare because he grinned, then pointed downriver at a group of children playing by the water's edge. "Now that looks like fun," he commented, as great handfuls of water were flung back and forth.

Just then, one of the boys slipped under the water. His

comrades quickly pulled him to his feet, then convulsed in laughter at the mud clinging to him and the weeds hanging from his head and shoulders. "You'd like to get muddy?" Katrina retorted, arching her eyebrows at him. "I'm sure that could be arranged."

His laughter warmed her through. "Oh, no, you don't." He tightened his arm against his side, trapping her arm against his. "I kind of like looking like something besides a desert soldier for a change."

"You clean up well," she teased. What she couldn't tell him was that he looked like her ideal of the casually well-dressed man. He wore a white short-sleeved shirt that had small navy stripes woven through it. A navy blue tie and navy trousers contributed to his polished appearance.

"Thank you. Yellow does a lot more for you than relish," he teased back.

She couldn't help laughing. "Relish" was the term the soldiers used for their everyday combat uniforms, which had been computer designed to provide the best possible camouflage, at least in a jungle setting. The fabric was designed with tiny rectangles forming random patterns in various colors, which looked just like a jar of sweet pickle relish.

The evening unfolded perfectly. Brian helped her with her chair but didn't try to order on her behalf. The string quartet provided just the right ambience, as did the ever-changing twinkle of lights outside as the boat slowly moved down the famous river. The other four people at the table were also UN personnel, so conversation flowed easily. When the meal concluded, all six of them trooped up to the observation deck to see if they could catch a glimpse of the Egyptian night sky.

Katrina was pleased with the others' companionship as it meant she and Brian could enjoy the experience together without raising speculation among their fellow travelers. She felt uncomfortable admitting it even to herself, but the more time she spent with Brian, the more time she wanted to spend with him.

As they got off the bus just outside the hotel shortly after 2200 hours, she noticed a number of their group setting off down the street toward one of the bars. She understood their desire to stretch out the evening, but their destination held no appeal. She wondered what Brian was going to do but refused to let herself ask him. However, just as she stepped through the revolving door of the hotel, he called quietly from behind her, "Ready to call it a night yet?"

Her face wanted to stretch into a wide grin, but she held her expression down to a friendly smile. "Not really, but bars aren't my scene."

"Mine either," he said. "Let's check out the café. I've heard they have a killer dessert cart."

"How can you even think of food after that dinner?" Before she realized what she was doing, she gave him a slow once-over with her eyes, barely managing to avoid tripping over her own feet. "You don't look like an eating machine," she blurted, then wished she'd kept her mouth shut. If he asked what she meant, she'd never be able to answer. In truth, he looked to her like a perfectly maintained human being should look. No extra weight, a solid-looking physique that suggested he spent time exercising, and a general look of good health. Were she to put those thoughts into words, he'd think she was flirting—or worse.

He chuckled as he held the glass door of the café open for her. "My metabolism has frustrated my sister ever since we were teens. As long as I go for a run every day, I can eat whatever takes my fancy."

Now that he'd introduced the subject of family, she could ask about them without sounding overly inquisitive. "Are you the oldest?"

The waiter appeared before he could answer. "What may I bring to you?" His English was excellent, though heavily accented.

What sounded good to Katrina at the moment was a cup of tea, but there was no way to guarantee it would be made with bottled water. Soda pop didn't hold any appeal at this hour of night. "Just a bottle of water, please."

"I'll have one, as well," Brian added, "and I'd like to see your dessert cart."

"Very well." The waiter gave a slight bow and moved away.

Brian turned his attention to Katrina, making her feel as though she were the only person in the room. "Yes, I am the oldest. My brother, Kevin, is three years younger than I am, and our sister, Jillian, is two years younger than he is."

"Are either of them military?"

"No, I'm the only one, which I'm glad for. I think it would be too hard on my mom to have more than one of us taking off for the various trouble spots around the world."

She waited until he'd selected a creamy-looking slice of trifle before continuing. "Where does your mom live?"

"In a seniors' complex in Ottawa, which is where I grew up." He took two forks with his dessert and handed one to her.

She let the fork lay in front of her, taking a drink of her water to cover her sudden discomfiture. "I grew up in Toronto," she offered when she could speak again. The two cities lay less than three hundred miles apart in a country where long distances were the rule rather than the exception.

"Did you really?" he questioned, sliding the plate of dessert toward her. "Go ahead. Just a tiny bite won't give you indigestion."

She couldn't tell him her concern had nothing to do with physical health. Sharing a dessert seemed like such a "couple" thing to do. "No, but thanks for the offer."

He looked like he might protest, then reverted to their previous conversation. "So tell me about your family."

She almost grabbed the fork and took a big bite of his trifle, just to circumvent having to answer his question. However, that might make him question her earlier refusal. Either subject was equally uncomfortable. She opted for a breezy, casual explanation of the situation, which still shattered her heart every time she thought of it. "We kind of scattered all over. My mom lives in Toronto, my dad lives in Washington, D. C., and my brother is a U.S. Air Force pilot currently stationed in England."

"Have you visited your brother since you came over here?"

Katrina couldn't believe he hadn't pursued the subject of her parents' separate lives—or that her brother served a different country. While she knew intellectually that parental divorce was something that had happened to many people, she always expected people to ask more questions about her family than they did. "I took my October leave in England, and I plan to go again in July when my posting is finished. He married another air force officer last Christmas, and they're stereotypically blissful."

Brian's lips twitched with amusement. "You sound like you don't entirely approve."

"Oh, no, it's not that!" Katrina toyed with her napkin while trying to figure out how to state her opinion without laying bare too much of her history. "It just scares me to see them so emotionally wrapped up in each other. I've seen what can happen when things fall apart, and it's worse than if they'd never fallen in love in the first place."

He didn't say anything as he cleaned the last crumbs from his plate and fork. Without meeting her gaze, he mused, "So that's why you're so skittish."

She couldn't think of a sensible answer, nor could she decide whether his insight troubled or comforted her. He'd read deeper into her soul than anyone she'd ever met, her brother included. Her first impulse was to distance herself from him immediately, before her vulnerability increased. But another impulse rose along with the first. What if she let the friendship between them remain? They'd be going their separate ways in six months anyway, and surely her heart couldn't get dangerously entangled in that short space of time. She lifted her gaze to his face, only to see him studying her. He raised his eyebrows as though in question but said nothing.

She let his dark gaze hold hers for a heartbeat, long enough to make her wish she were capable of trusting him.

Chapter 5

Katrina returned from the Cairo trip both refreshed and unsettled. On the way home, she and Brian had chosen seats across the aisle from one another and spent the entire twelve hours of travel talking. Was the connection she felt with him real or just the product of the close proximity created by the trip? How would she feel if it didn't carry over into daily life at Camp Ziouanni? How would she feel if it did?

Work kept her too busy to spend much time pondering. February brought more cool weather, and with it increased crises, particularly at the UN observer posts. Water pipes at one of the observer posts on Mount Hermon broke, while at one of the most southern posts, an air-conditioning unit quit working, leaving the military observers sweltering.

Just as she felt she was making some headway on the never-ending paperwork the next day, Master Corporal Leger, her most senior plumber, knocked on her doorframe. "Ma'am, you're not going to be happy about it, but I need you to sign this requisition."

She scanned the form he handed her. "A backhoe? Don't tell me we have drainage problems."

He shook his head. "Worse than that. As near as I can tell from the drainage diagrams we have, it's a freshwater pipe, rather than sewage, but we're going to need to let the staff in the headquarters building know that they should stick with bottled water. Until we see what's happened underground, we have no way of knowing if the main water supply has been contaminated."

"How much help are you going to need when the backhoe gets here?"

"I'll need someone to run it, and I'd like to have Corporal Ainsworth if we can get him. I'll also need at least one other person with a shovel."

Katrina mentally shuffled the rest of the day's obligations. Corporal Ainsworth had worked in his father's road construction company before joining the forces. Even though he'd become one of the best apprentice electricians she'd ever worked with, he was still the one called in whenever the CE section needed a heavy equipment operator. He could make a machine dig to within inches of a given point, which meant he rarely caused accidental damage to any of the underground pipes and wires that didn't need repair. One of her plumbers was on leave, and the other was still repairing the problem at the Mount Hermon observation post. "I guess we'll call in a couple of the refrigeration guys to work the shovels. Thankfully, they're not overwhelmed at the moment. Ask Master Corporal Little to take the requisition to Faouar, and I'll make a call to see if the force engineer will give us verbal approval so we can order the backhoe right away."

"Thanks, Ma'am."

Master Corporal Leger returned to the front office, and Katrina quickly dialed the number for the FEO's office. If the force engineer, an Austrian major, insisted on seeing the paperwork first, she wouldn't be able to order the equipment for at least four hours, which meant it wouldn't be on-site for another two hours, which would have her men working well into the evening. To her relief, the major realized the urgency of the situation and gave his consent for work to proceed. With the backhoe ordered and on the way, she put in a call to her refrigeration mechanical supervisor. "Can you spare one or two of your guys in a couple of hours?"

Master Corporal Green, a skilled tradesmen who usually went out of his way to assist her, cleared his throat. "No, Ma'am, I can't. One of them is on leave, and the other is over at the orderly room."

Katrina felt a headache beginning in her temples. "What's happening in the orderly room besides stocking up on bottled water?"

"Seems that's part of the problem, Ma'am." His voice held barely contained amusement. "Someone decided to defrost the refrigerator so they could fit more water into it. Since the conventional method would be too slow, the person under discussion decided to use his bayonet to chip at the ice. . . ."

Even before he finished, Katrina could anticipate the result. ". . .and broke through one of the refrigeration fluid lines."

"Yup." The master corporal chuckled. "Water everywhere,

and wouldn't you know it?—the CO walked in just then."

"Oh, no." Katrina could envision DCO Davis's expression. The commanding officer was one of the best she'd ever worked with, but he took a dim view of what he called "preventable accidents." Not only that, but she'd talked with him just yesterday afternoon about how thin her staff was stretched. He wouldn't be pleased at the latest developments. "What's the prognosis?"

"We'll have to bring the unit back here so we can take it apart for repairs."

"Which means the orderly room staff will be drinking lukewarm water by afternoon."

"Yes, Ma'am." Master Corporal Green chuckled again before breaking the connection.

Katrina wished she felt amused. The headquarters staff used the same refrigerator as the orderly room. If Major Davis had to drink lukewarm water this afternoon, she'd get a phone call for sure. Another thought made a private chuckle escape her lips. If she couldn't find someone else to help Master Corporal Leger on shovel duty, she'd have to do it. Heavy-duty physical labor would be a welcome change.

The telephone rang three times before she realized she was the only one left in the office. With an unladylike snort of frustration, she picked up the receiver. "Engineering. Captain Falkirk."

"Good afternoon, Captain." The DCO's tone couldn't have been friendlier or more casual.

Katrina felt her blood pressure rise three notches. "Hello, Sir."

"I was over at the gym last night, and I really appreciate what your guys have done with the ventilation system. It's much better."

She couldn't help grinning. So far, she hadn't had time to assign anyone to the work. The cooler weather was obviously making a difference in the amount of body odor being trapped in the gym, but she wasn't going to explain that to the major. If he was happy about it for the moment, she'd just be grateful for small blessings. "Thank you, Sir." She heard the front door squeak open and hoped one of her sergeants would appear quickly to take care of the visitor.

"There's one other thing I noticed, though."

She swallowed the groan that rose through her throat. "Yes, Sir?"

"The rest room over there is really cramped. I was thinking it shouldn't be too hard to. . ."

She heard the major's continuing babble in the phone pressed against her ear, but the individual words were lost as an Israeli civilian appeared in her doorway, bearing a plastic-wrapped floral arrangement. "Katrina Falkirk?" he asked.

She nodded, then gestured toward her desk. He set the arrangement down and left. With the DCO's voice still droning on in the telephone receiver, she tucked the receiver between her ear and her shoulder and used both hands to pull the plastic away from the flowers.

A simple cluster of three yellow roses surrounded by baby's breath and greenery sat in a crystal vase. A card stapled to the plastic read, "I've missed you. Friends, Brian."

"Captain?"

The DCO's irritated tone let Katrina know he'd been waiting for a reply from her. "I'm sorry, Sir. I'm afraid I missed that last bit. The office is rather hectic this afternoon." If she sounded at all coherent, it would be the best acting job she'd ever done. No one had ever sent her flowers before. A flurry of emotions, both pleasant and unsettling, swarmed through her. She forced herself to pay attention to Major Davis.

"We need more stalls and at least five showers. It would be good for our troops' morale to have a fully functional changing room as part of the fitness facility."

"I'll look into it, Sir," she managed to respond. Part of her still felt utterly numbed by the gift before her. The slowly returning rational part wanted to guffaw at this latest project to grip the DCO's imagination. The building he so grandly referred to as the "fitness facility" was nothing more than a warehouse with some sports and weightlifting equipment installed. The officers' quarters stood the farthest from the gym, and for her part, Katrina would rather make the ten-minute walk back to her own room than use a communal changing room. He'd obviously not thought about the need for two changing rooms—one for men and one for women.

At 1930, she finally forced herself to leave the office. The backhoe had arrived just before lunch. Adequate assistance had been found for Master Corporal Leger, so Katrina had remained in her office for the afternoon and into the evening, making the necessary phone calls and signing the appropriate forms to provide the parts needed to repair the water line. The orderly room's refrigerator had been reassembled but still required recharging. Master Corporal Green had all but promised her it would be back in service before lunch tomorrow.

Even though supper ended at 1830 hours, the mess stayed open until 2200 hours, making a few food items available after hours. Tonight's minestrone soup smelled enticing, and some dark rye bread had been placed on the sandwich table, along with white bread and a variety of meats and cheeses. When she carried her tray into the officers' dining room, she almost stumbled in surprise.

Brian paused in taking a bite of the sandwich he held. His grin looked like that of a ten-year-old boy who'd just executed the perfect practical joke. "Well, hello, Stranger. Care to join me?"

Opposing impulses again warred in Katrina's emotions, but the enjoyment of this man's company won out. "Sure. Eating alone gets old."

"You've been doing a lot of that?"

His tone conveyed concern, and she discovered she liked being at the receiving end of someone else's worry. "Most evenings, yes. It's rare for me to get away from my office before 1830."

He nodded. "I know what you mean. It's a struggle for me to get finished at HQ before Alpha gate closes. By the time I get finished catching up on what's happened at A-detachment, I tend to miss supper, as well."

They exchanged grins, and Katrina started to eat, trying to ignore the delighted rush that swept through her at being with him again. "The flowers arrived today. Thank you very much."

"You're welcome." His smile seemed to light up his entire face. "I hope you're not allergic or anything."

"No, they're beautiful. I had about three crises going when they arrived, and they provided me with a wonderful sanity break."

"I'm glad." He stacked his empty dishes together but made no move to get up. "Seems like we've hardly seen each other since the trip, and I wanted to let you know I've been thinking of you."

She didn't know how to reply to that, so she focused on scooping up the last of her soup.

"I have an idea," he announced in a casual, yet tense, tone. "Since we're always late anyway, how about if we plan to meet here at, say, 1900 hours on certain evenings? That way we'd both have company."

She took her time answering. Looking forward to seeing him again was one thing. Making concrete plans to be with him was another.

"If you're worried about fraternization, I doubt anybody is going to be in a hurry to charge the provost marshal."

Fraternization. It was one of the most serious charges that could be levied against a deployed soldier. With her instinctive avoidance of social connections, she'd not had to worry about this before. Now she had to let Brian know where she stood. "A fraternization charge won't stick unless someone can prove. . ." She almost choked but forced herself to say the words, "intimate activity, which just isn't an issue for me. Even if I were in a relationship, my beliefs are that certain activities are reserved for marriage alone." She kept her attention focused on her sandwich, not wanting to see the mocking look in his eyes. Without a doubt, she'd just poured cold water on any attraction simmering between them.

"Katrina." His voice was both gentle and compelling. "I agree with you fully." He paused until she looked up at him. "My earlier comment was an attempt at a joke and was inappropriate. I'm sorry to have embarrassed you."

She shrugged, not sure how to respond. She was relieved he wasn't about to dub her "the ice maiden" or one of the other monikers she still winced over when remembering college days.

His gaze still held hers. "You're a Christian, aren't you?"

She nodded.

His grin widened. "Me too."

"Then how come I haven't seen you at Sunday fellowship meetings?" she blurted, then blushed at her forwardness.

"Fellowship meetings here on camp?" he asked.

"Yes. Every Sunday afternoon right after lunch. There are about a dozen of us."

"I had no idea. Soon after I arrived at UNDOF, I happened to find out about a messianic synagogue in one of the little communities north of here. That's where I've been going."

Katrina felt like someone had just pushed all the air out of her lungs. Never would she have predicted this turn in the conversation. "I'd never even thought of that option," she admitted.

"It's amazing how much we've talked about, and yet we still didn't know one of the most important things about each other." His tone held no rebuke, just reflection.

"Sharing confidences doesn't come easily for me."

His eyes twinkled with amusement. "Really?" he teased. "Let me share a confidence with you." He waited for her nod of assent. "I was hoping to meet up with you tonight. If you hadn't shown up here, I was planning to go to the Officers' Club to see if you were there."

She discovered that she enjoyed the feeling of being sought after. "And if I wasn't there?"

"I would have sent someone to get you," he pronounced firmly. "I'd like to spend more time with you, Katrina."

A breathless rush of emotion swept over her again. Was it normal to be so delighted that a handsome man wanted to spend time with her? On the other hand, if she did spend time with him, wasn't she risking losing her heart to him and ending up as shattered as her mother?

Her thoughts must have shown on her face, because his next words were gentle, almost cajoling. "Once a week?"

He had her there. What harm could come from meeting him for a late supper once a week? "I'd like that."

Again, his eyes lit with delight. "How about Tuesday evenings? Tuesdays are usually my least busy days, which means I can almost guarantee being here by 1900."

"Me too," she replied, though she didn't really have any day that was less busy than another. Lately, they'd all been running together in a single blur of work. But maybe that would change. She had a feeling Tuesdays were about to become the highlight of her week.

Chapter 6

Katrina woke with a sense of anticipation. Yesterday a requisition from the force engineering officer had arrived, authorizing her section to conduct renovations on the MP headquarters building at Charlie gate. It had seemed as good an excuse as any to telephone Brian, and he'd immediately offered to escort her to the building for a preliminary evaluation. Despite the overlapping crises of the week, she felt energized and uncharacteristically cheerful for first thing in the morning.

As she showered and prepared for the day, uneasiness kept trying to break through her euphoria. She mentally slapped the emotion away. She'd enjoyed three Tuesday night dinners with Brian, and with each one, she felt their friendship deepening. What she felt this morning, though, couldn't be attributed to mere friendship, could it? She didn't want to analyze it too deeply. She still had no intention of falling in love with anyone, much less a man whom she likely wouldn't see after their time here in Israel came to an end in July. Her upcoming trip to Canada for two weeks' leave would give her plenty of time to evaluate her feelings and what she wanted to do about them. For now, she'd just enjoy the pleasure Brian's company brought her.

Promptly at 0900 hours, she heard his familiar voice greet one of her sergeants, then her clerk. She looked over the form she'd been studying, scrawled her signature across the bottom, and placed it in her Out tray, which for once contained more paper than her In tray. She stood and grabbed her beret from the shelf behind her desk just as Master Corporal Little appeared in her doorway. "Yes, I heard Captain Smith come in." She gestured to her Out basket. "These need to be sorted and sent to the FEO. There are a few leave passes in the pile that need to go to the CO. If anybody needs me, tell them I'll be back after lunch." She grabbed two bottles of water from the refreshment room, then returned to the office area where Brian stood waiting.

The stocky, dark-haired provost marshal turned to her immediately. "Captain Falkirk." He shook her hand, then held the door open. "I appreciate your taking time to do this with me. It sounds like another busy day for the engineering section."

The bright sunshine momentarily blinded her as she walked past him, though the ever-present wind was cool. The air almost felt like autumn back home. "It's actually a fairly normal day for us. Seems if it's not one disaster, it's three others. At least all of today's problems so far are on our side. It can get hairy if there's an emergency at one of the UNMO posts or at Faouar."

Their tan desert boots crunched in unison on the gravel pathway as they walked toward the front gates of Camp

Ziouanni. They chatted about nothing in particular, passing through the front gates, then turning a sharp left toward Alpha gate, which lay less than two hundred yards away. Katrina marveled at the sense of ease she felt. From high school days she'd realized that somehow the small-talk gene had been left out of her DNA. Making conversation for conversation's sake always left her tongue-tied. But with Brian, there never seemed to be enough time to discuss the many topics in which they shared an interest.

Together, they reached the guard shack at Alpha gate and showed their orange UN identification cards that authorized their entry into the Area of Separation. Another five minutes took them to Charlie gate, the headquarters of the UNDOF Military Police Force.

Katrina looked around the simple one-story building with interest, wanting to catch every detail about Brian's work environment. He showed her through the front area where two corporals sat at desks, generating the typical piles of paper. His office and a large conference room lay just beyond the front area, with a central hallway leading to basic sleeping quarters for four in a common room, a small kitchen area, an equally small recreation area, and the requisite two washrooms, complete with shower stalls. He wanted an addition along one entire side of the building, allowing for another separate office, more sleeping space, and a larger recreation area. "With four people living here full-time, and always the possibility of a couple of people having to spend the night, there simply has to be more living space," he explained.

The job looked straightforward enough, though eight

months' experience in this position had taught Katrina that any job had the potential of being anything but simple. "Barring any crises, we should have drawings ready for you at the end of next week," she told him. "Construction might begin as early as June."

She saw the grimace cross his face, but it was gone when he turned to face her. "The wheels of bureaucracy grind slowly, don't they?"

"And none more slowly than the UN's." She kept her expression carefully neutral. She appreciated his understanding of the restrictions under which she worked and wished she could communicate it with at least a smile. But with all the people around, she didn't want to give any indication that she felt more for him than professional respect.

She busied herself taking notes and drawing diagrams. They again passed through the lounge area where a TV displayed a news channel. The broadcast was in Hebrew, so Katrina could do little more than guess what was being said. However, the video shot of an exploding car, followed by video shots of people lying like so much litter on the streets spoke for itself.

One of the MPs uttered a mild oath. "They got the orphanage!"

Instantly, Captain Smith's attention veered to the person speaking. Rather than reprimanding him for language, as Katrina expected, he simply asked, "What was that?"

"Sorry, Sir, Ma'am," the soldier replied. "Shouldn't have said it like that, but I can't believe the car bomb took out the orphanage." He pointed to the screen, where a stone building displayed a gaping hole in one corner. "I recognize the statue on the rise right behind it. That's the orphanage I was telling you about, Sir, the one we went to when I was here in '93."

The camera angle changed to show a cluster of weary-looking children shepherded by three or four nuns. Had a movie director set up the scene, he couldn't have more vividly portrayed the combination of innocence and destruction.

Katrina knew if she looked any longer at the images, she'd begin to weep, behavior she'd long ago learned to avoid in public. The circumstances of her life had been less dramatic but no less devastating. How well she knew the feeling of having home and security destroyed. She blinked, then studied her notes. Though the marks on the paper made no sense, the effort helped her find composure. She glanced at Captain Smith to see if he was ready to continue the tour.

His gaze collided with hers. His eyes shimmered with what might have been unshed tears before he blinked quickly and cleared his throat. "Sorry for the interruption, Captain. Shall we continue?"

It took some effort for Katrina to bring her thoughts back to the subject of renovations. Though they discussed details for another hour, the demolished orphanage took first place in her mind as soon as she left the MP HQ for her walk back to camp. Childhood memories assailed her. Often she and her mother had lived in buildings so poorly constructed that snow blew in under the door, and loose ends of siding banged against the house on windy days. No matter how often they'd requested repairs, the landlords just hadn't cared. She still easily recalled how it felt to be without the advantages of money and position, which made the necessities of life something to be taken for granted. Though she'd been self-sufficient for well over a decade, she never let herself forget those who were most dependent on the caring and concern of others. As she approached the gates of the camp, she forced the memories and emotions back into hiding.

However, the afternoon proved to be a continuous challenge to keep her thoughts focused on the work at hand. The Jerusalem orphans represented her motivation for becoming a peacekeeper. Filling out forms for the DCO's latest scheme seemed like a waste of time while those children's home remained a heap of rubble.

Welcome relief from her thoughts came at 1500 hours. Every Friday afternoon, Katrina met with her troop for a discussion of their projects and plans. She saw reflected in the men's faces the exhaustion she felt after week upon week of trying to keep ahead of various crises. They were fine soldiers as well as skilled tradesmen, and she valued their efforts. Some soldiers came to Camp Ziouanni expecting their tour of duty to be a six-month vacation. Her guys took their work seriously, even putting in fourteen- and sixteen-hour days when necessary to make sure the camp stayed functioning efficiently.

When they'd all settled around outdoor tables in a fenced area adjacent to her office, she began her briefing. "I can start with some good news. The CO has authorized an extra day of short leave for our entire troop in recognition of your outstanding work since Christmas." The men cheered and applauded.

"For those of you who didn't hear, there was a grease fire

in the kitchen this afternoon, which was mostly extinguished by the time Sergeant Dyer got there. The kitchen is still functional—" Here she was interrupted with a few groans. "But the section of wall behind the stove is going to have to be repaired. You didn't have anything else to do next week, did you, Corporal Douglas?" She grinned at the only carpenter in the room. There were two carpenters working for the CE section, but the other one had been living at Camp Faouar the past month while doing renovations to the recreation building. That left Corporal Douglas solely responsible for any carpentry work at Camp Ziouanni as well as any required by the observation posts.

Corporal Douglas leaned back in his chair in a pose of exaggerated relaxation. "I'm just on holidays here. Sure, I don't mind a little something to keep me busy."

After the chuckles and smart comments died down, she continued outlining the work to be done in the following week by the four plumbers, three electricians, and four refrigeration mechanical technicians. She concluded with, "Anything else we need to discuss?"

There was a pause, but no one seemed eager to fill it. Finally Sergeant Dyer spoke up. "There's something I'd like to talk about informally if you don't mind, Ma'am."

Katrina nodded her consent.

"Most of you have heard by now of the orphanage that was bombed in Jerusalem earlier today." The men nodded, and Katrina leaned forward in her eagerness to catch every detail. She hadn't expected anyone other than herself to be concerned about this. "You're probably not aware that this orphanage has been a special project of the Canadian contingent since the early years of UNDOF. During my first tour here in the early eighties, the CE section actually spent a few weekends down there building beds and doing other repairs. If any of you feel inclined to donate, I'm starting an unofficial collection to be sent down to them to help with restoration."

"If there were a work party put together, I'd be glad to volunteer," Corporal Douglas responded. Several others agreed.

Katrina felt a lump of emotion rise in her throat. She'd had no idea that the engineers had a history with the orphanage and felt proud that it was her unit that had first seen the need. That her troops would volunteer their rare off-duty time to continue that tradition made her prouder still. She had to swallow hard more than once before she could speak. "Since Jerusalem is out of bounds for recreational travel, I'll have to talk to the CO about getting special permission for a work trip down there."

"In the meantime," Master Corporal Little said, "I'll put a coffee can beside the pop cooler and toss a quarter in there for every can of pop I buy."

"Hear, hear!" the rest of the men encouraged him. "Same here."

With the official part of the meeting out of the way, the Friday evening "patio" commenced. Someone at some time had scrounged or purchased a barbecue that was used to grill burgers, steaks, or hot dogs obtained from the kitchen. This became a time for the members of the construction engineering section to interact informally with one another in a relaxed environment. Particularly since the travel restrictions imposed by the political unrest in the Middle East, any opportunity for recreation, no matter how simple, was welcome. Katrina always enjoyed these events. It gave her an opportunity to listen to her men discuss the topics of interest to them. Most often, the conversations centered around a North American sporting event, but sometimes tales of home and family would be woven into the discussion. Often through observing body language and listening to what wasn't said, she learned about details that affected her soldiers despite, and sometimes because of, their distance from home.

A trip to the pop cooler revealed a considerable amount of money already in the coffee can. She tossed in the Israeli equivalent of a dollar, paid the requisite amount for the pop, and turned back toward the tables.

Later that evening as she relaxed in her room, two images took turns intruding on the story she tried to read—the cluster of orphans huddling outside their mangled home and the soldier with a heart big enough to hold tears for children he'd never met.

Chapter 7

T uesday evenings had become the highlight of Brian's weeks, but tonight held the potential for more than pleasant companionship. Katrina would be leaving tomorrow for two weeks' leave in Canada. He thought she'd mentioned going to visit her mother, but he couldn't recall any other details. Details didn't matter much, he reminded himself as he made a short stop at his quarters for a quick shower and change of clothes. The important fact to him was that he would have to wait three weeks for another dinner with her. He wanted tonight to be special, a memory to make her look forward to coming back. Dressed in a freshly ironed pair of casual pants and a short-sleeved button-down shirt, he tucked a small package into his pocket. Her response to this gift should give him a clue as to whether she might be open to a change in their relationship.

He couldn't deny the fact he was falling in love with her. That wasn't to say he'd already fallen in love, just that he felt himself leaning over the edge of the precipice. Would she even consider the possibility? He hoped tonight would tell.

Katrina sat at a table in the officers' dining room when he arrived. Unfortunately, two other officers also sat nearby. While Brian usually didn't mind if their Tuesday suppers weren't completely private, tonight he'd hoped to be alone with Katrina. He hid his dismay as best he could as he set his tray down across the table from her.

"You look spiffed up," she said in greeting. "Something happening tonight I don't know about?"

"You might say that," he replied, giving her a teasing glance over his ham-and-Swiss sandwich. "How was your meeting with the FEO today?"

Disappointment flashed in her eyes, replaced almost instantly by the neutral expression he'd come to recognize as her means of concealing her emotions. He felt pleased she seemed to want to pursue the more personal discussion. Once the other two officers left, he'd explain why he'd chosen the more neutral subject for now, and hopefully be forgiven. "It must have been a long one," he offered. "I noticed you didn't make it back through Charlie gate until almost 1600."

That brought the smile back to her eyes. "Checking up on me?"

"But of course! I need to make sure the addition gets built on my HQ building."

She laughed then, and to his relief, the other two officers finished their meals. As soon as they were out of earshot, he leaned forward. "I wanted to tell—"

Simultaneously she said, "I need to ask you—"

Again, they laughed together. He welcomed the sound more each time he heard it. Katrina rarely laughed at all, almost never in public. He didn't yet understand her reserve, but he knew her laugh meant she felt at ease with him. He thought again of the box in his pocket, then gestured to her. "You go first."

"No, you go ahead." Now she seemed uncomfortable.

He waited until her eyes looked into his. "I'd like to hear what you were going to say. I promise I won't forget what I was going to tell you."

"Okay. It's just that some of my guys approached me on Friday about getting together a volunteer work troop to spend some of their leave time in Jerusalem helping out the orphanage. It seems the orphanage has been an unofficial project of the Canadian contingent for several years, and of the engineering section for even longer than that. We'd—I mean they'd like to continue the tradition." She flashed him a grin that reminded him of his younger sister when she wanted to talk him into something.

For many reasons, Brian devoutly wished he didn't have to obstruct her plan. "Have you talked to the CO about it?"

"No." The shake of her head revealed the loosening of the twist in which she wore her hair while in uniform. The slightly mussed appearance made her look young, much too young to be carrying her load of responsibility. "I plan to ask him tomorrow. I just thought it would lend more weight to my request if I'd already received informal approval from you. I know Jerusalem is not an approved destination for us right now." She grinned again.

Had he been standing, he would have shifted on his feet so he wouldn't have had to look at her while he replied. "In principle, I support your plan. I think it's a wonderful idea, and it's exactly the kind of thing I wish we could do more of." He could tell by the look on her face she knew what was coming. "Unfortunately, I can't approve a trip into Jerusalem, even for such a worthy cause. It's just too risky."

Dejection flickered in her eyes as she looked away from him. When her gaze met his again, it was devoid of emotion. "There's no chance of getting a different answer?"

He shook his head, hoping his eyes conveyed his empathy. "Even if the CO did approve the trip, I'd have to refuse. Since we're here as peacekeepers, not peacemakers, it's my job to keep our soldiers safe. Jerusalem is anything but safe right now."

"If we wanted to stay safe, we shouldn't have become soldiers." Though her face remained impassive and her tone bland, her eyes once again gave him a glimpse into deep, long-buried hurt.

"I wish I could tell you otherwise, but I can't. I really am sorry." He wanted to reach across the table to clasp her hand, but such a gesture could be misinterpreted by anyone who might see them. Despite what he felt for her, they had to avoid the appearance of romantic involvement until their deployments ended.

Her smile appeared and disappeared just as quickly without affecting her gaze. "There's no chance at all of changing your mind?"

He hoped his answer wouldn't ruin the rest of the evening. "If it were possible to change the policy, I'd want to be part of the work team." He looked directly into her eyes, hoping she'd believe him. "However, the guidelines I've been given say no one goes into Jerusalem unless they're on official duty."

Before she could shield her gaze, he saw how much the trip meant to her, more than he would have expected. The question popped out of his mouth before he had a chance to stop it. "Why did you become a soldier, Katrina?"

Her face showed her surprise at his question. "Do you want the real reason?"

"Sure." He shrugged as if to communicate that it didn't matter one way or the other, not wanting her to guess that her answer might mean a great deal to him.

"Initially, it was because it was the only way I could get a university degree."

"And now?"

"Now I stay because I hope that somehow, somewhere, I'll be able to make a difference as a peacekeeper. I'm proud of Canada's record of peacekeeping, and I'm proud to be part of it. So far, I've just done the routine stuff my job requires. It doesn't feel like much, but I'm convinced that by doing my job the best I can, one of these days I'll be able to make a real difference somewhere."

Her response so closely mirrored his own motives, it left him speechless. It would have seemed corny to tell her "me too," so he just nodded. "It's hard to see the innocent suffer and be unable to do anything about it, isn't it?"

For the first time since their conversation began, she held his gaze with her own. "I know what it's like to be on the other side of the fence, Brian. People have a thousand and one reasons for not helping those who need it most desperately. They have no idea how much a warm bed and a decent meal can mean."

"What was your childhood like, Katrina? Can you tell me?" He held his breath, wondering if she'd just walk out on him.

At long last, she lifted her gaze from the tabletop. "Until I was five, it was idyllic. Mom, Dad, Tim, and me—one happy family, or so I thought. The day after my fifth birthday, my parents told us they were separating. They'd decided Tim would go with Dad, and I'd stay with Mom. For the first few months, Mom and I stayed in the house I'd grown up in. I missed Dad and Tim, and I cried for them every night. So did Mom. Then one day Mom told me we had to move. I found out later it was because she hadn't been able to keep up with the mortgage payments. Dad's leaving stripped the soul right out of her. We moved every year or so after that, each place more shabby than the one before it. Things got better when Mom got on welfare, but that just barely kept food on the table."

"Where were your dad and brother in all this?" Brian felt ready to strangle the pair of them. How could any father have let his daughter live on the edge of poverty if he had the power to do something about it?

"I didn't hear from them again until I was a teenager. I thought they'd forgotten about me. I only found out later that Dad had received a job offer from a company in the States. I guess we moved so often they weren't able to keep track of us. I still don't know the whole story, even though Dad and I have formed an amicable relationship in recent years."

"And your mom?"

Silence stretched between them so long he wondered if she'd ever answer. This time she didn't look at him but picked at the tablecloth while she talked. "Mom was so totally crushed by Dad's leaving that she never recovered. A registered nurse lives with her, and from time to time, she ends up hospitalized for depression. She hates for me to be out of the country, so she's always worse when I'm deployed."

Brian wanted nothing more than to gather her in his arms and promise nothing would ever hurt her again. "Is she in the hospital right now?"

Katrina nodded. "That's why I'm going a week earlier than I'd originally planned. Maybe if she sees I'm still alive and well, she'll find the strength to function again."

The agony in her eyes made breathing painful for him. What an easy life he'd had, and how much he'd taken it for granted! He now understood why she always seemed so self-contained, so aloof. He'd heard all the things she hadn't said, knowing somehow she'd been the caregiver, even as a child. "Katrina." He spoke her name softly and waited for her to look at him in response. "Thank you for trusting me with your story. I can only imagine how hard it must have been for you." He paused, hoping his words would sink into the lonely, vulnerable place in her heart that didn't know what it felt like to be secure and cared for. "I'm going to be praying for you while you're gone, every day, several times a day."

She nodded and whispered, "Thank you." Tears trembled on her lashes, making her eyes look bluer than ever.

He reached into his pocket. "I originally bought this to

make up for that awful Christmas present, but now I want to give it to you to remind you that no matter what happens, you aren't ever alone. I'm your friend for always, Katrina."

Tears filled her eyes and spilled down her cheeks as she opened the small box. He'd seen the hammered gold maple leaf lapel pin at the goldsmith's shop one day when he stopped to pick out some jewelry for his sister and mother. The minute he saw it, he knew it was for Katrina—beautiful enough to convey his feelings, yet not loaded with connotations that might frighten her into complete withdrawal. She dabbed at the tears with a napkin and sent him a watery smile. "It's gorgeous, Brian. Thank you."

Chapter 8

Two thoughts dominated Katrina's mind during her entire leave—the Jerusalem orphanage and Brian. As she walked the halls of the psychiatric ward with her mother, discussed medications with the doctor, and—two days before her departure—helped check her mother out of the hospital and get her settled at home, she reached a difficult conclusion. Though letting herself fall in love with Brian, and him with her, tempted her to her core, she mustn't let it happen. From the number of fully functional people she knew, some people obviously weathered the falling in and out of love process. Watching her mother, however, reminded Katrina that she harbored a genetic weakness. Losing love had made a mess of her mother's life. If Katrina wanted to remain strong, she had to avoid emotional entanglement. She would enjoy all the richness Brian's friendship had to offer, but she would not let either of them fall in love.

The solution to the orphanage problem came to her during the fourteen-hour flight back to Israel. Enthusiasm for the project had her stumbling over to the engineering section the next day for the Friday patio, despite a serious case of jet lag. Master Corporal Green gave the work briefing, which sounded as though the engineering section's workload had continued unabated in her absence. He then turned to her. "Good to have you back, Captain. Anything you want to report?"

"As a matter of fact, yes, though forgive me if I sound less than coherent." After the laughter faded, she outlined the idea that had come to her. "Next month is the anniversary of the Canadian Military Engineers. How do you feel about putting on an 'Engineer Day' to both celebrate and to raise funds for the orphanage, since we can't go down there in person?"

The silence scared her for a moment. Did they think the idea too lame for words? Then response began to build.

"What about a three-legged relay race to show how well engineers cooperate with one another?"

"We could give tours of the CE section and charge admission."

"What about a bridge-building challenge? We'd show them how it's done, and the other sections could try to duplicate it."

Within an hour, the troop had the entire day planned. Some of the events would require after-hours preparation from the men, but every one of them agreed willingly.

Three days later, she told Brian during their supper, "I knew the guys were concerned about the orphanage, but I was just overwhelmed at how enthusiastically they supported the fund-raising day. When I asked the CO about it yesterday, he was just as enthusiastic."

His eyes twinkled at her. "Does that mean you've forgiven me for not giving you permission to take a work crew to Jerusalem?"

She pretended to consider. "Hmm. Maybe." Despite her best intentions, she couldn't help feeling delighted at being with him again. She'd never had a best friend, she told herself. Wouldn't anyone blessed enough to have such a friend be thrilled to be able to spend time with him or her?

"I have an idea."

Brian's exclamation pulled her out of her uncomfortable introspection. "Yes?"

"How about if we have a baseball challenge between the engineers and the military police? Each participant can contribute, say, two dollars, as a participation fee, and we can charge admission for spectators."

"Your guys would do that?" Katrina couldn't believe others might pick up the cause so quickly.

"Around here, anything different from the ordinary gets people enthused."

Engineer Day dawned with bright sunshine and perfect temperatures. Katrina escorted group after group through the CE section office and shops, delighted with how many showed up simply to support the fund-raising effort. The "tour" itself wasn't that interesting, and any of them could have stopped by on their own at any time. But having seen the posters the CE section had distributed all over camp, people came to the section, deposited their "admission" in the coffee can provided, and pretended deep interest in everything she showed them. The other activities proved similarly successful. By the end of the day, the troop had collected over $600, as well as bragging rights for having defeated the MP baseball team.

Following the game, Katrina used the camp public address system to thank everyone who had contributed, announcing with glee, "Thanks to your generosity, we've raised over $728 for the Jerusalem orphanage. You should be proud of yourselves, Canadians!"

To her surprise, a dear and familiar voice followed hers. "To add to what Captain Falkirk has just said, I'd like to announce that the military police are contributing $100 from their canteen toward the orphanage, and that the force provost marshal has agreed to deliver the funds in person to a military observer whose weekly duties take him into Jerusalem."

After a moment, Captain Galenza from the maintenance section announced a $50 donation from his troop's canteen, as well as a $100 donation from the officers' mess. A representative from the warrants and sergeants' mess made a similar announcement, followed by one from the junior ranks' mess. In a space of ten minutes, the orphanage fund swelled to over $1,200. Katrina couldn't stop the tears. She felt as if a neglected little girl from many years ago had finally found someone who cared that she'd had to do without for far too long.

The euphoria might have carried over into her relationship with Brian but for one thing: the arrival of posting messages. For those who were part of UNDOF for one-year postings, April and May brought the messages from Canada indicating where the next posting would be. Katrina learned she'd be going to Gagetown, New Brunswick, as part of the Canadian

School of Military Engineers. Brian's posting would take him in the opposite direction, to Edmonton, Alberta, where he'd take over the military police platoon.

Though their informal dinners together increased to twice a week and Brian often joined her on her run around the perimeter of the camp, Katrina held her emotions firmly in check. Anytime she felt herself becoming too giddy over his companionship, she reminded herself of their impending separation.

If Brian noticed her withdrawal, he said nothing about it. Rather, he seemed to delight in surprising her with flowers or little gifts. The top of her dresser now boasted a varied collection of items, some as goofy as the singing toy and others as endearing as the little plush beaver he brought back from his leave.

❦

Katrina's subtle withdrawal frightened Brian. He knew there was nothing he could do about it. Life experiences had convinced Katrina that falling in love would be dangerous. Though she opened up to him a little more after the Engineer Day, he still felt her reserve. He did the only thing he knew to do—he prayed. "God, You told me to be her friend. I did that, and now I'm in love with her. I know she's afraid of love. Have You led me into a hopeless cause?" He asked the questions over and over, while he was driving or walking, during his devotional time, and during the day anytime Katrina came to mind. He knew he needed to quiet himself and listen for God's answer, but the turmoil in his heart just kept spilling over. As their postings drew closer to an end and Katrina continued keeping him at arm's length, he became increasingly more anxious.

Less than a month before they were due to return to Canada, he exited the MP detachment at Camp Faouar in time to see a dearly familiar figure leaving a nearby building. He lengthened his stride to catch up with her.

"Captain Falkirk!" Regardless of how deep his feelings were, in public he took care to keep his demeanor strictly professional.

She turned toward him with undisguised delight in her eyes. As always, she quickly shrouded it behind a more neutral expression, but as always, that brief unguarded moment gave him hope. "I didn't expect to see you here."

"Didn't you know it's part of my job to be where I'm least expected?" he teased as he matched his steps to her shorter stride. "Are you over here for the day?"

"No. I just finished a meeting with the force engineering officer and am on my way back to Ziouanni."

A risky idea suddenly took root. "Might you have time to have tea with me at Khan Uraynibah?" The little town sat just shy of the Syrian border and boasted several shops specifically set up to attract trade from the peacekeepers passing back and forth between the two camps.

"I didn't know there was a tea shop there." She looked puzzled yet pleased, as well.

"Actually, it's a goldsmith shop, but Elias always serves tea when peacekeepers stop by."

"I noticed that the couple of times I went shopping in Damascus. We get treated like honored guests rather than mere customers." She grinned. "Actually, the goldsmith shop would be perfect. I've been wanting to pick out something nice to take to my new sister-in-law. I'll follow you there."

Anticipation surged through Brian as he started his white UN car, pulled out into the lane, and waited for Katrina's similarly marked vehicle to catch up. He hadn't even had to cajole her into taking a look at the goldsmith's wares. "Father God, thank You; this is just perfect!" He found he had to keep a close eye on his speedometer. When he didn't, the needle crept above the legal limit. The last thing he needed was to be pulled over for speeding.

Elias greeted them with the graciousness and enthusiasm for which he'd become known throughout the twenty years of UNDOF's presence in the area. "Welcome. Welcome. May I serve you tea?"

"Yes, please," Brian answered for them both as Katrina bent over the glass cases displaying an endless variety of jewelry.

Elias motioned them toward two high wooden chairs. "Sit. Sit. I will bring you whatever you like."

They sat, and he set small cups of steaming liquid in front of them. They each sipped and pronounced it delicious. Only then did he ask, "What does the lady want to see?"

Katrina tilted her head to one side in thought, a gesture Brian found endearing. "Bracelets, I think."

Elias retrieved several black, felt-lined trays and placed them in front of Katrina. "Pick them up. Try them on," he urged. "They're the best quality. You won't find better anywhere."

From Elias, this was more than a sales pitch. Having purchased jewelry from him in the past and had it appraised in Canada, Brian knew the quality of the gold and of the workmanship surpassed much of what was readily available in North America.

It took Katrina just a few minutes to select a tri-gold bangle set. "This is perfect," she declared. "Thank you for your help."

"Anything else?" Elias looked at Brian.

"Yes. I'd like to look at this tray, please." He pointed to the display in the glass case immediately to his left.

Elias's eyes began to twinkle. "This is special? I am glad you come to Elias." He set the assortment of diamond rings in front of Katrina.

She started to push it toward Brian, then stopped as understanding dawned. Her face drained of color. "No, Brian. No. Don't do this, please." Tears filled her eyes, and she stood abruptly, striding out the door.

Brian sat in shock. Elias, to his credit, said nothing for a few moments before picking up the tri-gold bangles. "Shall I hold these for the lady?"

Brian blinked the moisture out of his eyes and cleared his throat. "No, I'll take them to her." He extracted the appropriate number of Syrian dollars from his wallet while Elias wrapped the jewelry in a soft cloth bag.

He drove the few minutes back to Charlie gate, his soul as torn as it had been euphoric less than an hour ago. "Lord God, how did this go so wrong?" He strode past the corporals in the front office without speaking and shut his office door behind him. Lowering his head onto his hands, he asked again, "What did I do wrong?"

Slowly, the answer dawned. He hadn't been listening. He'd spent the last weeks pummeling heaven with his questions and requests, but he hadn't stopped to listen for a response. He'd assumed no response meant approval on his plans. "Father God, forgive me for rushing ahead of You." Tears of contrition dripped through his fingers. "What do I do now?" He let quiet seep into his grieving heart, and after a moment, felt the answer.

"Wait."

"Wait for what? How long? In three weeks we'll be at opposite ends of the country." Again, he forced himself to let go of the questions and wait for whatever God wanted to tell him. The answer didn't come in words but rather as a knowing in his soul. God had led him into friendship with Katrina. Her rejection of his romantic love hadn't released him from God's directive to be her friend.

"But, God, if I know Katrina at all, she's not going to want to speak with me again. How do I be her friend if she wants nothing to do with me?" He sat back in his chair and stared up at the ceiling, wishing an answer could be written plainly there. He let his hands fall into his lap and encountered a bulge in his uniform pocket—the bracelets.

Renewed purpose took the place of the grief. "Thanks, God. This time I'll try to wait for You."

Chapter 9

Katrina avoided Brian as much as she could for the next three weeks. She couldn't just stand him up for their next supper date, so she met him at the dining hall long enough to explain that she couldn't stay. "I have twenty personnel evaluations to complete before my replacement gets here next week," she explained without meeting his gaze. The explanation sounded hollow, even to her own ears, but she couldn't think of anything better.

To her astonishment, he nodded with understanding. "I know how it goes," he assured her. "There's a multitude of little details to tie up before we leave. By the way, you left something at Elias's the other day." He handed her a cloth-wrapped package.

Half afraid of what she'd find, she opened it, then sighed with relief. "Oh! The bracelet I picked out for Cathy!"

He shrugged and nodded. "I figured it was the least I could do since I upset you. I didn't mean to."

"I know. How much do I owe you?" She didn't want to discuss it.

He told her the amount in Syrian pounds, then suggested, "Or when you get back to Canada, you can just mail me a check for $50 Canadian."

"Thanks. I'll let you know before we leave how I want to handle it. I'd better get back to the office if I want to get anything done tonight."

Sadness lingered in his eyes, but he didn't try to detain her. "Have a good evening, Katrina."

But once back in her office, Katrina found concentration impossible. She hadn't expected such kindness from Brian after the way she must have embarrassed him at the goldsmith's shop. Even now, she couldn't bring herself to explain to him the panic that had gone through her at the sight of those diamond rings. She knew her feelings for him went beyond friendship. A big part of her had wanted to pick out a ring with him, to say "yes" to his unspoken proposal. Memories of her mother's suffering remained too vivid. The feelings between her and Brian felt strong enough, solid enough, to risk a future on. But would they withstand the inevitable separations brought about by their respective careers? Would they even endure through their next postings, virtually at opposite ends of the country? Better to extricate herself now while she could, than risk getting in any deeper and finding herself unable to cope with the consequences.

Or so she told herself at least a dozen times a day. How he managed it, she couldn't guess, but Brian seemed always to be nearby. More often than not, he was already in the officers' dining room when she arrived for a meal, and came in just after she'd seated herself. Unable to tolerate being alone with her thoughts, she ventured over to the Officers' Club three different evenings, and two of the three times he was already there. They exchanged pleasantries, but their earlier camaraderie had vanished.

Nothing in his eyes or his demeanor ever reproached her. He seemed, rather, to be waiting. *Waiting for what?* she wondered. If he was hoping she'd change her mind about their relationship, he'd just have to be disappointed.

Her last week in camp brought a sense of relief. She took the officer replacing her through all the procedures and ongoing projects, as well as on a quick trip to Faouar to meet the new force engineering officer. A pang of disappointment seized her as they passed Khan Uraynibah, but she ignored it. There was no point in wishing for what couldn't be.

The morning of her departure, she awoke at 0400. Her ride to the Tel Aviv airport would leave at 0530, and she still had several last-minute items to pack. At 0515, she hauled her luggage over to the waiting bus, only to find Brian already there.

"Good morning." He greeted her as if there'd been no strain between them.

"You're flying out today, as well?"

He grinned. "Yeah. You're stuck with me until we get to London's Heathrow Airport."

She couldn't decide how she felt. It would be nice to have a traveling companion, but could her heart endure postponing the good-bye? No matter how she felt, it wouldn't change the fact that Brian would be nearby for the rest of the day.

Having a companion did make the six-hour flight to

London much more pleasant. Katrina even felt comfortable enough to fall asleep, only to find upon awaking that she'd ended up resting her head on Brian's shoulder. "I'm sorry," she murmured groggily as the plane slowed to a stop on the runway at Heathrow.

"For what?" The tenderness in his eyes made her want to throw herself into his arms and apologize for ever pushing him away.

Instead, she busied herself folding the blanket she couldn't remember having requested. "For draping myself all over you while I slept."

No other word could describe the look on his face but love. "No apology necessary. I enjoyed it."

Passengers began filing off the plane, saving her the need of a reply. She and Brian walked together up the passageway and into the huge, brightly lit airport. He draped his arm across her shoulders and guided her off to one side out of the way of the milling crowds. He turned to look into her eyes. "This is where we go our separate ways. Good-bye, my friend." He pulled her into the tightest, warmest, most secure-feeling hug she could ever remember.

She returned the embrace, suddenly unable to speak past the lump in her throat. Tears tried to push into her eyes, but she refused to let them gather. When he finally released her, his eyes held the shine of unshed tears, as well. He touched her cheek gently. "Take care."

Her lips trembling, she walked away from him, toward the hallway leading to the baggage claim area. With each step, she fought the urge to turn back. Then she turned a corner and, with the turn, resolved to put Brian out of her mind.

The reunion with Tim and Cathy more than met her expectations. Confidence still emanated from Tim's every word and gesture, but now gentleness accompanied it. Even when he embraced Katrina and inquired about her trip, his attention still clung to Cathy. For her part, Cathy watched him with undiluted affection as though he were the absolute center of her world. Their absorption in one another and sparkling happiness made Katrina wonder once again what she might have lost. She refused to let herself dwell on what-ifs.

Throughout the two-hour drive to Lakenheath, she made herself focus on Tim's and Cathy's comments to the exclusion of all else. The only way she would get over Brian was to refuse to let him occupy her thoughts. Upon arrival at their cottage, Tim and Cathy showed her to a small but cozy guest room. "Feel free to take a rest before dinner," Cathy told her. "I know how exhausting travel can be."

Whether it was travel or her own turbulent emotions, Katrina didn't want to say, but exhaustion dragged at her. As soon as the door closed behind her brother and sister-in-law, Katrina sank down on the bed and kicked off her shoes. She pulled the colorful fleece blanket over herself and willed herself into the welcome oblivion of sleep.

Sleep refused to come. For well over an hour, she lay hovering in the fuzzy zone between full alertness and unconsciousness. She finally gave up and began unpacking her bags for her three-week stay. As she made one last check through the pockets of her carry-on, she encountered an unfamiliar package. Drawing it out, she saw a box similar to the one in which Brian had given her the maple leaf pin. She opened the lid to find a tightly folded piece of paper.

Dear Katrina,
This gift is to remind you of the friendship we've shared. Time and distance will not ever make me less your friend. If ever you need me, or just want to talk, please phone. Until I get settled in Edmonton, you can reach me at my cell phone (416) 347-8923.

Love,
Brian

Beneath the piece of paper lay a puzzle ring. Four interlocking bands fit together to form an intricate design. She'd seen people disassemble the rings and fit them back together, but she didn't dare try. The last thing she wanted was to render the ring unwearable. She slid it onto the ring finger of her right hand, where it fit perfectly.

Over the course of the next week, Katrina found herself with plenty of time to rest and think while Tim and Cathy worked. Her body seemed to need an enormous amount of sleep, but when she wasn't sleeping, she felt as if her mind were stuck in overdrive. No matter how hard she tried, she couldn't eliminate Brian from her thoughts. Even when she wasn't consciously thinking of him, she felt his absence as keenly as she'd felt her father's and brother's absence all those years of her childhood.

Finally one afternoon, she sank to her knees in desperation. "Heavenly Father, I don't know what to do. The longer I'm away from Brian, the more I miss him. Have I already lost my heart irretrievably? What do You want me to do now?" Tears began to flow—all the tears she'd held back since that afternoon in Khan Uraynibah. She sobbed until she felt spent. She didn't know Tim and Cathy had come home until she felt their hugs surround her from either side.

They held her until her sobs abated. Then Cathy asked, "Can you tell us about it?"

To Katrina's amazement, she felt able to tell them about Brian. She started with their impromptu duet, then told the entire tale without a pause until their separation in the airport.

"Why are you afraid of loving him?" Cathy asked.

Before Katrina could reply, Tim offered, "It's because of Mom and Dad, isn't it?"

She looked at him through still-teary eyes. "That's it exactly. During my last leave, I had to go get Mom out of the hospital again. I won't let myself be that vulnerable. I just can't."

Tim sat back on his knees and reached for her hands. "Kat, I don't think Mom's problems have had much to do with the divorce."

The idea was so contrary to Katrina's long-held assumptions, she could only gape at him.

He nodded but with sadness in his eyes. "I can remember things from before Dad and I moved out—things you wouldn't know about. I remember a nurse living with us for months after you were born, and Mom rarely coming out of her room."

Confusion warred with anger in Katrina's thoughts. "If

she was that unstable, then why did Dad leave me with her?"

Tim looked down at their joined hands, his thumb rubbing across the uneven surface of her puzzle ring. "The truth, Kat?" When she nodded, he continued. "Mom threatened suicide if he didn't."

Katrina felt as if someone had suddenly tipped her universe on its side. "It doesn't make sense."

"No, it doesn't." Cathy massaged Katrina's shoulders lovingly. "Tim and I have talked a lot about your parents' marriage because we don't want to make the same mistakes. We've decided we'll never know for sure what went wrong, that we can only promise ourselves and each other we won't let anything come between us. When we encounter difficult spots, we have God to turn to, and your parents didn't."

Peace began to settle into Katrina's spirit. In all her thoughts about love and its risks, she'd never factored God's love into the equation. Over the next few days, she spent hours with her Bible, reading every verse she could find about marriage and about God's love. To her amazement, she saw for the first time how often Scripture teaches that the love between husband and wife should be a mirror of God's love for the church.

She'd been in England just eight days when she found the courage to pick up the phone and dial the number she'd been given. When Brian answered, she didn't even identify herself. She simply asked, "Shall I come to Canada or do you want to come to England?"

Epilogue

With the swell of organ music, Katrina gripped Tim's arm, and the two stepped through the doorway of the small Ottawa church. Christmas greenery had been secured to the end of each pew with white and navy bows. Through the froth of her wedding veil, she could see Brian standing beneath a greenery-covered arch at the front of the church. The twinkling, clear Christmas lights above him couldn't compare to the love she saw shining from his eyes as he watched her progress down the aisle.

He hadn't even hesitated when she'd phoned him six months ago. Within twenty-four hours, they met once again in Heathrow Airport, except this time, there were no strangling good-byes. She would never forget the crushing hug he'd given her or the butterfly-light kiss he'd placed on her lips.

The next six days had been exactly what they'd both needed. Free from the demands of work and the restrictions of deployment regulations, they spent every waking hour together. When they boarded the plane to return to Canada together, Katrina's right ring finger bore the diamond solitaire in a filigreed band Brian had chosen from Elias's store.

Tim's gentle tug on her arm stopped Katrina just two steps away from her goal—Brian's side. A grin twitched the minister's lips. "Who gives this woman to be married to this man?"

"I do," Tim declared.

Brian stepped forward and Tim placed Katrina's hand on Brian's. Throughout the rest of the ceremony, Katrina's gaze never left Brian's face. She had no doubts about the durability of their love. The career manager had found an opening for Brian in Gagetown rather than Edmonton, which had enabled them to spend the past six months working near one another. From here on out, they'd be bound together, regardless of where life might take either of them.

They exchanged vows, then rings, and the minister prayed a blessing over them, followed by the words Katrina had waited a lifetime to hear. "What therefore God hath joined together, let no man put asunder."

JANELLE BURNHAM SCHNEIDER

Writing fiction has been a passion for Janelle since she was a teenager. She spent several years doing freelance reporting before finding her creative home in fiction. Her first book was published by **Heartsong Presents** during its first year of existence.

Janelle is married to her best friend and favorite romantic hero, who is also an engineering officer in the Canadian Forces. They have two children and two dogs, and in the eight years of their marriage have lived in New Brunswick, Alberta, and Ontario. As a result of their military postings, they've also visited Egypt, Syria, Israel, and Greece. Though they've spent many months separated by military duty, she tells anyone who will listen, "I'd rather have Mark part-time than any other husband full-time."

A Letter to Our Readers

Dear Readers:

In order that we might better contribute to your reading enjoyment, we would appreciate your taking a few minutes to respond to the following questions. When completed, please return to the following: Fiction Editor, Barbour Publishing, Inc., P.O. Box 719, Uhrichsville, OH 44683.

1. Did you enjoy reading *Christmas Duty?*
   ❑ Very much—I would like to see more books like this.
   ❑ Moderately—I would have enjoyed it more if _____
   _____
   _____

2. What influenced your decision to purchase this book?
   (Check those that apply.)
   ❑ Cover   ❑ Back cover copy   ❑ Title   ❑ Price
   ❑ Friends   ❑ Publicity   ❑ Other

3. Which story was your favorite?
   ❑ *About-Face*   ❑ *Seeking Shade*
   ❑ *Outranked by Love*   ❑ *A Distant Love*

4. Please check your age range:
   ❑ Under 18   ❑ 18–24   ❑ 25–34
   ❑ 35–45   ❑ 46–55   ❑ Over 55

5. How many hours per week do you read? _____

Name _____

Occupation _____

Address _____

City _____ State _____ Zip _____

E-mail _____